SCAR CULTURE

SCAR CULTURE

Toni Davidson

First published in Great Britain in 1999 by Rebel Inc,
an imprint of Canongate Books Ltd, 14 High Street
Edinburgh EH1 1TE

10 9 8 7 6 5 4 3 2 1

British Library Cataloguing-in-Publication Data
A catalogue record for this book is available
on request from the British Library

ISBN 0 86241 892 5

Rebel Inc series editor Kevin Williamson

Typeset by Hewer Text Ltd, Edinburgh
Printed and Bound by R. R. Donnelley & Sons,
Crawfordsville, Indiana

For my family,
all my family.

'Scars are created within and without, a culture of scars cultivated in petri dishes, welded onto our skins and etched undeniably into our minds.'

REX OTTO *The Maelstrom of Memory*

CLICK

Note. The following written notes and
photographic images were found by the
authorities at the scene. They are presented here
in the order they were found.

I heard the groans first, 17 whistling, chesty groans, the
familiar rumble of my father's tones, seeping out the cracks in the
wooden slats of the hut. I nursed my slight injuries from the fall –
grazed skin on my arms and legs, a deeper bruise on my back
where my T-shirt had been torn and inadvertently camouflaged
and a throbbing head from numerous root thuds – but the grazes
and bruises were nothing, I had the resilience of expectation, an
incredible, believable shield that was such strong armour.

Then.

I knew this was where my father had disappeared to every
day for the past week for hours on end, vacating the close
quarter intensity of our movable beast, escaping incarceration
in our battered caravan, nestled uneasily with the three of us.
And in my sensible, near-grown-up state I could only agree
with him. There it was, back up the slope, the blackened,
rusty, four-wheeled bucket that I had called home since my
head camera first clicked. Oh God there it was, back in the
viewfinder, taking away the hut from my eyes. And there she
was. Exit scratching the windows to get out, Exit taking her
arms around her chest and goosestepping her legs into a
strange quick step or mangled foxtrot, pacing back and forth
between the eight-feet gap that separated one wall from the
other, viewing herself, her manic reflection in that cracked old
mirror that hung always at an angle because no one had the
time or the inclination to fix it. There she was marching with
her own reflection, uncertain whether to be proud or

disgusted. There she was. One, two, three HIT, one, two, three HIT.

How she laughed.

*

Inside the hut I could hear the groans grow louder, the momentum of thuds and thumps growing stronger as though furniture was being pushed out the way. Space being cleared for an alien autopsy. It could be anything. Would be anything.

Count the number of times I have run away from the thoughts in my head.

But the head camera can lie. My father was dancing, my father was *dancing*. Not the rigid, mechanical movements of Exit's march but the fluid swerves of a dancer . . . I couldn't help the big smile that broke across my face. With my eyes two centimetres above the window ledge I watched him and his miraculous dance. He whirled and thrashed in time to some silent tempo, silent for me but perhaps not for him. I cannot describe the form, the style; the movement seemed both wild and in control; uneven yet seamless. But what I saw I liked, what I saw burst dams of emotions in me, that sprang me into such hopeful action and I raced round to the door of the hut ready to burst in and join in this unexpected jig, join my father in a different kind of movement. Everything that had gone before had been preparation for this intimate father/ son moment. Then I understood, now I understand.

HEAD PHOTO

Exit knelt at the bottom of my bed. I looked up from the haze of half-sleep and saw her face framed between my feet. I asked her what she was doing. The caravan was quiet, a time before the dancing, the marching began, a time when my father would sit quietly in his chair reading. A time when Exit had her real name. Mother. A time when she would spend hours with me, awake or asleep. And sometimes she would just stare as though communication was taking place with me not

hearing a thing. I felt the touch of the wet flannel that slid between my
toes, one by one, pausing to eradicate every last bit of fluff or dirt. I
watched her reach the last toe, watched her leaning back, arching the
stiffness out of her spine and perusing her work. My head slumped back
onto the pillow, fazed with tiredness but I could hear my mother's voice
saying over and over again, oh dear . . . oh dear . . . oh dear. And the
flannel resumed its short stroking movements between my toes.

My hand was six centimetres away from the handle before
I jerked it back. The sound had suddenly changed from inside
the rickety walls. From groans to shouts, from moans to
screams. The chairs were kicked not pushed, the table thrown
from one wall to another. Three metres, I estimated. Perhaps
three and a half. Something, maybe someone, had changed
tempo inside the hut, broken the ballet and now, and now
there was not a dance any more, at least not the sound or feel
of any dance I had seen. It was a cardiac jerk, his limbs moving
without fluidity intervened by a sporadic, fitful rigidity.

There were no words just sound, his long black beard
became entangled in his mouth, so that each scream, each
piercing cry, blew the long black strands out then back into his
mouth. He launched himself at my side of the hut and I ducked
a quick 50 centimetres of fright below the window ledge
shaken by the force of the thump on the rotting slats. Between
one wall and another he threw himself with increasing violence, and I was floundering in my attempts to define what I
saw, to rationalise this sudden turn in events, in images . . .

I crept back from the window and took flight rushing to
scramble back up the slope, slipping and sliding on the wet
moss, barely keeping a grip on the ground, barely keeping a
grip altogether.

HEAD PHOTO

My mother is at my father's throat. I am six years old. Sitting
with my new teddy bear fresh from a toy shop we had ambled through,
the caravan behind us, lurching in fits and starts over the cobbled

streets. I don't have much feeling for the teddy, at least not as much as my mother seemed to have when she bought it. She pressed its new-smelling synthetic fur against my face, took its paw in her hand and brushed it across my lips, pushing its soft pads into my mouth in slow, gentle movements, laughing with short gasps of breath. When I took it into the caravan it seemed more hers than mine and it lay unmoving on my chest as I watched my mother's teeth scraping against my father's long neck. I knew all about kissing. There were days when I seemed to drip with my mother's saliva, my cheeks, my neck, my arms and legs, wet and shining with that strange feel and smell that I didn't know whether to like or hate. After kissing there was no perfume smell about my mother, the tell-tale signs of hairspray or soap. There was only the sickly sweet smell of saliva. I couldn't tell if my father liked it either. He stood leaning against the caravan door with my mother pressed against his neck, her hands pushing his chest further into the wall. He would stay silent while my mother would moan between slurps. She saw me watching and she turned herself and my father round so that I was in her sight directly over his shoulder. She caught my eye and held it and I felt uneasy, trapped as she continued to chew her way over my father's face.

PHOTO 1   MOTHER AND SON

The caravan is a haven for no one; if there was a tranquil idyll in place before it had been shunted out the way by that grubby shell on wheels, heaving as it was from side to side, with its familiar distraught, syncopated rhythm then there was no telling that now.

'Come and play with me, son, you never play with me any more.'

I framed Exit in my hands, focusing my eyes on just her, zooming into the long brown hair falling onto her shoulders, the hand held out for mine.

'I have a present for you.'

Her smile was believable, the hand behind her back even more so. I walked over to her and she took me onto her lap, her arms wrapped around my waist.

'Do you want to know what it is?'

I could smell our dinner on her breath, sulphur mixed with smoke from her cigarette burning on the work surface in the kitchen area.

'Who's it from?'

Her arms dug into my ribs, spilling my breath out of my mouth.

'What do you mean who's it from? What sort of question is that to ask? Do you think it's from your father? Do you?'

Her voice changed, her mouth came closer to mine and I could feel the veil of hair brushing in front of my eyes. These were not good signs. I knew about them. But she was right. It was as black and white as this photograph, except that's not true either, what I mean is that this photo is grey, a hundred shades and tones of grey and the truth is this, my father wouldn't have given me a present.

'No,' I said.

'I didn't think so. Well, here you are.'

Her other hand appeared in front of me, in its palm a small Instamatic camera, a black case and brightly coloured strap.

'Don't tell me it's not what you want. I know it's what you've wanted for a long time.'

She was right, of course, she had seen my hands, my fingers squaring everything from the countryside around us to every movement she or Panic made in the caravan.

The camera as far as I was concerned offered the best possible view of the world around me.

'What can I take pictures of?' I asked her.

She laughed and let me go, standing me in front of her, still close to her face, our foreheads close to clashing, our noses close to fighting for the same air.

'Why, what you always take pictures of, of course.'

I smiled this time. She didn't mean that. She wouldn't want the photographs I had taken or could take with my head or my fingers. Neither would Panic, he would run or walk or swim a mile before he would look at them.

'But let me take the first one.'

She pulled me against her, taking the camera in one hand, my waist in the other and we both stared at the little black box shaking in her hand. Click.

'There. Don't I deserve a kiss?'

I put my lips together and touched the skin on her cheek. It felt dry and powdery. She laughed again, tossing her head back so the hair went out of both of our eyes.

'You're a funny boy. You kiss the cheek of a friend. You kiss your mother on the lips.'

She gripped me by the waist again meeting my lips halfway and I felt sulphur trickle and smoke work its way down my throat.

'You come from me, remember, this body and my eyes have seen everything there is to see of you. Everything, you understand. Now, go and play with your new toy.'

She had her eyes, yes, but I had the camera.

Click.

HEAD PHOTO

My mother was screaming at my father. Her mouth centimetres away from his ear. There was no volume in her voice – I was lying on the floor in the living area and they were in bed and I could barely hear any words that didn't end in a long hiss, a drawn out venomous snarl. There were no words just a deep resonance that seemed to vibrate its way through the thin flooring to my thighs, which glued themselves to the floor, my arms outstretched in front of me, free-falling with nowhere to go. There was a feeling which spread beyond the vibrations I felt in my body, a tremor in my heart, a pain in my head . . . If I hadn't been glued to the spot I would have run. If I hadn't seen my mother tug at my father's long black hair and then shake it off her hand like it was the remains of a dead rodent, then I might have been okay. As it was, and maybe as it is, I felt tears coming into my eyes that had nowhere to go. My father didn't react, she pulled his head towards then away from her, his hair a limp lever that he could not stop. There was no resolution as far as I could tell, the pulling and low-volume hissing continued long after I buried my face in my hands.

PHOTO 2 SELF-PORTRAIT: ERECTION

I can hear Exit whispering, the words are blanketed and muffled but the edge, the sharp scythe of her tone, reached the fusty air of the caravan all the same. The night is pulsing with the family's noise. Like any other night, it is a night of sound after a long silent day. The staccato hiss of my breath through my teeth, the low groan and choked coughs of my father, who tosses and turns in half-sleep trying to escape a few centimetres closer to the wall, trying to evade the pinpricks of endless harshly spoken words, the hum of the fridge, the whine of the wind outside. The sound of something. I'm counting the tap of a loose branch on the window above my Zed bed. Two hundred and fifty eight so far. And counting. Its brief scraping sound brings a smile to my lips, a reassurance to my heart. I hurl myself out the window and onto the branch, one swift, dream-time movement, head camera intact, in action and I am scrambling for balance, my arms outstretched like a tightrope walker in jeopardy. The caravan looks so small from my perch, an off-white stain on the blackened land of the night landscape. It creaks and groans as it shifts, its breathing sleep merges with the rustle and tussle of the branches as they collide and move apart.

With my Instamatic securely in my hand, I take another photo, knowing but ignoring the fact that I should be careful about squandering precious film. But I can't resist, cannot lose the tempting lurch of my own body as it swells in the night air. It, all 11.2 centimetres of *it*, pokes through my thin cotton pyjamas, a blimp on the landscape, shadowed sporadically by the listless branches, waving with its own momentum up and outwards. With difficulty my legs straddle two branches, the balance precarious but held long enough for me to angle the camera down and frame myself for some curious posterity. Not that much can be seen. An extra twig in the trees, a bud beginning to flower . . . It makes me laugh. Click takes a pic of dick . . . Precious moment lurching into celluloid memory.

HEAD PHOTO

I can hear my mother and father whispering in the kitchen. Their ears and mouths are locked together, one head turns to a mouth, then the other mouth turns to the other ear. And so on and on. I don't know what they can be whispering about but I can feel the short hairs on the back of my neck, feel them rise, the skin tightening while I try and concentrate on the puzzle in front of me. Fifty pieces, none of which seem to fit. I feel like I want to throw the whole lot into the air and watch them scatter around the caravan. Instead I can hear my mother rush over to me, I see her arms reaching out towards me, her hands under my arms, and I get a view of the caravan I had threatened the jigsaw with. She picks me up and rushes me past my father who turns his head away, his eyes turning to the food cooking in the pan. Six sausages, two eggs, three rashers of bacon. My mother puts me in front of the sink and pulls my hands from my sides and thrusts them under the cold tap. The water pours out splashing everywhere, and her own hands meet mine, frantically scraping at the skin, under the nails, between the fingers. 'Must I tell you again, must I?' I'm not sure what she is telling me but my hands are getting numb from the cold water pouring onto them.

PHOTO 3   NIGHT VISIT

Exit got out of bed and I lay stock still. She walked to the food preparation area and ran the tap into the sink. I could hear her drink from the tap, the slurping noises drowning out everything else temporarily. And then I heard her drop to her knees, her hands slapping onto the vinyl floor and she slithered out of the kitchen into the living accommodation area where I slept on a rickety old Zed bed.

If I hadn't heard her then the smell of smoke would have alerted me to her approach. This was a game to be played at night, just like years before when I could sit on her lap without the awkwardness of weight and we would watch horror films while my father, who had just begun to wander, was out. I took comfort in the situation, another diversion into celluloid, but Exit always knew the films and just before the music slid up to a crescendo she would poke me in the ribs, bite my neck, squeeze my thigh. And I would jump out of my skin while she rolled about, tears rolling down her cheeks, saying, 'That scared you didn't it?'

She got me every time.

She slid her body to the bottom of the bed and I waited for the shock with knowing not helping since I could never be sure what the shock would be and I was always, always awake. When it came I jumped out of my bed, out of my skin, out of my breath, so that I gulped for a few seconds. She burst with laughter, glad that she had given me a rerun of all the Hammer House of Horrors we had watched but then she thought the shock of being woken had been enough for me, that it had been fright enough to get the joke across. But it wasn't her presence, it was the touch of her icy cold hands on my bare shins that had catapulted me out of bed. And I realised that it was not just her mouth she had held under the tap but her hands. All part of the game.

She was so full of laughter as she walked back to bed that she didn't hear the click of the Instamatic poking out from under the duvet.

HEAD PHOTO

It's the middle of the night and I am in the bathroom again. I feel dizzy. There are spots on my arms and an ache in my stomach that won't go away. I moan for attention, someone to come in and take me away from myself, I lean over the toilet bowl wondering if sickness at least will come.

Then my father parts the curtain of plastic beads and steps in. His eyes are foggy from sleep and it takes him a while to focus on me, his eyes screwing up against the bare shine of the bulb. He is naked but all I see is how long his hair is, its black fibres cascading down his back. Without a word he lifts me away from the toilet, his strong hands burning the skin under my arms, and he sits straddling the toilet. And then the only sound is his toilet sound, the only movement his bowels descending loosely and hurriedly into the bowl. He doesn't say a word to me as he sits, his face reacting with pleasure and relief as the loose stools pour into the water. There are beads of sweat on his forehead and he looks as ill as I feel but he doesn't mention my spots, my hands pressed to my stomach, my pain manifesting itself graphically for his benefit, his attention. But he says nothing. He tugs at the toilet roll, the sound of the roller the loudest thing in the caravan at that moment. He stands up and stretches. I watch with strange fascination the drop of liquid at the tip of his thing. When he closes his eyes and stretches his arms I know for a second or two that it is okay to look. As his body relaxes and his eyes inevitably open, I wonder how it can just hang there. But then my father's indifferent movements that take him out of the toilet without a word answer that question. The yellow drop jumps from him to me, lands on my arms, a yellow spot surrounded by red blemishes and I let it lie there, the pain in my stomach forgotten about temporarily.

PHOTO 4 EXIT AND PANIC

I could still hear whispers. But this time there were words on the breath.

'Not now.'

'Please . . .'

'It's not the right time.'

'Please . . .'

'Just wait . . . another time . . . soon.'

'Why?'

Panic, four strides away from my bed, is talking to Exit. If I could not hear the words I could tell from the mist above their bed, their stifled to and fro lost in vapour lit by the small strip light that hung between them, its cord swinging from one to the other in the exchange of their breath.

'I don't understand.'

I couldn't see his face properly but I heard his voice. It was such a strange tone, thin and melancholic, proud and confused. Then a brief silence. A calm followed by a sudden, staccato screech as he lunged and kicked the duvet hard, his feet chopping frantically at the foam inside, so that in the darkness of the caravan I could see the duvet float, suspended by two white lines attached to my father. Then it came, the slow rumble of his earthquake, a murmur turning to a roar. He swore and cursed under his breath, his legs beating the duvet with increasing vigour.

'Stop it,' I shout to him.

But he has only just begun. Like other times, other thrashes in different locations, he will keep going. He couldn't stop himself. When he shouted my mother's name it was not in anger but in expectation of her calm. But she was off into the bathroom, the door slamming behind her, the snib being rammed into its hole. His shouting, his tearful rage, tore through the caravan, his fingers frantically slashed and sliced at the cotton of his pyjamas, the material wrapping itself in knots around his body.

He kept the momentum going for what seemed like hours, the sound of the pummelled foam adding slowly to the background hums and throbs of the caravan. I sank further into my Zed bed, hiding out even more but I left just enough room for the camera to poke through.

Click.

PHOTO 5 THRASHING

This is a blur this photograph, the image but not the memory.

Exit shouts from the bathroom, 'Ride 'em, cowboy !'

And the show is on, myself the audience, the silent witness to the caravan's pandemonium, an urgent clamour rushing to challenge the noise of the restless trees outside.

'Have you not done yet, for God's sake? How long does it take for you to get it out of your system?'

I shouted at them both, something feeble, something that would never get heard above the tumble of sheets and blankets or Exit's curses and insults, so I crawled over to Panic to grapple with his legs but not before I framed his legs in my new viewfinder. He was tiring now and I clicked before he stopped, before things got too quiet. Then, I pulled the duvet tight around his body and pinned the edges down with what weight I had. I didn't look at him, he didn't look at me. It had finished. Like before, like countless times before, he had gone from machine to cocoon, his long black hair falling over his bare legs as he grasped them to his chest. I looked out the window and found the branch I had been on many times with my head camera. I looked at the gnarled twisted bark and began to count the notches I could see through the window.

There was not a sound from Exit in the bathroom.

PHOTO 6 SELF-PORTRAIT: CHEST

I lay on top of the duvet while my father was dragged into sleep and shifted my gaze from the trees to watch the goose bumps speckle my body. I sat the camera on my bare chest pointing towards my face.

Click.

Portrait of . . . six taken, six left if I included the one from the tree outside. And I did. That Click was as real as the one playing races between goose bumps, his finger skidding round moles and recent, reddening scars.

HEAD PHOTO

I saw her in the pokey bathroom of the caravan, angry at me. She pulled me in and stripped me, tore the muck-caked clothes off me and lifted me, my eight-year-old skin blue with cold streaked by red veins, patches of brown mud, into the bath of steaming water. There were no bubbles, only a quickly surfacing scum that left my skin the moment it made contact.

'Why oh why oh why must you always get so dirty?' she said to me pushing my head into the water. She stopped for a moment and tied her long straight hair back, rolling up her sleeves to reveal mottled skin, the white of her bones showing through.

Then she upturned me, my face suddenly pressed against the walls of the plastic bath, my arse sticking up and out into the air. With a hand that was both familiar and firm, she rubbed vigorously, with the ardour of someone intent on removing even the slightest stain, the smallest unsightly blemish. I was silent. There was little to say that hadn't been said before. At five, at six, at seven. This was routine. To protest merely increased the velocity of the rub, to cry out or complain meant hot water poured into the most sensitive areas. 'You have to be clean, if nothing else, you have to be clean.' At the age of eight she could pull my arms above my head and lift me out the bath, spinning me around 360 degrees checking for any missed dirt. If she was satisfied she would bring out the towel and rub me dry.

One time, after a dizzying revolution, she confided in me with a deep sigh, 'It's a simple life for you isn't it, your father makes you dirty, I make you clean.'

PHOTO 7 INSIDE THE WOODEN HUT

The lead up to this was strong. A good photographer knew the photograph even before it was lined up, could feel it before it was even framed and this one was hanging over me. Thick. Heavy. Inside, the atmosphere in the caravan matched my mood, a blunt edge dragged through the air with the sluggishness of morning. I slid out of bed quietly not wanting to disturb a rare peace. Panic was not in his bed and Exit was nowhere to be seen.

I scrambled into my clothes and stepped back for a suitable panorama. My novice eye framed the domestic scene with intuitive zeal. Click and it could be done; but I chose not to. Already the discerning image maker, I decided the light wasn't right. The fledgling photographer seizes his trusty tool and makes off for the woods.

I hopped, skipped and jumped around the hut. Five hops, five skips and one long jump. In athletic tribute I moved to the rhythm of Panic. In the green glade, in the early shadows of the morning, we struck a tempo all of our own. I paused only to line up the shot I had not dared take, the lens to the glass of the cracked pane of the hut. Inside the hut I saw the rhythm I had heard; I saw the movement of Panic's black hair swirling around his bare shoulders and chest, his hands clawing his skin, dragging some unseen object from his head and throwing it to the ground in front of him. At one point his feet stopped and his upper body took on their tempo, pumping and slamming in agitated aerobics, his head reaching for his toes, his arms swinging, keeping time. Five swings to the left, five to the right. And then he was off again, jumping on the spot, grabbing at his head and throwing it in all directions.

Somehow above all the noise of his feet, his singing, his grunts and groans, he heard the click of the shutter. Time froze as did his stare, locking in an instant onto my startled eyes as they peered through the glass. I didn't know what to do. Instinct told me to run, to beat it back up that slope, rush across the brief clearing to the caravan, hop into bed and snore with the rest of them, feign sleep with the best of them. But I could not move. I was a stealth burglar on my father's intimacies caught with camera in hand, my fingers wrapped around the evidence.

The door burst open and I was hauled in. A cartoon yelp, animated trails and a slam of the door.

I was pulled into my father's dance, his strong arms held me to his chest, his black hair veiling my face. I could smell his sweat, feel the moisture of the beads, soaking my shirt, tickling my spine as they poured from his face. I could barely breathe the grip was so tight, I could barely see the spin was so fast. All the time, his mantra went on, more a drone than mystical words, reverberating from one ear to another. Four lines, eight verses, no deviation, simple repetition, and I was lost. If I closed my eyes I didn't feel so sick, if I closed my eyes I forgot where I was, except that I was scared to be in my father's dance. His hands bundled me higher on his chest so my head drooped over his back, the black hairs sprouting from his back tickling my nose, his fingers tingling my spine as they chased and counted vertebrae.

I can smell the image in my hands.

'Dad . . .' I say quietly, 'I'm feeling sick . . .'
'Dad . . .' I say loudly, 'I'm going to be sick.'

'Nausea makes us all strong. Let it go. Free yourself.'

'Dad . . . I really am.'

A trickle, then a jet, of vomit hosed my father first then spattered the floor, the walls, seemingly everything around me as the spin picked up rather than lost speed. *Ishi ta, ishi ta ishi ta, ishi ta* . . .

He held me above him, the last spurts of sick dripping onto his face, onto his skin, half chewed food lodging in his hair. He held me out and away from his body and at first I thought he was finally going to put me down, but he held me like a trophy, held for all to see, except there was no one to see. Just me and him. Even my camera lay abandoned on the floor near the door. I was close to the roof, his strong arms never flinching, and then as the sick changed to bile he pulled me downwards, my face to his, his mouth to mine. A furtive and strong kiss. And the taste was more than I could bear, the movement more than I could understand and I fainted like the novice I was, a crumpled, stinking bag of bones encased in his arms, wrapped by his hair.

PHOTO 8 MOVING LOCATION

This was one of many moving photos, some developed, all ingrained. The sensation of moving on hung over any location our battered caravan found itself in. Everything was temporary, roots didn't come into it. One morning my father roused me by a fit of anger. In one swift moment I went from my dream to Panic's rant and then to Exit's attempt to put her palm over his mouth, her knee into the back of his thigh. In my hazy state I saw both of them wrestle to the ground, an untidy heap spilling into the debris in the food preparation area. My waking thought was not of my father, though, not of his tumultuous morning call or the vicious kicks he aimed at the carrier bags brimming with rubbish, but of my camera, my film. All used up and nowhere to go. I needed more film. Now was not the best time to ask.

'Get up, get up, get up, get up.'

The irritable and urgent mantra went on and on until it was impossible for me to ignore it. Cans and tins flew over my head as strings of rotting cabbage hung like streamers in the still air of the caravan. Our mobile family was thrown into consciousness, stunned by my father's dangerous spontaneity. If only I had a film. The ticker-tape parade of rotting kitchen debris would be caught for posterity.

'We've got to go NOW.'

My father shouted at the top of his voice, scanning and rootling the formica surfaces for the keys to the car.

'But what's the hurry?' I heard myself say as I scrambled for clothes and cover from the kitchen top fallout as it spread in all directions.

'The hurry is the hurry is the hurry. That's all it is. We need to move. Move on. Another place, another time. Everybody must get up and out. Into the car. So we can go. Now.'

HEAD PHOTO

My mother is huddled in the living area with my father, each holding the other's hand. I wasn't supposed to be listening. I knew without being told, I knew the look my mother sent over to me every so often, checking to see if I was still playing with my toys, my proud furry bear sitting ridiculously on the Tonka truck waiting for theatre to begin. But I was too busy trying to listen and watch, surreptitiously trying to understand the conversation. My father leant across my mother's lap, bending his head as if he was atoning for something, ashamed to carry the weight of his head on his shoulders. But that wasn't it. 'Let me see, let me see, I'm sure it's nothing.' This was an inspection. She ruffled his lustrous black hair, parting it with her fingers, pressing the flyaway strands with her fingers. She peered at his scalp, used her other hand to run her hand over the skin. 'It's only small, it's nothing to worry about. You just want something to worry about, don't you, you'll find anything to worry about. It's nothing. Don't think about it.' . . . But there was something else I thought, my hands deep inside the bear's zip up stomach. I could tell so easily.

There was the glance she threw across to me seconds after she finished speaking, wondering if I had heard her words, understood the fragility of truth in her tone. Then there was my father, unreassured, putting his hands to the back of his head, pressing and brushing his skin. And there was something else, unspoken, unseen.

My father had already assumed his usual white knuckle position, a rigid posture that hunched his back and rounded his shoulders while his long hair fell forward with each wrenching gear change. Whatever journey this was, whatever time it would take . . . His eyes were grimly on the road ahead and he said nothing, not even a twitch or a cough. Everything was concentrated, controlled. On the quieter roads, at least. When he reached the main road it was a different matter. He wrenched first left, then right, then left again and with break-neck, body-jarring speed we found ourselves on the road being tooted and abused by other motorists as we swerved from one side to another, my father wrestling not so much with the wheel but with his temper. And losing, I thought. For a moment it seemed that our home was on two wheels, impossibly gripping the road. I looked at the scenery getting blurred and hid from the anger of the road users who screamed in car loads at our frightening launch into civilisation.

'White knuckle it is.' I said out loud.

PHOTO 9 WASTELAND

We drew to a grinding halt, the tyres of the car spinning briefly on the gravel, the caravan behind us tilting dangerously.

'Oh God,' Exit said surveying the scene as the dust settled around the car.

'Why here?'

It was a good question. We had travelled 36 kilometres, 300 metres from our scenic country spot to the desolate wasteland we now found ourselves in, that Panic had now placed us in with a sudden jerk of the hand brake. Everywhere there were craters filled with oil and mud in between burned out shells of prefab factories surrounded by a tangled mesh of wire, save for the gap my father poked the car and caravan through. I could hear the gate close behind, the cold sound of a bolt being drawn and Panic's feet churn the gravel underneath him as he walked in front of the car and rested on its bonnet. Somewhere a siren went off.

'Its safe here.'

Out front, seemingly impassive on the warm bonnet of the car, Panic's head jerked unsettlingly from me to the world around him and then back to me. I christened the film that had been bought for me 15 kilometres back. Even before the viewfinder was pressed against my eye, I could see the image of Panic, a face and an expression which blurred the difference between the camera in my head and the one in my hands. He was silhouetted against the brilliant sky and I remember that all of us, not just him but Exit and me too, were dark shadows toppling into the craters.

HEAD PHOTO

'Where's your father? Where in this godforsaken world is your father? I've been stuck in here for hours with nothing but you to keep me company and I've had enough. Some life. Where is he?'

My mother, I think, was addressing me but I did my best to convince myself she wasn't. I played with my Lego, the type of house I saw other children make whenever we stayed in a place long enough to go to school. A door and four windows, a slanting roof and a chimney and, if there was enough Lego, a garage with a swing door. I knew if she wanted to confirm that she was talking to me, she would come much closer to my ears and emphasise her point with volume. He had been gone a long time. He had sneaked out hours before, just after dawn, but I didn't feel I wanted to tell her. It was a question of loyalty but there was no answer I could give.

Exit couldn't wait. For something. She was scratching at the door to get out, kicking at anything that was near, punching the air, then

the wall, then back to the air again. I could feel her glance swerve
towards me and I just kept on looking at my Lego house, adjusting the
windows so that they swung out the way.

'Do something,' I heard her say, her stare locked on my hand
movements. I thought the tiles on the roof of the house were squint so I
carefully took each one off until I discovered the problem.

'Do something.' I heard Exit shout and she came and stood over
me, her stockinged feet less than 30 centimetres away from my house,
the hem of her dress 20 centimetres away from my face. I matched the
walls of the house with the lines on the earth coloured threadbare carpet
but, as I admired the structure and form of my Lego house, it was
demolished by stockinged feet and the bricks went flying into my face,
half the chimney lodging in my mouth, while the windows so carefully
adjusted were thrown clear across the room. My mother bent down,
leaning into my face so that her familiar, smoky smell smothered me.
She picked up the door to my house and laughed, the punch of her
breath making me blink the hair out of my eyes.

PHOTOS 10, 11, 12 SEARCHING

Home was where the caravan was. The heart didn't get a
chance. I stepped out the caravan in the fading twilight,
breathed in the remnants of the day's noxious fumes and
stared out at land that used to be something, used to be used
for something.

I wandered as far as I could, pressing myself to the mesh of
fence, turning my skin into a prickly grid, a stinging reminder
of my limits. But not my father's. I had plotted the route from
caravan to the furthest extent of the land. Six hundred and
fifteen strides, one and a half times my normal step and as near
as I could get to his walk. There were only really three possible
ways he could have gone.

The first was unlikely, for there was simply nothing to
walk to. You could stand as I did for a whole twenty minutes
and watch the grey potholes and vehicle tracks that started at
the wheels of the caravan and went on until the perimeter
fence. If my father had gone in that direction he was lying

between the ruts left by some heavy lorry, or perhaps in an extended pothole. But it didn't seem likely. There was no room to dance.

I clicked the first view.

The second direction was more likely – there were no trees, no huts, no secluded groves, but there were two sizable mounds, side by side; large enough to hide my father's movement, distant enough for no sound to carry to my ears. But there was a large pool of mud between the caravan and the fence with no other route to take that wasn't embedded with barbed wire or putrid heaps of rubbish. And like the boy scout I never was, like the Indian savvy I wanted to be, I could tell he hadn't gone that way. There were no footprints to be seen.

I clicked the second view.

And then there was a block to my detective thrills. Seven steps and three and a half strides in front of me was a tunnel. I wanted to step closer over the last few sprouts of barbed wire, I wanted to inch my way past the torn-down fencing which protected the tunnel's mouth, and listen. Listen because there was nothing to see. The tunnel from where I stood nursing the scratches on my knees, that had reopened the wounds from the woods of a different world a few days before, could have been endless. The horror films came jerking back into memory and I shivered at my mother's ghostly touch. It stuck out of the grey oily earth like a worm bisected, and disappeared into the ground with no end in sight either above or below. I listened for his voice, his movement, his words that made no sense. But there was nothing.

I clicked the third view.

HEAD PHOTO

When I was nine years and sixty-three days old my mother took me on a rare journey away from the caravan. We walked past the school where, since my father had stopped long enough, I went to school. It was a Saturday morning and I even recognised other children walking with their parents and for once I felt on an even keel with them. I lingered at windows displaying toys or chocolate. I felt injustice at the sight of the growing number of carrier bags in my mother's hands and nothing in mine. And there was a sense of revenge too when my bladder began to burn, necessitating a stop at a public toilet. I knew, just knew that she wouldn't like this stop but I also had begun to recognise that she couldn't stand by and ignore the need, since the accidental consequences could send her into a boundless rage.

But it wasn't that simple and I hadn't understood or thought through the ramifications of my actions. I had thought I could escape into the cold dank walls of the gents' toilet and be separated blissfully for a short while from the pressure of my mother's hand. But it wasn't like that. She wasn't about to let me loose in such a despoiled facility as a concrete convenience.

'You're not going in there alone. You never know who's in there and I would never know if you had done things properly and washed your hands.'

So she came in with me to my utter embarrassment. There was a strong smell not of urine or unwashed men but of pine disinfectant, and the only person inside the small building was an elderly attendant mopping the floor. I went towards one of the vacant cubicles but my mother grabbed my hand and pushed me in the direction of one of the urinals on the opposite side. 'Not there, there. Less things to touch. Less things to dirty your hands with.'

The old man looked vaguely affronted by her comment, which seemed to echo around the bare walls, and he gave her a long stare that betrayed his anger as well as his puzzlement when he took in the sight of my mother's arms folded resolutely against her chest. I stood with my back to her, terribly aware of her stare. I was tall for my age, taking after, no doubt, my father's unravelled genes, and I easily reached the mouth of the porcelain. Nervously, I unzipped my trousers and pulled out what my mother told me was my penis.

'I don't want to hear any other name for it.'

But nothing happened, even though there had been a genuine need, it had gone in the instant I stood there exposed. The longer I waited for the jet of urine the more I became aware of my mother's eyes, the clattering sound of the attendant's mop against the door of the cubicle. I thought of gurgling streams I had seen on our travels, I *thought of the water fountains in school, I thought of the film I had seen of a man in a barrel floating on the rapids of a river before it fell hundreds of metres over a waterfall. None of it worked. Then I heard my mother tut in impatience and heard her footsteps behind me. She looked over my shoulder, at my hands holding my sadly dry penis and shook her head, her grip on patience becoming less secure.*

'For goodness' sake, would you stop wasting time.'

She reached down and with one hand held my penis towards the urinal and with the other she reached behind and pressed her hand between my legs, between holes. Miraculously a steady stream of urine spurted out into the white urinal and she did not let go until the very last drop was shaken into the porcelain. But her help, surprising and effective as it was, didn't stop there. She wouldn't let me touch anything, wouldn't let me put away my little man, as I had heard it wrongly described. She raised my hands above my head as though I was under arrest and marched me to the basin. There she scrubbed my hands until they were sore, took a wipe and patted away any trace of urine. Then she tucked away my penis, zipped me up and proceeded to wash her own hands with the same resolute firmness. I could see the man looking at me but I couldn't been to look at him. I was nine years old and my mother had to help me do the toilet. That's how it seemed to me and, what was worse, that's how it must have seemed to him.

PHOTOS 13, 14, 15 THE TUNNEL

I took a photograph of the tunnel's entrance. A non-sensical waste of precious film but the urge was too great, the symbolism burning into me, a tentative fear that this black hole could be my last photograph. And I rushed another one, spurred on by the intoxicating feeling of my own mortality. I balanced the camera on a drum which lay in front of the tunnel and searched for a suitable stick or wire; then, I posed like a proud Scott in an Antarctic bliss, or a Sunday angler with his biggest and best catch, in front of the hole, the intrepid explorer framed for history to recognise his sacrifice.

The tunnel's entrance was almost exactly my size. If my father had made his hiding place in its depth he would have been bent over, restricted and curtailed in his dance, his movement. But as I stepped into the tunnel, listening to the quick click of my shoes on the metal I could not hear a sound. There was the distant drone of the wasteland, a background industrial noise clamouring for attention. But at the mouth of the tunnel there was nothing except my own breath in my mouth, my own pulse at the side of my head.

Of course I needed a flash. I had seen them. Big bulbous lights the size of a plate or small cubes of crystal. I had seen and loved the films that had some star quaking under their magnesium glow, old black and whites that had me crying but my mother rigid with boredom, *smile for the camera, Mr. Crystal, smile . . .* But the lucky bag camera Exit had bought didn't amount to that standard and the hole was all the darker for it. I would have to rely on my other camera, I decided. The one that didn't need film, didn't need flashlight.

I heard something ahead of me, just as I found it impossible to grip the tunnel with my feet. The surface beneath me had grown slippery, the air dank and colder and, on my knees in the tunnel with no light ahead or behind, I heard the sound of my father. Not an anonymous sound that might have curdled my wits and left me frozen with fear but a familiar, rumbled tone – a scent, of sorts, that I could follow, a picture I could see clearly, that would lead me straight to him.

Easier said than done. In the end I had no choice whether to walk or roll, the dilemma was solved. I slipped and tumbled, creasing my skin on rivets and grooves, burning my shins and thighs on the metal sides. I could have sworn there were sparks leaping out at me, shards of light jumping from my skidding feet; sparks that glittered in front of my eyes, all around my head.

And I woke up at the bottom of something.

Instinct was first. In the gloom, with fingers that felt that they had been bent and twisted, I squeezed a shot out of my camera which lay – thankfully – intact, close to my chest. There he was, larger than life, his long black hair sweeping around his shoulders, falling over his bare chest, sliding through hands held out in front of him. There was a low drone coming from somewhere. Could have been his mouth but I wasn't sure, it didn't sound like his mouth, didn't sound like it was coming from him at all.

He was sitting in a circle of candles, small white ones with dried up fountains of wax caked to the floor. He had been here a while, I thought. Since he had pulled on the hand brake and slammed the car door.

'Just in time,' he said, his voice choked, coated with dust and deepened by smoke.

'Just in time for what?'

He lifted me up, ignoring the blood oozing from one deep cut on my leg, and hoisted me over the circle of candles. He placed me in the circle, appraised my position and then rearranged my legs so that they crossed identically to his. Then he took my bare arms and again imitated their position. He stepped out the circle and looked carefully at the arrangement. With one last artistic touch up he stood back and said, 'Fine.'

'What's fine?' I asked.

'You are, son.'

I didn't understand. He started dancing around me, following the perimeter of the circle of candles; dancing just like he had in the ramshackle shed of a few days before, a few worlds ago. His voice echoed in the tunnel and bounced its way back up the shaft, his voice softening *ishi ta ishi ta ishi ta,* then growing in volume, in velocity, *ishi ta ishi ta*. He bowed my head and I covered my ears when he got too loud when the stamping stomping feet got just too close, the dust choking my cries. But he wouldn't let me not hear, not be there. 'Open your eyes,' he shouted, and he reached across the circle of candles and pulled my hands away from my face and replaced them in the position he had arranged them.

He skipped, hopped, jumped and jived for an eternity, long enough for me to feel the pulse of my wounds, long enough to be mesmerised by his body, his hair as it flew out in the darkness playing tricks with the light strobing it, filtering it before it smashed into my eyes. He leant forward, across the candles, right into my face.

'Sleepy?' he asked, and before I could answer he was off on his revolution again.

'Yes,' I replied and lied but what else was there for me to say? Again he swooped to within five centimetres of my face.

'Then sleep.' I looked up at him, into his eyes mad with darkness, and me falling again. For real, for certain. The bristles on his chin scraped my cheek, the soft wet tip of his tongue poked my lips, his large hands wrapped themselves around my rib cage. He stopped his movements, knelt beside me putting one hand over my eyes, the other between my legs.

'Yes,' I said again weakly and then there was no difference between the darkness in the tunnel, in his eyes, in my head. It was all the same.

PHOTO 16 SOMETHING HAS HAPPENED

Something had happened. I found myself staggering back to the caravan just as last light floundered over the wasteland. In the distance I could see an oil drum burning just outside the perimeter fence and behind me as I stumbled and raced in and out of the petrol coated potholes. I could hear music, muffled and indistinct, closer inside the fence. I felt tempted to take the camera and take a look. I thought I should be on the spot to record anything that my senses picked up. It was my duty as well as my ambition. But the sight of the darkened caravan distracted me from my vocation.

It was too quiet. I had been gone so long, Panic even longer, that I expected Exit to be patrolling the outside of the caravan. But she was nowhere to be seen. She could be brooding I thought, shackled to the table, pen in hand, vitriol in mind and steam coming out of her ears. I could see her too, sharpening the wedding knives that had played such an important part in their marriage; a wedding present that had lasted beyond their giver's modest expectations. Or she could be in the bathroom, scrubbing or rubbing or cleaning until there was nothing left to gleam.

Click. The sound of the shutter was the noisiest thing about being around that caravan and that scared me so much, filled me with such jittery dread that I almost hightailed it back to the tunnel, to its gaping bisected worm mouth, to look for my father again.

'Mother,' I half-shouted, standing on my tiptoes, and peered into the caravan. It seemed strange to use her given name.

There was nothing but gloom apart from the LED glow of my father's alarm, its blinking non-time telling me nothing about what was going on inside. The darkness was not unusual in itself. In our caravan, each one of us, at some point, had hidden ourselves in some fusty corner wishing the world, or at least the immediate one, to hell. But there was an edge, a twisting turning cut that worked its way into my stomach. I wished for a torch, a flash, a flood of lights to ease my guts but instead I girded them. No choice.

I heard Exit's voice first.

'Just you wait, you idiot, you fuck
one of these days you'll run out of luck.'

The chant continued as I shut the door as quietly as I could. Exit was sitting cross-legged in the middle of the living accommodation area, her brown hair everywhere but straight down, and while I crept across the room behind her, to hide behind the kitchen counter, I could see her pulling at its roots, twisting and turning it in spirals, screwing it tightly to her scalp. She was literally tearing through the family album, snapshots she had taken of the early days before I had been born, when there had been an unmovable house and mutual dreams. I had seen the album, at least its cover, many times. It had been brought out at times like these before, when my mother would sit in the caravan while my father drove maniacally somewhere or anywhere, and I saw her in the caravan through the back window of the car, turning one page and breaking down into a crumpled heap, eyes streaming, and then a few minutes later turning the page, with the same result. Sometimes, she took it into the bathroom and then I would hear the sounds but not see the movements. But this time, coming in from the wasteland, I had both sound and vision.

When she heard a careless movement she spun round, her hair barely following her and she shot me a stare that froze me to the spot.

'What the fuck do you want? Why oh why oh why must you always sneak up on me? What are you watching, what are you spying on me for? Go and play, just go outside and play and leave me alone.'

If her tone was menacing, then her attempt to get up, the slow coiling of her fist, the tightening of her neck muscles, was even more so, and I left. Through the window I saw her mouthing words I had heard her say to me before. *If it wasn't for you . . .*

HEAD PHOTO

When my mother fought hand to hand combat with my father, she never seemed to hold back. There was never just a slap, or a brief punch; there was always a volley of curled fists, always a cycle of slap, kick, slap, pull, that would go on until my father ran out the caravan to wherever.

'Get a job . . . clean yourself up . . . wandering to nowhere . . . stinking the whole place out . . .' were the snippets I caught. There was a sight which was repeated in various ways right up until the moment she left. She would hold my father's soiled underpants up to the yellow light of the room, swinging them like some terrible flag for an unmentionable country, shouting into his ear as he turned away from her onslaught.

'This is disgusting . . . do you think I want to be around you when you're like this? This room, this whole caravan, you, smell like a toilet. You and your son smell bad, turned bad. Your special son . . .'

And in a fit of anger or maybe it was just simply an urgent need for things to be different, to be clean, she unscrewed the top from a bottle of disinfectant and threw it liberally around her, on the clothes, on the walls, on my father, who curled up into a ball and rolled under the bed, away from the stinging shower. And then in a last desperate act before she too crumpled like my father onto the floor, she would pour the remains of the disinfectant over her head rubbing the liquid into her skin, tonguing it into her gums and between her teeth. And I remember the pause, the sobbing moment when all I could hear was bird song and the sounds of Panic and Exit crying, the pause that was broken by Exit tearing towards the bathroom, screaming in pain, clawing at her skin.

HEAD PHOTO

Here's another. There was a screaming match going on, a very one-sided event with me the sole audience, the lone frightened spectator. It could have been funny at first, some worn kind of slapstick that all three of us at some point had sat in front of the television and laughed at, as first cushions then books were thrown at Panic, who was standing forlornly in the middle of the living area. But it didn't stay funny. He was, as always, rubbing his head, pulling the long strands of black hair through his fingers. He was standing there taking each object that was thrown at him with cowering bewilderment.

'And what did they say, what did they say to you when you went up?'

My mother was in full flow, her arms gesticulating wildly when they weren't throwing something through the air.

'Let me get this right. You went up to the social work department. You told them that you hadn't received any letters because you don't have a home and that your child hasn't been at school because you never stayed in one place long enough. Is that what you told them? Is it? You're an idiot, that's what you are. An unthinking, uncaring fool who hasn't got two pence to rub together, who never wants to work and now, to make matters worse, you babble a lot of dangerous nonsense to some social workers. I should have gone, of course, but then that would leave you to stay here and look after the kid and that would probably be worse. You know what's going to happen now, don't you? Don't you?'

Exit raised her voice even more, hoping to get some kind of response from Panic, but all he could manage in the face of this barrage was a simple and quiet 'No.'

My mother went straight for him, trampling my teddy's soft stomach.

'They're going to start to take an interest in us, snoop around to see what kind of place we are bringing up a child in. And you know, at this point, I don't know what to say, I don't know what kind of home we are bringing up a child in. Do you?'

My father didn't say anything, he just fled from the caravan. Mother stared after him, shaking her head, then she saw me, reaching for my teddy trapped by her foot. She kicked the brown bear swiftly and viciously across the living space area. She walked into the bathroom, locked the door, slammed the lock on. I cried.

'I will not keep on protecting you,' I heard her shout from the bathroom window.

I didn't understand what she meant.

PHOTO 17 THE STRANGER

I went back after several hours in hiding, waiting for exhaustion. Not mine but Exit's. When I got there something was still not right. There was someone outside the caravan. Although it was dark, although I didn't have a complete view from my hiding place inside a tunnel fragment, I could tell there was someone there. There was the feel of a shadow, not just the sight nor sound of a shadow, but its feel. It was not my father, I knew that for sure, there was not enough height, not enough mane tumbling from what I assumed was the stranger's head. I shut my eyes, fingered my camera, useless in such dark conditions, and counted to ten. At five I heard the sound of shuffling feet echoing across the pools and puddles to my hideout; at eight I heard the door of the caravan open, and at ten I heard it close, then still. Deathly still. If I had a flash I would have caught everything, not just the shadow, but the caravan, the orange glow from the city beyond the one fire left burning at the perimeter of the fence. All of it would have been caught. Suddenly, after such a short time of naive joy at having a camera at last, I was struck by the limitations of such amateurish equipment. I wanted more. I had recognised limitations and I wanted a new and better camera.

I didn't go up to the door. There was no such confidence there and I was too tired from the long day, the early rushed start to gird my courage into some form or other. The window it was and I crept up to it through the darkness, watching for debris that might give away my approach.

At least I knew the distance between my head and the window. I was ten centimetres too tall for the sill, meaning that I ducked down in my stealth until the very last moment, when I raised my head so that my chin leant on the cold metal, and let my eyes peer into the gloom.

I saw Exit first, sitting cross-legged as she so often did, motionless in the centre of the living area of the caravan with its thin rug and worn couch; sitting and staring straight ahead towards the sleeping accommodation. At first I couldn't see what she was seeing, with my head camera zooming into one implausible situation after another. It was a stranger from the perimeter burning oil drums, a sentinel of the night garbed in weird and wonderful clothing, who had come to tell us stories of old and about the strange life of a different family of nomads with tattered clothes and unkempt hair; but then it was a man in a suit with a long metal lead attached to Exit's neck . . .

A light went on, the lamp beside my father's double Zed bed, in fact, and both suggestions proved to be wrong. Panic was standing facing Exit, stock still and naked; not a thread on him. Exit was staring back, equally naked, her head fixed towards a static television picture until Panic put his arms across his chest and bowed his head. Exit leant over to pick up my disfigured toys, most of which I hadn't played with in years – melted toy soldiers, battered old Dinky cars – any-thing that was within easy reach on the caravan floor – and threw them at Panic. My head camera was becoming unbalanced with surprise and shock and I reached for the Instamatic, even though there was not enough light. Somehow I had to catch the image of the bear with a deranged look on his face sailing through the air and landing on Panic's chest and staying briefly, fur sticking on hair, before falling to the floor.

This went on until Exit ran out of things to throw and it seemed then that her choice was to either retrieve the objects lying around Panic's feet or look for new, more dangerous objects to throw. I could see her put a hand on the lamp beside the couch, its stripey shade hanging limply to one side.

'No,' I heard Panic say.

'Yes,' I heard Exit say.

But she changed tack suddenly and rolled Panic's filthy white socks into a ball and threw them so that they momentarily paused on my father's straggly hair before falling to join the other debris. Then she fell about laughing, a rare sight, tears streaming down her face while my father stood there impassively, the look on his face not having changed from the moment I reached the window.

When I changed my view, when I moved from window to door as I clicked my way into this showing, a third-rate paparazzo trying to capture any action he could find, when I made my grand entrance on the farce played before my eyes, everything changed.

'Oh, here's our little man.' Exit said grabbing my legs.

'Don't . . .' my father began to say.

'Don't what . . . this is a family moment, a time for us to be together, to play a game together. Where shall I touch him? Is there anything you wouldn't like me to touch?

'No . . .' my father stammered.

Like a flash, Exit threw the lamp at him anyway, the shade colliding with his arm, the thin china falling and smashing into a hundred pieces on the floor.

'It's okay for you is it, it's okay for you to play games with our son, but not me, is that it? Well, more than two can play at that game . . . In fact, it's better when more than two play, isn't that right, isn't that what you always used to say until you got scared, scared of being caught? *Can't we play with our son together dear . . .?*'

She grabbed me and pulled off my shirt and vest then, tore down my shorts and pants, throwing them all into a heap in the food preparation area. We were all naked now, I thought. A splendid family snapshot.

'Go and stand beside your father,' she said firmly, without shouting.

I just stood there, frozen to the spot, my hands trying to cover everything I didn't want to be seen.

'Go and stand where I told you,' she screamed into my ear, smoke from her cigarette going in one ear and out the other.

She pushed me and I bumped into my father, who stood with his head in his hands saying over and over again. 'No, not now, not now . . .'

'Catch.' A book, an atlas of the world, flew through the air but I couldn't catch it, my hands were too busy trying to obscure my skin, my everything from sight.

The book fell between my father and me, our feet touching the coastline of Africa.

'Catch it, I said. And stop trying to cover up your genitals. I've seen them, son, I've washed them, from the year dot. You haven't got anything that I haven't seen, touched or smelt. Understand? Play the game and catch this.'

She reached for an empty baked-bean tin and I caught it tightly in my right hand. The jagged lid of the can sliced into the palm of my hand and as my fingers clenched the metal I felt the warm trickle of blood run across the lines on my hand.

'Oh God.' Panic ran from his spot and dived into the sleeping area, pulling the covers over his head.

Exit walked on her knees towards me, taking my hand in hers and gently turning the reddened palm towards her. She smiled and took my hand and placed it between her breasts, the blood smearing her pale skin.

'*You* understand, don't you? There is nothing of you that I haven't seen, touched or smelt. Nothing. Your father's an idiot, eh? He doesn't understand. What's a little blood between family?'

*

There's still more for this photograph, the image and the memory are there as intact, as sure as they ever were. I don't believe this photograph will fade with time, I don't believe the words or actions will ever diminish. How long has it been – six years, forty-five days and counting, since they took me, took all of us, away, and there it is in my head, here it is in my hand.

'Go away, go away,' he screamed at me from under the covers. I put my toilet-paper-wrapped hand to the rough material of the blanket and was about to pull it away from his trembling body when I heard footsteps outside the door. For some reason, out of some kind of scared instinct, I dived for cover.

'Is there anything wrong?' I heard a man's voice say. The stranger I had spotted from the tunnel had returned. A backpacker, an all-purpose passer-by peered into the gloom of the caravan. And for a moment it seemed he was on the verge of exclaiming something. A naked boy under a table with a blood-soaked temporary bandage, a trembling man under a duvet cover and a naked woman laughing on her knees surrounded by children's toys. But if he was going to say something he didn't get the chance. In a flash, Exit, shocked out of her manic reverie, jumped up and kicked the door shut in the stranger's face.

(Just before the door shut I had made a move for my camera and without time to even position myself or the photo, I clicked and hoped that intuition would guide the viewfinder.)

Everything changed in the caravan again, the game well and truly over. Exit pushed herself into her crumpled clothes and threw mine to me under the table and Panic wound himself up into a pre-flight frenzy.

'We've got to move. That idiot . . . nosy bastard . . . stupid fuck . . . it'll be them, come to get us, come to take us all away . . . Oh God, oh God, oh God . . .'

'Enough.' Exit shouted at him, first running across the living area to slap him on the face then secondly clutching her remaining clothes and rushing into the bathroom.

Panic rubbed his cheek and searched around him for his clothes.

From then on, whenever any stranger came near, it was a case of everybody to the floor until the danger, the strangers, had passed. It could have been bird watchers, anglers, trekkers, any number of people could have been walking past our battered tub of white metal. But it didn't matter, my mother vocalised my father's paranoia and everything was thrown into turmoil. We were waiting for the bomb to fall on us.

HEAD PHOTO

I remember this one well, another photo taken in the dark, another time when my head camera tried to influence my Instamatic one. It was too dark. There is nothing on the paper in my hands but it is still there in my head. There is nothing missing.

All the lights were turned off in the caravan. My mother had got up and ran about the living and sleeping accommodation areas and clicked them off. It could mean only one thing and I buried myself deep into the Zed bed's thin mattress, one eye poking out before the last light went off. Usually a light or two was left on to fend off one or other of our fears but when it went dark it meant grunts and groans . . . But it wasn't as dark as my mother thought. I could see her run back into the bed, her nightie riding up the back of her legs. Her shadow gave away her activities. She pulled the little used curtains beside their double Zed bed tighter together but their fit was imperfect and no matter how much she arranged and rearranged them, still a crack would allow the moon to light her face, her quivering shoulders. She straddled my father with a sigh, not of sadness but of relief, and she began to slowly move up and down. Panic was silent. If this was an effort for him, if this was even desirable for him, it didn't show. The only movement, the only sound came from Exit as she rode him, the pace remaining the same.

The sound of skin against skin slid its way across to me.

At first there was no other sound apart from this soft grinding but then I heard a growling monologue emerging from Exit.

'You can still fuck, can't you? You can remember where to put it, can't you, move your hips for Christ's sake, do you have to be always a lump of lead . . . God, as always, as usual I have to do the fucking work, don't I? But maybe I should give you more warning, give you time to get to the bathroom and wash. Jesus, do you ever think of taking a bath, of cleaning your penis even? It's disgusting, the smell makes me want to heave. Is that all you do when you wander the fucking countryside is tug at yourself and let it dry on you? Or our son, our son! It's like the dried up icing on a fucking Christmas cake. Or a wedding cake. Well, here's my present to you, darling.

In the half light, I saw Exit's body rise up above Panic's and then slam down so hard that I heard a gasp of air escaping from him while his body scissored, his head jerking up towards Exit's face. She repeated this again and again and the rasp of air coming from Panic turned into a cry of pain. But she didn't stop, and put one hand between his legs, the other on top of his face, holding him down and holding him in.

It only stopped when Exit pierced the caravan with a shrill cry, not a scream or a shout but something that I wasn't sure how to describe, and the head photo doesn't bring anything back to me apart from the violent momentum, the vicious tango being danced in front of my eyes.

But at least the rest was familiar. In a sudden movement Exit leapt off Panic and scrambled off the bed, running into the bathroom, slamming the door while Panic turned over onto his side nearest the wall and sobbed until either he or I drifted into sleep.

PHOTOS 18, 19 A BEAUTIFUL PLACE

Another location, another place for our home. We had arrived somewhere deep in the country. The photo brings out the sound of the caravan desperately clinging to loose stones, the sound of Exit's snores as her head bounces from left to right, limp with sleep. Panic's hands are still gripping the steering wheel, white-knuckle position secured, and then there's me in the back clicking this particular photo without thought for the jerky movement of the car. Within barely minutes of us arriving, with Exit beginning to rouse herself from sleep, Panic had jumped out the car not even bothering to shut the door, and made off up a steep path. Within two minutes of the engine being turned off, he had disappeared from sight.

There were two thoughts in my head. The first was more photographs, being suddenly inspired by the fading light of the day, the purples and reds of a dramatic sunset in such beautiful country. The second was a determination not to be around when Exit was fully awake.

I scrambled after Panic. Twenty steps to his sixty and there was still no sight of him . . . I was hot on the trail with the scent still warm. But my twenty steps to his sixty became slower and slower as the path he had taken stretched tighter and tighter over the curve in the hill. I took my camera out and turned around on the spot with little breath in my lungs but a pile of images, potential photos, a parade of panoramic landscapes in my head. But I reined in the ideas, linked my desire to the realities of my equipment and snapped one behind and one in front.

I sniffed the air expecting a scent, a linger of aftershave, a dose of sweat, a hint of direction. But in the end, there was only one way he could have gone – he had not passed me and either side of the path was a perilous roll into oblivion, a terrible somersault that would have kept him moving well beyond dusk. I picked up my pace, tried to make up for his longer strides and soon I was jogging, stones pushing into my soles through my soft shoes, bracken tickling and the gorse scratching my legs. In search of Panic, the scars of nature ever increasing.

PHOTOS 20, 21, 22 IN THE POOL

And there he was. It was his long hair I saw at first, his head framed in the middle of the image in my hand. A raft of black plants floating on the green water of a mountain pool. I hid behind a rock, 250 metres from the water. I noticed his clothes had been scattered, a sock hanging from a bush, his shirt stamped into the mud at the water's edge. There was no time and no desire to arrange his clothes into a neat pile. There was no point.

For Panic everything that mattered was impulsive.

I clicked first with my head camera, zooming into the pool, diving under the water, weaving my way through his legs and popping out the other side gasping for air. Then I clicked with the Instamatic. In the water Panic plunged under the surface, his legs kicking up, then disappearing from view. I crept closer, stalking to the point where I reached his shirt. And then for some reason I clicked again, the dislocated sleeves of the shirt rooted in mud catching my eye. Not a landscape nor a portrait but an abstract. And without thinking. In my pride I failed to notice Panic surfacing at the far end of the pool.

'Come on in, the water's fine.'

I practised an old trick, one I had done many times before the Instamatic and maybe even before the head camera. In the past I dived and ducked and whirled around, suddenly coming to a halt with my two thumbs and fore-fingers framing a sight at the edge of the road. A hitchhiker, a dead hare, anything that I could quickly get into my fingered viewfinder before my father blurred it with speed. This time, with Instamatic in hand, I turned quickly on the spot and clicked.

'See, it's lovely and warm. Take your clothes off and jump in.'

I looked around for other people but Panic had found a secluded spot off the treacherous path. I looked around too for a hut where Panic might dance or chant or pull at the back of his head, and then the more I thought about it, the more I got lost in my daydream. The camera, the photos, my art suddenly forgotten, I saw him swinging me about or leading me into a tunnel filled with candles, holding my hand telling me *everything's fine*. I saw him, felt him lying beside me, his eyes wide open, staring straight ahead. An arm outstretched, reaching, touching. Me.

He dived under the water again, his back arching, then disappearing, leaving the ripples to make their way to the muddy bank. I took my clothes off, quickly stripping to my shorts and raggedy vest. I wanted to take the camera with me, submerge my images, go where my head had already been, but I knew that Exit's first and last present to me would not stand the strain, would break in the depths, and waterlog my ambition with leaking memories.

One step at a time. Five steps and the water would be at knee height, a further seven and the lukewarm water would be flattening my shorts, shocking my stomach, and beyond these twelve steps I didn't know, didn't want to know in many ways. It was impossible to estimate, for after twelve steps the water changed to a dark green and I could no longer see the bottom.

Then my legs were brushed by something and I feared a carp, or a shark for that matter; a steady stream of warmth flowed through my legs, inside my thighs. Then Panic jumped through and up out of the water, barely 20 centimetres from my face. His long black hair swatted me off balance so that I fell backwards as he surged through the water.

'The best feeling in the world,' he shouted.

And I fell backwards, the sky, the world, in fact, rushing to the horizontal until it stopped or I stopped, the water saving me, floating me. (The focus is fuzzy here for some reason.)

Panic lay on his back while his long arms stretched down to grab hold of my ankles and we were off, a slow moving punt through the pool to the far side. While I sailed across the water my head camera zoomed above me and I loved what I saw. A moment of peace, no Exit turning me inside out, no tumbling games or caravan fumbling, no strangers throwing cans after the car. *Never come here again. We'll set the dogs on you if you do.* Just Panic, just my father pulling me across the water, synchronised to fate. Fifteen ripples, ten of his strokes, and we were at the other side of the pool and I felt his arms lift me towards him, his callused skin chafing the skin under my armpits, his beard scratching my shoulder blades.

On his back, my legs resting against his hips, knees bent either side of him, I saw a view that must have been snapped by a hundred photographers but never by this fledgling clicker, never by my head, which zoomed and panned taking in a panorama that struck me dumb. I wanted to touch the back of his head, the place I had seen him claw and tear at with his own hands, but when I tried he took my hands firmly but gently and pressed them against my chest, spreading my fingers one by one until each thumb touched my nipples. Gazing at the pattern the fingers made, his eyes lingering and lingering until his voice broke the silence.

'Never touch my head,' he said gently.

HEAD PHOTO

'You're not going out like that.'

An inspection was needed before any attempt was made by me to contact or see or be in the outside world. It wasn't simply a case of a quick clean-up, a brush of the teeth, a comb of the hair, and I was free. She would strip-search me for signs of grime, my best clothes held up to the yellow light of the caravan and checked for holes.

She was as thorough as a doctor looking for disease. She made me raise my arms above my head while she peered closely under my arms. She stroked the skin at first, tugged the hair that had started to grow and then put the tip of her finger to her nose. Dissatisfied with the scent she reached into her bag, and pulled out a deodorant stick which she applied roughly to both my armpits. She told me to brush my teeth, wash my hair, and then I would be allowed to put on my clothes and go out. Then she checked the nails on both my feet and my hands.

'How could you let this happen?' she suddenly shouted, the power of her voice pushing me back onto my heels, my balance saved only by my mother grabbing my hands and clipping the nails. I was petrified by this point, petrified by embarrassment. Firstly, because I was concerned that people passing would look through the uncurtained window and see me lined up for inspection. We were not in the country this time, there wasn't just the possibility of a lone backpacker peering into our caravan world. The whole town could have seen and I imagined a crowd would gather and in my head the photograph was already taken. A hundred, maybe two hundred, people pressed against the window laughing. Secondly, I could feel the cold air of the caravan around my genitals, the rush of blood to and fro as it decided just how excited it should be.

But by this point I was losing the erection battle for some reason – no matter how much I kept my mind blank or full of mundane thoughts, the blood seemed to flow forward – and outward. My mother stood in front of me, looking straight into my eyes. I couldn't return her look, there was something about the direct stare which pinned me, rooted me to the spot with inaction. There was a smile on her thin lips and then I felt her hand on my penis, a gentle touch that peeled back my foreskin slowly. The she bent down and for a brief moment I could feel her breath.

She stood back up, letting my still-semi erection fall awkwardly back to its resting place.

She was looking into my eyes but all I could see, all I wanted to see was the brickwork on the wall that ran the length of the lane outside.

'You need to wash that.'

I could see her smiling and looking down at me again.

'You never know, you might meet some nice girl while you are out.'

I didn't understand her. What girl would pass her inspection?

PHOTO 23 MOUTH

I shouldn't have been out so late. No one told me this, no one shouted this until they were blue in the face or otherwise. I just knew. I just knew that trying to find my way back to the caravan through the dark with treacherous drops to the left and right and an unmarked, uneven path in front of me was going to be hard.

This photograph is of my mouth. I remember stopping suddenly on the path and taking the camera out from the waistband of my trousers and holding it up to my face. There was hair in my teeth. Long strands of black hair, flossing my teeth as I ground them together. The rest of the hair, the rest of my father was back here in that mountainside lagoon. At least I thought so. In truth, I didn't know where he was. One minute we had been staring at the evening sky in silence his arm around my shoulder, mine around his waist; a brief moment of peace and quiet and then the next moment he was gone, ducked under the surface of the water and without a ripple he sped away. He was like a deer, frightened by the slightest rustle of a bush, and I was suddenly marooned, or rather, bereft and adrift and left to my own devices, with a bunch of black hair wrapping my fingers together.

There was nothing else to do except take the path back down to the caravan and trust that Panic would make his own way there. He always did, these excursions away from his family were second nature to him after all these years on the move. Maybe they were first nature too.

HEAD PHOTO

My mother is cradling my father's head. He is lying on the couch in the living accommodation area, his long legs sprawled over the faded material, his arms stiffly by his side. She leans so that her hair falls into his face, a veil that obscures my sight. But I know what is happening. I always know what is happening. For them it's hidden, for me it's clear; clear then but even clearer now. She massages his scalp, kneading the skin through the long black hair. He winces when she gets to the lump. 'Ssh,' she says and he quietens to a whimper. It sounds as though he is crying and he probably is. I look at my mother but I don't expect to see tears. Her hands are attending my father, but her eyes are somewhere else, perhaps looking out the caravan windows to the black wall of trees surrounding us at that particular moment, at that particular stop. But the stare doesn't seem to be going anywhere, at least nowhere I can see.

PHOTOS 24, 25 THE CHASE

I was being watched. Alongside the path in the trees and gorse bushes someone was matching my pace, step for step, pant for pant. I just kept going, thinking of the young backpacker for some reason, who had come back to spy on us. Stupidly, I tried to take a photograph of my flight, holding the Instamatic in my hand and clicking wildly from left to right in some attempt to capture the movements of whoever was in the bushes. Exit ran out in front of me, her eyes bright even in the moonless night, and she bent down to grab my legs as I ran into her. She upturned me so that my legs gave way and my head came crunching down onto the path. She tried to lift me up but by then I was getting too heavy for her to simply lift me into her arms. I couldn't be carried so easily any more.

'Idiot, look what you've made me do.'

I could feel a wound at the back of my head, a dampness that could have been blood or mud or both.

I asked her why she did that.

'Why were you running from me?'

'Have you been with your father again?'

There were too many questions and Exit smacked my face, not liking either the questions or my tone.

'You're coming back right now.'

I asked her where she thought I would go anyway.

She slapped me again on the other cheek and I got up and started to run down the slope. Back home was all it could be, the battered caravan, the tiny Zed bed, the thin sheets, the flattened pillow was all there was. But Exit stuck her foot out and I tripped over it, taking a dive onto the path and this time I felt mud and blood coat my chin. My jaw felt suddenly numb.

Exit crouched down beside me, her mouth close to my ear.

'Did I interrupt a cosy little evening swim with your father? You think I didn't know what you were doing, what *he* was doing. It's disgusting, revolting, and I'm not going to stand for it. Do you hear me, do you understand me?'

My ear went as numb as my chin felt but there was hearing enough left to isolate footsteps running from the path further up the hill. With an effort I turned my head to peer back up the hill and saw a shadowy figure that could only be Panic, his long hair in motion with his frantic step.

'Oh, here he comes.' Exit said standing up, turning to face him, her hands curling tightly into fists. 'Here comes the fucking cavalry!' I wished I had strength enough to reach for my camera that moment, I knew in my naive photographer's heart that this was a good image, as dramatic as they come, as atmospheric as can be, and yet I was stiffly glued to the ground, pinned down with both pain and Exit's left foot.

Panic was almost beside us when Exit shouted, 'Why you charging to rescue your son? Eh? Why you worrying about him?'

But Panic didn't stop, he jumped over my body and kept on going down the hill, with only the smell of his sweat and a few loose hairs lingering above me. There he goes, I thought.

'Typical, just bloody typical. Where you running to?'

But her scream fell on distant ears and she bent down and said in such a different voice that I felt she had slapped me again, 'Come on, dear, I'll help you up and we can go back down to the caravan ourselves. We don't need him. He's a fool. It can be just you and me.'

PHOTOS 26, 27, 28, 29, 30, 31 PANORAMA

Caravan boredom.

First I was pressed against the window, tonguing the glass, playing with the mist that formed, then fled; then I was taking a panoramic view of the darkness with my head camera. It took six shots, I had worked out, to take in the full shape of land that was barely visible beyond the drift of light from the caravan. My head in exact eight centimetre shifts revolved from extreme left to extreme right, my eyes opening and shutting with each precise movement. With precious shots remaining I combined my cameras, synching one movement with another, combining one viewfinder with the other. It had taken a long time to work out the distances, but then time was something I had plenty of. My eyes were locked steadily ahead, my body an inelegant tripod, so that there would no gaps in the vista, no jumps in the smooth panorama.

My father was somewhere. Again. Perhaps he was back up the rocky path, at the lagoon, swimming at the midnight hour, chanting, pulling, tearing. Something. Anywhere.

In the flicker of video light, Exit was transfixed by a film. She had her back to me and the only movement taking place was her left hand taking long draws on a cigarette while her right took sweets out of a wrapper. One sweet every forty seconds, one drag every ten.

HEAD PHOTO

And then another midnight inspection. They happened infrequently, never at regular intervals. They happened when my mother's large brown eyes got wild. And they were wild now. It's late, the time being well beyond midnight, but the principle remains the same, the actions routine and efficient. I wake to find her leaning over me, sniffing the air above me. As I am wrenched from dreams, she pulls back the covers and touches my pyjamas, feeling for wetness, for the tell-tale signs of spilt urine. Or worse. Even if there is nothing there and there never has been, she raises me so that I am sitting dazed in the Zed bed. She unbuttons my top and discards it, she pulls the trousers down and squeezes them over my feet. She pats my skin with the palm of her hand, pushing me to one side to touch the cotton sheets and all this is done in silence. She presses firmly on my shoulders which I know means 'don't move', and whether it is the dead of winter or not, I am left with goose bumps rippling over my skin as she gets another pair of pyjamas and puts them on me. She presses my shoulders back down and I lie on the mattress thoroughly awake while she tucks the sheet tightly over my chest and goes back to her bed. Soon I can hear her snore, while all I can do is count the taps of a branch on the window, the barks of a dog, the revolutions of a can in the street.

All this time my father has stood in the shadows in the kitchen, hiding behind opened cupboard doors. Watching, unmoving. He had said nothing, not interrupted my mother's ritual and nor had she interrupted his. This was our family, I thought.

PHOTO 32, 33 MOVING AGAIN

A photo for motion, an image from motion. I heard a bang, a car door slam, and assumed it was the film, but Exit didn't jump or stop eating or smoking. Then I heard an engine start and I knew it wasn't the film.

The caravan lurched forward three times, each sudden movement keeping us off balance and then with one more vicious spurt we felt ourselves moving, turning a tight corner, the video sliding off its stand, the cigarettes spilling from their packet, the sweets spewing their contents onto the floor. Exit jumped up in a state of confusion and threw her cigarette down, still burning, while she rushed to the window of the living accommodation area. As did I.

Exit and I fought for space at the window, arms and legs clashing as I tried to see past her.

'What is he doing, the fucking idiot? He just ups and leaves without a word.'

But there was nothing she could do. We were already moving fast enough to make any kind of attempt to reach the car impossible. This was not the movies and there were no stunt men around to do our job for us.

'I'll kill him if he doesn't kill us first.'

She moved away from the window long enough for me to press my face to the glass and get dizzy and frightened by the swirling branches colliding violently with the side of the caravan.

I thought I knew what had happened. The young backpacker again, the brief interlocutor of our caravan domestic had returned to take us away on his journey, to take us onto the open country roads back to a house I had not known, shrouded by years from my memory. He was a smiling saviour hijacking us back to the past. *Take me away from here.* But then the smile was replaced by my father's. It was not the same smile. It was full of teeth, a jungle of hair obscuring most of his face. He was driving the car out of the clearing, onto the track road, precariously fast down the steep track we had ascended.

There was nothing I could do. We sped down the track towards the tarmacked road, with my father seeming not to care about the potholes and bumps which nearly tore the caravan from its link to the back of his rusty car. While Exit went into hyper mode, hitting the kitchen units, punching the air, I strained out the window, no longer trying to communicate, realising that I could not get through to Panic even if he heard me. This was worth a photo, I thought, even with precious few left, this pandemonium inside and out had to be recorded. First I trained the viewfinder on my father's hunched back, quickly having to decide when to snap. One moment both hands were on the wheel and the next both were off and clawing at his back or pulling his hair and wrapping it three times around his head before stuffing it in his mouth. I chose the latter, I was after all, hanging out the window, my head close to being severed by wayward branches, and I was not going for any ordinary image, somehow I had to capture the moment of relentless confusion. And his hands frantically attacking his back seemed appropriate.

Turning to the interior of the caravan I caught Exit in

mid-air leaping from a unit in the kitchen area to their Zed bed in the sleeping area. Then I tucked the camera into my shorts and ducked down between the humming fridge and the cooker, feeling something like safe between the white metal, while to the right of me Exit collided with furniture and threw herself around, acting as if there was no tomorrow.

HEAD PHOTO

Motion was always there. Early, early memories of my mother holding tight onto my father's waist as the car raced around a country corner. My mother was calm but her inner peace was beginning to fray at the edges while my father's mania was growing. Every five seconds he would look over his shoulder, his hair sweeping across the back of the driver's seat, his eyes scanning the view out the back window.

'There's no one there, there's nothing to worry about, just keep your eyes on the road in front.'

Each word was almost spelled out by Exit, her voice simmering with control. My father blurted out semi-sentences, phrases badly constructed, construed by fear.

'There were two men . . . I'm sure of it . . . there were two men driving a car . . . they looked like police, the ones from our last stop . . . I'm sure, I'm sure, I'm sure.' My mother petted his head, carefully avoiding the lump,

'You're not sure, you're just scared. Nothing's going to happen. Everything's all right.'

While they found some way of comforting each other, all I could think about was the road safety talk I had at my last school, at the last long enough stop. Stop, Look and Listen. It seemed to me my father had forgotten all about that.

PHOTO 34 BY THE SEA

As I clicked the view, Panic spoke to me in a voice I barely recognised, could only just remember. He was calm.

'They're on to us,' he told me.

CLICK   47

I asked who.

'*They* are,' he replied watching the pebble fly further than the previous one.

Again I asked who they were. I persisted, slipping my hand into his pocket. He tensed almost immediately, surprised, I think, by the touch.

'Don't touch the stones,' he said.

'Why?' I asked, taking my hand out of his pocket.

He turned around on the spot, a twirl from his dance, a spinning Panic only I had seen in all its glory. He was quick, quicker, I thought, than Exit knew, since I had never seen him dance in front of her. It was our secret. Our secret. He reached out and gathered me roughly into his arms, holding me by the belt of my trousers and the collar of my shirt. He was joking.

'Always with the questions, always with the questions. And a one . . . a two . . . a three . . .'

I felt myself getting dizzy, the belt chafing my waist, the blood rushing and staying in my head as the collar tightened around my neck. I could see the ground rushing towards me then the rotten wood of the pier ten centimetres away from my face − if I'd had time to stick out my tongue I felt that I could have licked the salt from the planks.

'. . . And a four . . . a five.'

And then he let go. I couldn't believe it. In that split second before I hit the water, I thought of myself above his head in the battered hut, underground in the dark tunnel, underwater in the mountain pool, between his long arms as they thrashed the air . . . I saw his hair falling in front of his shocked expression, his face looming towards me, and I felt everything was being lost. Especially touch.

The water was so cold as it poured into my open mouth. I knew there was a dent in my head where I hit an oncoming wave, or perhaps it had been a rock hidden beneath the surface of the water. But there was no time to judge anything. I flapped and screamed and shouted and for a moment, looking up through the crash of water, I thought I could see my father looking down at me from the jetty above, his legs buckling and bending, his arms up around his head. And *now* he dances . . . I thought, but perhaps it was just the waves pushing and pulling me, for within 30 seconds I felt his arms grab hold of me, felt the palm of his hand pushing my chin out of the water.

Everything was a haze. As he bundled me out of the water and ran towards the car, the world seemed to be going haywire, a confusion of colours and sensations; I felt cold, chilled to the bone, yet it seemed to be warmth that flooded my body; I could see nothing of the beach or the sea, yet I could see Exit staring at me, her face close to mine. She had not been there and yet suddenly there she was, intimate in a way only she knew. A brush, a nail brush, that lay beside the bath, an adult cleaning utensil that I had not yet endured was suddenly all over me, on my chest, between my legs, then vigorously between my buttocks, and all the time her face, a gaze of unwavering concentration, pressed against mine. I thought to myself, how could I be dirty?

No one had given me the kiss of life.

She put soap into my mouth.

'Sea water is filthy.'

My father slapped my face, then brushed my hair with a gentle stroke.

I couldn't answer.

'What happened?' Exit demanded

'He's been in the water,' Panic replied while slowly but surely backing away from Exit's frenzied movements, as she rubbed my skin deep into the bone. Within eight seconds he had surveyed the chaotic scene – thrashing arms, pools of sea water, my squeals – and run out full pelt without a backward glance.

'That's right, your son's half-dead and you run away.'

She cursed him and knelt down beside me, stroked my hair gently with one hand, placing the other onto my face so she could jerk my eyes round to hers.

'Did you jump or were you pushed?'

PHOTO 35, 36   SENSING THE END

My mother got her name Exit on a strange day. My
father had parked the car on the flattest ground I had ever
seen, two strips of tarmac as far as the eye could see, our
shabby hull of a home a striking blemish on the landscape. It
was a beautiful day, blue skies, no clouds and a gentle breeze.
There was an idyll there, I just had to look, just had to feel to
find it. There was a sense of calm while I watched the world
from a rug my mother had put out on the grass at the edge of
the tarmac. I was counting the reflectors at the side of the old
runway, counting them as far as I could see in either
direction. It was taking a long time. Each time I managed
to get a little further, imprinting the red reflectors in my head
but after twenty-two or twenty-three I would lose my
perception, horizons shifting with the confusing glint of
the sun, and I would return to the beginning. I counted
out loud and for once Exit didn't complain. She seemed to
be somewhere else, even though she was right beside me. I
clicked the view of the runway and sensed Exit moving
behind me, the cold touch of sun cream on my bare back,
her smoky breath whistling in my ears.

'It's going to be up to you from now on, up to you.' I
didn't know what she meant but could find no question that
she would want to answer. She squirted the cream onto my
bare legs and rubbed it down to my ankles and up to the top of
my thighs, lifting the thin cotton of my shorts so that she could
spread the last drops.

'Do you know what I'm saying?' she said. I didn't and she
got up abruptly.

'You will,' the gentle tone elevating her voice, 'You will.
Everybody has to know when to go through the door marked
EXIT and that time, for me, is now.

I watched her walk into the caravan. I saw my father, a
small speck in the middle of the nearest runway. I could see his
arms waving in the air, as though he was semaphoring an
incoming plane, planting his hands on top of his head and

grinding his palms into his scalp. His signals were confused. The plane will crash.

The last time I saw her, there were no arguments, no shouting, or hitting or intimate inspections. She walked out of the caravan, a bag in her hand and without a backward glance walked down the runway, the opposite direction from my father's position, and from me, gleaming with cream in the sunlight. I took a picture of her walking into the sun. Then I understood. My mother's lips were mouthing the word EXIT when she passed, a strange half-smile on her lips, her face as resolute and as impassive as I had ever seen it. She always meant what she said, always carried out her threats, and never did anything she didn't want to. And exit she did.

HEAD PHOTO

My father laid his head next to mine on my Zed bed pillow. I was nine going on ten, my father sad going on to cry, his head shaking, big teardrops splashing down onto the pillow. Somehow I felt I was expected to take an arm and pat his face or wrap it around his shoulders in some kind of embrace. But it seemed strange, my tall, huge father to be cuddled and held like a baby. It felt confused. In between sobs he said to me, 'You're everything to me.' He slid his arm down my chest under the waistband of my pyjamas and cupped me in his large hand. 'I mean here,' he said into my ear while he slid the hand back up to my head, his palm encircling my scalp. 'And I mean here.' All I could think of was to say 'I know, Dad.' And that seemed enough to stop his tears but when he had gone back to his bed it was nearly enough to start mine.

PHOTO 37, 38 THEM

This should be a striking photograph, full of strong tones and pathos, but it has developed into a muddle of greys, sharp edges softened into nothing.

They came for us, just as Panic had promised.

He had not said a word to me. He either didn't care or he cared beyond words. He didn't dance but neither did he cry.

He stayed in bed most of the time, rolling from side to side, chanting rhymes and rubbing his scalp, pressing down on the lump that could be seen through his thick black hair. When eventually he did get up 36 hours later, he found me still sitting on the rug, my Lego house built into a mansion, unhampered, unkicked by Exit's legs. I lay down on my front, burying myself into the rug, and watched him through one of the upstairs windows. He moved slowly, an awkward mechanical step, and after eight he fell to his knees, letting his fingers burrow deep into the dry soil. He was smiling strangely, a prelude to something usually, and opened his mouth about to say something but nothing came out. He didn't take it well. He crammed his fingers down his throat until he retched. *You have to speak your mind at all times,* Exit had always said when she held me upside down, when she pinned me to the floor, scrubbing brush in one hand, my bear in the other. And this is what she meant. In order to speak your mind you have to reach into your mouth and pull it out, grab a hold and let truth come out. It wasn't coming easily for Panic. Whatever he needed to say had got caught in his throat and seemed to be slowly choking him.

He stopped abruptly and rushed over to scoop me up into his arms carrying me to my Zed bed. His hands pressed into my chest, his long fingers slipping between my shirt buttons and his head tilted to one side as though he was trying to see something lurking on my chest. There were still no words or chants, only a low groan that found no sense in my head, and when our eyes met there was nothing but confusion in his stare, but he was brimming with something, I could see that – whatever was stuck in his throat was cutting off his air supply and he went redder and redder as he leant over me until I heard something pop. I still don't know what it was, but he ran inside the caravan and the next thing I knew, the next thing I saw, was Exit's clothes flying out the caravan door, shirt sleeves taking in air and taking on life, tights wrapping themselves around hats as they hovered above the tarmac in the breeze. The clothes were followed by bottles and jars and tubs – all of Exit's cleaning materials along with buckets and brushes and cloths, hitting the tarmac, cream from plastic bottles spilling over the bristles of her favourite brushes. In between spasms of clearing out, Panic would peer out the door and look past the rundown airport buildings to the main road.

Them.

In the distance a car kicked up dust and I turned the attention of the camera to the oncoming cloud. I focused on the cloud rather than the car racing towards us and I watched with a strange sense of calm the way the dust blocked out the horizon behind the car. Panic stopped his clearance and jumped from the caravan. His face was boiling, and there was a thin streak of blood coming from his lump, the target he had aimed for at other times, in the woods, in water or in tunnels deep beneath the ground.

'We have to get out now. Right now, right this second.' He lifted me and threw me into the caravan.

'You . . .' he said to me, looking at me directly . . . 'put your back to the door and if they start to push it you push back.'

He made it as far as the battered car when the car with two men and one woman inside screeched to a halt beside us. They jumped out and started running as they saw Panic get into the car, the men clasping their suit jackets as they ran with the woman maybe two metres behind – it was difficult to tell looking out the small caravan window. My father managed to get inside the car and was about to start the engine when one of the men stood in front of the car, his hands on the bonnet, while the other pulled at the driver's door. The woman went past them and ran to the caravan door. I did what I was told and dug my heels into the thin carpet.

I could feel the weight of the woman's shove increasing, the thump of the door echoing slightly from the thump of the car door as the taller of the two men wrenched it open from my father's grasp. He reached inside and pulled my father out from behind the wheel, the other man joining him to quell my father's long arms as they lashed out, hitting both of them at least once. And while I held firm, doing my duty as I far as I knew it, I saw a flash of metal in the dim sunlight and two bands of silver, one wrapped around my father's wrist, the other, I assumed, locked to the steering wheel. With an unsteady hand, bumped and jostled by thuds against the door, I captured a sad moment

With a sinking heart I watched my father slump over the wheel, as though his usually ultra taut body had suddenly been broken, and then I saw the two men make their way to the caravan to add their weight to the woman's shoulders.

Click. A last image shot from the hip as the world crowded in.

*

I heard what they said. They didn't really make any attempt to lower voices or wrap in whispers their theories about me. As Exit would have said – if you are in deep water you are not expected to be able to hear anything going on around you, you're meant to be too busy drowning. They watched me clinging to my teddy bear, stroking its furless body, kissing its eyeless eyes and they smiled.

The affection he's showing for the bear is classic really, isn't it. There is always a sense of reassurance in self-induced regression. He knows he's too old for the comfort of such a childish toy and yet he will gladly embrace what he sees as better, happier times as represented by the bear.

I was saying nothing. I had been separated from Panic and placed in some concrete building with its bare rooms and hospital-like atmosphere. I had no idea where he was. My last sight of him had been the back of his head, his hands clamped to his lump while he shook his head in disbelief and deep agitation. He was watching the social workers put all his belongings into white bin bags while the few things that we could call our own were thrown into black bin bags, but not before they noticed the camera round my neck.

Is this your camera? Did you take pictures with it? What sort of pictures did you take? And what about your Dad, did he take pictures with it? What sort of pictures did he take?

Where are the other films?

I was still saying nothing. I just hugged the bear I felt nothing much for, checked the zip on his back and fingered with satisfaction his full belly. I was saying nothing.

FRIGHT

Note. The following tapes were found by the
authorities at the scene. They have been
transcribed into chronological order. Long pauses
or mono-syllabic utterances have been taken out
and the remaining audible sections numerically
identified.

TAPE 1 SECTION A

'Get out the car, get out of it now.'

He slammed the door, missed my fingers but got my toes.
I had ringing in my head and bells in my ears.

'Don't scream, don't shout. People will hear and we don't
want people here.'

'Get out the car and shut your mouth. Or I'll squeeze
more than your feet.'

Me and brother Jake. A fine young man, a good dear
brother, a young soul with everything to live for.

'Get out the car and take your clothes off.'

I laughed. Ha ha. High-pitched barking. I couldn't stop. I
can't stop.

'Get out the car and take your clothes off.'

'Ho ho.'

'And stop laughing.'

Jake, silly Jake, didn't take his clothes off. Wouldn't take
one sock, one glove from his person. Deep mid-winter,
doctor, deep mid-winter when all the trees shook with snow,
dangled with ice.

'Take off your clothes and lean against the car or I'll give
you such a hiding your head will spin.'

Head's spinning now, Jake's was spinning then, poor boy,
poor brother. Just a kid. 'You're an idiot, d'y' hear, a complete

and utter nincompoop. I'll make you wish you'd never been born.'

And he did. He did make Jake wish he'd never been born. Made his ears into cauliflowers, their leaves dripping; made his nose a tomato, overripe and soft; made his mouth pulp with dental seeds seeping out. He was a man who knew how to use his fists.

'And what about you?'

'What about me, doctor? Am I all right?'

'And what about you?' he said to me.

'I'm naked,' I said to him.

He licked his lips, smoothed his moustache and said, 'So you are.'

'You must stand. You must stand and listen.'

I held Jake. Jake couldn't stand. Jake couldn't see.

'Take the rest of his clothes off.'

And I did. I took both socks, both gloves, trousers, shirt, pants. All off. Service with a smile, doctor, always service with a smile. Jake didn't seem pleased. But Jake didn't seem much at all.

'Stop crying, or you'll get more of the same.'

'Stop crying, Jake, please, stop crying or you'll get more of the same.'

'Stand and listen. Not a whimper, not a sound.'

Jake in my arms, my brother in my arms. Where is God? Where was God? Not in the car. Not outside the car with us. Me and Jake against the car, Jake on my shoulders, Jake everywhere dripping and bleeding, everything freezing. Deep mid-winter, doctor, deep mid-winter.

'You're my sons and you will do as I say.'

We were his sons and I did what he said. Jake didn't. Wouldn't. Maybe couldn't. Who knows?

He knew.

'Are you listening?'

Babies are slapped awake, aren't they, doctor? Can you remember your first slap? Giving. Receiving. When Jake was slapped he didn't wake. Jake went to sleep. On the frozen ground. In deep mid-winter.

He said, 'Useless.' He looked at me and licked his lips.

'Still, I have you though, don't I?'
Yes, he still had me.

And he said, and he said,
'Typical.'
Jake was out cold.
And he said,
'Leave him, just leave him where he is.'
So I did. Jake's bruise was blue, like his skin, like the sky.
Deep mid-winter, doctor, crisp and clear. But cold. Goose
bumps all over, everywhere.

'I'll warm you up,' he said and took the thick belt from
around his waist. Thick belt, big buckle. He licked its leather
strap.

'A taste of things to come.' He laughed, so did I. Jake didn't.
It was funny. But it wasn't. Jake would never have laughed.
Never would have taken his clothes off. I did and I did.

'You need some backbone boy,' my father said.

I needed to get back in the car. So did Jake. He was going
bluer than the sky.

'Turn round, bend over and lean against the car.'
'Like this?'
'Like that,' he said licking the leather, making it shine.
'Spread your legs.'
And I did.
'Wider.'
And wider they went, doctor.
'Don't shout out, remember, keep it tight shut.'
I bit my lip, bit my arm, bit the metal of the car roof.
'The first one is for me,' he said, 'the second for you.'
I bit hard.
'The third is for Jake because you must take his.'

Tears in the eyes, doctor, turning to ice and stabbing my
feet as they fell. Deep mid-winter tears bouncing off the
ground onto Jake.

'Are you listening?'

I wasn't.

'The fourth, the fifth, the sixth are for not listening.'

He was counting numbers, I was counting heat. Each wrap of the belt brought a strange heat, a tropical breeze on to my cold skin. Jake was flinching out of his sleep. Don't wake up, dear brother, don't wake. Stay where you are.

'If he wakes up, then we start again,' he said and he smiled.

I didn't but Jake did. He sat up, his hands on his bruise, his eyes on our father.

'What's the look, eh, what's that look you're giving me, boy!'

He licked the belt again.

'This is a different count. This isn't the same.'

And it wasn't, doctor, it wasn't the same at all. One, two, three, four, five, six, seven. Seven blows. Seven blows for one brother. He didn't even get the chance to get off the cold ground, poor Jake, poor dear brother. What a world, eh, doctor, what a world when you can't even get a moment to get up off the ground.

'Stay where you are' he said and Jake did stay where he was. Firm and silent, knees arched and back bent. Seven reels for one brother, seven scars on the blue-white skin. Then he was flat out, head back under the car, legs wide apart. What a day, doctor, what a day. It was so beautiful, so brittle and cold and fragile and empty. Day trip to the country with brother Jake. Except he saw none of it. My father was having none of it.

'Where were we?'

Seven, I said. Seven and I don't know why. Didn't say that though, just seven but I still don't know why. There was Jake bluer than ever under the car, for seven too. His eyes were open, mine were shut, doctor. He saw what was coming, I didn't. Older and wiser was our Jake.

'Yes, seven. Eight is for your soul, nine is for your heart and ten is for . . . and ten is for . . .'

He didn't know. Or I can't remember. One of the two. Doesn't matter. His arm was heavy, my back red and Jake blue.

'Wait there,' he said, and walked away into the country. 'Don't move,' he said.

But he did and so did I. Out of ear and eye shot I got under the car with Jake, getting heat from the engine, Jake getting cold from the cold. I touched his skin, I touched his eyes, touched his mouth. Signs of life, stirrings from something deep. He was alive if not awake. There are more tears somewhere, if I can find them. There are so many to be used. Rationing, doctor, that's what it's called. Sometimes you have to decide whether to cry or not; who to cry for and why. This was a moment under the car with Jake, this was a moment I decided was a moment for tears. For both of us. Let them come, Jake, I shouted into his ear. He smiled and on they came.

He turned his back to us. My father. Our father. Except Jake said he never was. Swore he never was. 'I came from outer space.' Of course he did. Where else could Jake be from? Anywhere was better, doctor, anywhere was better than under the car, choking on oil and mixing with tears. Cough and splutter, hack, hack, hacking our throats. Terrible. Poor Jake, I got it worse, he took it worse.

'Shut your racket and be still.'

But there were no more coughs anyway. Jake had buried his face in the dirt. He knew what was coming. Didn't want to see. Neither did I. I still looked. Maybe it's him that comes from outer space, I say to Jake's trembling back.

'I'm nearly finished,' he shouted, red in the face. Like beetroot. No, like blood. Like Jake's dripping back.

First he was twenty metres away. Then fifteen, then ten, then five, then above us dripping with everything. Splatter onto our legs. Jake flinched. I didn't. Jake didn't need to look. I did. What does it mean, doctor, what does it mean? Jake must have felt it on his bare shins, I felt it bouncing from my legs to my chest. I saw it. He didn't want to imagine it. Old news to him.

'There,' my father said.

'Oh God,' Jake moaned.

'All done,' he said zipping and wrapping himself up again.

'That wasn't too bad now, was it?'

Jake moaned louder.

'Now out from under there, both of you.'

Both of us didn't move. Jake was rigid like a board. Both of us, in fact. Taut as the skin on the drum.

'Do I have to pull you out of there?'

Yes, he did. He did have to pull us out of there. Me first, leg first. Jake next. One quick pull, one swift slide and we were out in the mid-winter air.

'Cold now, I'll warrant. Put your clothes back on,' he said to me.

'You better do as you're told next time,' he said to Jake, kicking his feet.

Maybe it was the tap, doctor, the nudge, the push from shoe to sole. But Jake broke, and breaking was what Jake did best. From calm to storm is a short route. From pain to tears is longer. Jake knew. I knew. We all knew. My father too. From inside to out, anger found a way. Jake jumped. Feisty and bleeding. Tear and blood stained. A sight on a cold mid-winter day. A sight to behold. And behold my father did. A kick in the stomach, a slap to the side of the head. Jake was quick. But my father bigger.

'And now we see some life, is that right?'

Jake tried a punch but my father caught his fist in his palm and turned his palm to a fist. There was a smack that broke the call of nature so it did, rang out the glades, doctor, a new call. Not a tweet but a thwack. And Jake went down.

'You're my son and you will do what you are told.' Another hit, not a thwack but a crunch as something on Jake's face broke. Not the ears or the nose, they were too soft to crunch. Something new had gone to pulp and seed, pulp and seed with brother Jake. I was ashamed, truth be told, shamed and ashamed by my white body pimpling and ripening. For all my sins, doctor, were taken there and then with thwack after smack after hit after crunch. Poor Jake. What a world, eh, what a world where a face can be smashed in a side so full of country. Beautiful but cold.

'A good day to die on, son, is that what you want. For surely that is what you shall get. Get up. Get in the car. Your choice.'

I chose to get up. Jake chose not.

'Not your choice, I should say,' smacked my father.

My choice was to help drag Jake to his feet. Into my arms heavier and older but after all he had done for me. All I had done for him. Nothing. This was the least, the very least.

'Head for home, eh, boys, too much country air and all that.' He headed for home but Jake was heading for outer space and I was going with him.

'Where are we going?'

'Home, of course,' my father said.

'Where are we going?' I asked Jake.

'Anywhere but here,' Jake mumbled through the mush in his mouth. 'Anywhere up there . . .' and he strained his head to the window.

'Look at the sky, brother.' And I did and we lay back in the seat and held each other until the sky went darker and smaller into nothing at all.

TAPE 1 SECTION C

And so to home and so to bed and so to sleep off our wounds, our hurt. We throbbed and we cried. That's what we did, doctor, till the cows came home. Or got up. No cows anyway.

All night Jake throbbed. All night I lay beside him and watched. There were lines on his face, lines on his face that shouldn't have been there, not on one so young, not on anyone, truth be told. My father had put the lines on his back but Jake had put the lines on his face.

'You'll worry yourself sick, Jake.'

'I don't want to hear a sound in there or you'll know what you get.'

He biffed the curtain, the orange and brown flowers flying over dear Jake. I laughed at the flowers, so stupid-looking, so unreal. But Jake didn't laugh. Too busy throbbing, too busy flinching from the touch of cotton petals. That's how bad it was. For a strong boy, doctor, a strong boy to flinch at the touch of cotton flowers. That's as bad as it gets.

Jake punched the curtain back to the other side of the room. My father's side. Neither of us could go near. Neither of us could even look. Drawn tight. Shut and closed and never to be entered.

'What was that, did someone touch the curtain?'

'It was an accident,' I told him. 'My knee . . . my elbow, my something somehow touched the curtain.'

Jake looked at me and without saying anything asked me why.

'What's the use, Jake, what's the god's earth use? This is the only way.'

'It's the wrong way,' was all he would say, the pillows eating his words.

'No more accidents, boys,' was all he said. Was all I wanted to say as well. No more accidents, please.

'What's behind the curtain, Jake?' He didn't answer, wouldn't answer. And Jake knew. He was older than me. Had his wits before me. Had his wits taken before mine. He knew but wouldn't say.

'Maybe I should take a look,' I said, but Jake was lost to something. Maybe sleep. Maybe grief. Maybe both. The tossing and turning of dreams, doctor. Can happen awake, can happen asleep. He munched and munched on that pillow. Must be hungry, for something. Gave me an appetite for something too. But not sleep. That was far from me. Too many bruises shouting at me, crawling over my body like ants in the dirt we had eaten in that field. Ants and dirt we had both eaten. So we were full up, a stomach full all right, a head full too without a shade of doubt.

'I'm going to have a look.' I told him even if he was asleep. And I did and what a sight, doctor, what a sight for a young boy to see, drained of innocence, a fast disappearing swirl of dreams and hopes rushing towards a deep dark plughole. Jake's were in the pipe, in the system gone beyond redemption. No U-bend in this family's plumbing is the most profound thing I can say at this moment, in this time and state.

I saw, doctor, but I did not believe. I came, I saw and I conquered my fear of the flowered curtain but I still did not believe. There was nothing in the room. Nothing left of my mother, nothing left of my father. Everything had been pushed to the side. It was so dark. One lamp, burning oil, burning the air. A smell of thick smoke. A smokescreen behind the flower curtain. He was on the floor. Didn't see him at first. A dark shadow maybe, a black bulk possibly, could have been a chair, a cupboard, a loving father. Anything could have been in that room and I wouldn't have seen.

And then, doctor, and then and then. He moved. An arm at first stretching out above him, then the other replacing it high in the air. Then a leg and then the other. He was walking slowly on his back without swimming or maybe swimming without moving. Either way, any way, he was a puppet, a marionette with no strings attached. Not like me, not like Jake. Strings on both of us since the day we were born.

I felt arms around my stomach, a grip on my shoulders and I went flying into my father's forbidden face.

'Impossible, impossible,' I shouted to Jake, to my father, to anyone that might be listening. How could he, how on God's earth could he do that? But it wasn't him.

'What are you doing?' a voice said to me. A voice I had never heard, a face I had never seen loomed into mine. Still couldn't see. Too dark. Lamplight not enough for me to see the strange face at the end of the arms that held me.

'Curiosity got the cat,' said my father's voice and I saw him sit up. But it hadn't, curiosity hadn't got the cat. It had got me. Tight around the waist.

'Very inquisitive, aren't we?' My father smiled and laughed. But it wasn't funny. And I wasn't laughing.

'This is what happens to boys who are too curious for their own good.' And that is what happened to boys who were too curious for their own good. Had happened to Jake, I reckoned, and now it was happening to me.

'Jake!' I shouted.

'Jake's asleep,' the strange voice answered, 'Just like you'll wish you were in a minute.'

And I did but before that, the voice was wrong. I wanted to be asleep that very minute, that very instant. I wanted to be in the pillow chewing land of Jake. For ever.

TAPE 1 SECTION D

And my mother, she sang me to sleep, one arm for me, one arm for Jake; wrapped around her body, legs over legs over legs, peering out from the holes in her crocheted shawl. A close-knit family, doctor. Ha, ha, close-knit, tightly packed, a loving, caring unit of joy.

Her voice would whisper into our ears, one line for each ear, two for each son; back and forth, a reassuring stereo before frightening mono set in. Frightening mono.

She would sing, *Somewhere . . .*

He would shout, 'What's that racket?'

She would sing, *There is a place for us . . .*

He would threaten, 'And you'll be going to it soon.'

And we would listen, claw at each other's bodies, a tickle here, a thump there. Ordinary boys. Larking, just larking. Till the song stopped and she would pick us up, one by one, Jake first, of course, he was older but not wiser – yet. He hadn't been taught that yet. Experience wasn't in his life. Yet. She would pick us up and tuck us in and it was smiles all the way from the last note of her songs to the last touch of her lips on our birthday suit chest. Not lips for her sons, lips were not good enough for them.

She said, 'Can you guess where I'm going to kiss you tonight?'

And we never could, although we always tried. She rotated her love, doctor, whirled it around our tiny bedroom and we could never tell where the moisture would appear, where the soft touch would be felt.

He said, 'Can you guess where I'm going to hit you today?'

And we could, doctor, we could guess where he was going to hit us.

She said, 'Close your eyes and you will find out.' And we did. Jake first but only when he would lie still.

'Stop fidgeting,' she said, 'or nothing will happen.' He was laughing, a high-pitched squeal, a shrill sound that still rings somewhere. In a land deflowered of curtains.

'How can I kiss you if you hide under the cover?' He squirmed in delight. He wanted to delay the moment as long as he could. He hid at the foot of the bed and Mother ducked under the covers and touched a knee with her lips, an elbow jutting out, or a shoulder blade.

'Ah,' she said, 'Caught you.'

Then she caught me.

He said, 'When I catch you, I'm going to kill you.'

She said, 'When I catch you, I'm going to kiss you.'

Simple, doctor, rimple simple dimple. As far as I am concerned, as far as I know, see and believe. There she was in our beds, tickling us with warm lips and there he was in the other room, the other world, kicking us with cold kicks. So simple it would make you cry. And it did when it happened, when the dreadful day happened. The first dreadful day, I should say. Not the only one, though, of course, but it was the first, a very special, frightening day.

There we were in the country, close to woods that would make you cry.

'Sycamore splendour,' she called it.

'Hmmph,' my father called it.

'Don't run too far, Jake, there's a good boy.'

But Jake was already away, down the slope, scurrying between roots, ducking under branches, chewing leaves as he ran down and down the slope. He couldn't stop himself, from running, from laughing, and neither could I. His shirt tail slipped thorough my hands and he was away, his blond hair spiked with the adrenalin of the new. An adrenalin, doctor, that few ever know. But Jake did, Jake knew all about that, tearing down the slope.

'And don't *you* go too far,' she said. And of course I did.

He was panting and heaving when I caught him. I can feel it now, poor Jake, I can feel his ribs moving as if it was right now, fitting two fingers between his bones, grasping and gripping on for dear life, *his* dear life I should add. My chin on his neck, my legs around his waist until we tumbled and fell onto twigs and leaves, laughing and crying like there was no tomorrow.

There was a scream.

'A bird,' Jake said.

'Mother,' I knew. Somehow. Instinct, guts. Whatever. The first scream went over the tree tops, brushed the outer leaves and whistled and faded off into the sun, into her sons. The second scream dipped and dived through the trees down to us, the edge and shrillness of the sound not dulled by dampening wood. You could hear a pin drop. You could hear a scream cry.

'What do we do?' I asked Jake.

'We go back up.'

'We should hurry,' I said.

'We should fly,' was all he would say. Didn't know what he meant. No wings, how could we fly? No, how could we ever have got there quickly enough? No speed had been invented for our necessary journey. So we settled for running. Jake first because he was the older, clearing the way for me, hacking everything in his path. Just like the moment before, when he had crushed the wood with his laughter, now he stamped it with some anger. His anger, my bewilderment. Our fear.

The third scream slammed into our chests, nearly sent us back down to the bottom of the slope. 'We have to get there,'

Jake said. But the scream was freezing me solid, rooting me firmer than the trees.

'Hurry, hurry, hurry.' Jake pulled and tugged, wrenched and forced me up the slope to the top, the clearing, my father wailing into the summer air. A world at full sun.

He said, 'Not a word, not now, not ever. Say a word to anyone and it will be your last.'

And we believed him.

TAPE 1 SECTION E

And my mother, and my brother, and me all rolling about the floor, laughing so much we were crying, streams pouring out onto our arms, dropping onto the wooden sticks. Crying for good reasons, doctor, not crying for bad. Never knew the difference then. Know the difference now. One knots your stomach, the other churns it, like cement, thick greyer than grey cement.

It was an old game. Even then. A jumble of sticks sharpened both ends dropped from a height of twelve inches into a scattered pile on the floor. Six bands of colour at their tips – red 6, blue 5, green 4, yellow 3, purple 2, orange 1. If you wanted to take a stick out of the pile and get the points, then you weren't allowed to move any of the others. Do that and you lost your turn. Jake was good at it. He would look at the chaotic pile from all angles, with all possibilities for movement estimated in his mind. I would go for the easiest. If an orange stick lay on its own out-with the jumble, then I went for that, an easy point, but not Jake. Never took the easy option. Never got an easy option, doctor. While my father rampaged around the room, shouting at our stupid games, he would take his blue eyes, flick the hair out of the way, and analyse the pile. Then, his long skinny fingers would find a blue or a red balancing somehow in the middle of the pile and like a surgeon doctor, like a knife wielding operator, he would take the stick out without moving a thing and would hold up the stick with pride and joy.

Mother was terrible, worse than me. Her hands would not

stay steady and a trembling hand was not a good thing for this game. She would reach for a green and a whole stack would shift and fall. Jake would blow on her hand and try to put her off and she would push him away, gently, of course. Always gently. Not a smack nor a hit. A playful push. When my father had played the game once, he had thumped the floor to get the stick he wanted.

'All part of the rules,' he said. Of course it wasn't.

'Your turn,' my mother would say when she caught me dreaming about something. And when I was in difficulty, when I was in difficulty she would hold my hand – two trembles make a steady doctor, always've said that. White on white should, bone against bone would guide my hand and I would make a yellow, maybe a green, if luck was with us. Jake the confident, smirking, toothy Jake would laugh at our efforts, then glide in on his turn, angle his way and another five or six points were his. My mother laughed with his skill.

She was not laughing when Jake and I reached the top of the slope. Her smile was askew, not warm and inviting but cold and repellent. Smiles are strange things too, doctor. The smile when she tucked me and Jake into the same bed, before she played her kissing games, her smile made us laugh. Now it made us cry. Jake fell onto his knees beside her.

'What happened, what happened?'

'Not a word,' my father said. 'It was an accident. You came back up the hill and saw the result of a terrible accident. That's right, isn't it, boys?'

But there was nothing right about it. Her head couldn't be like that, not if it was all right; her arms wouldn't be bent under her if they were all right; her legs wouldn't be spread out like that if everything was all right.

'But how did it happen?' Jake wailed to the sun.

'We have to go now,' my father said, 'tell someone about this terrible accident.'

I couldn't move. I remembered my heart beating, after Jake and I had tumbled down the slope, the feel of adrenalin everywhere, but I couldn't feel my heart any more, everything had stopped. I was caught in a limbo I didn't understand. You would say shock, doctor. I would say misunderstanding. I didn't understand that she was dead.

'It was an accident.'

I had thought people don't get hurt in accidents, they only get hurt when they are killed. Stupid, stupid me. I scraped a knee and my mother would clean and bandage it; Jake sprained an ankle and she would bathe it till the swelling went down. They were accidents and the hurt didn't last.

'Let's move. Now,' my father said.

'We can't leave her,' Jake said screaming at my father.

'We have to go and tell someone what happened.'

'But what did happen, what did happen?' Jake leapt up at my father, who smacked him on the back of the head.

'Into the car.'

I tried to get her head to go back into position, the way it should be. It was heavy, her skin warm, her lips, her game playing lips waiting for us to turn home and put us to bed. Cold.

'You too, hurry up.' I tried to change her smile, to a good smile from a bad, but I couldn't change it. Every time I moved her lips upwards they would curl back down. My father dragged me to the car and I could hear Jake crying on the back seat.

'But what about her smile?' I said to my father.

'She won't be smiling any more, son.' And he was right.

TAPE 1 SECTION F

And the engine, the spluttering engine, was all we could hear. Bombs could blast, guns could shoot and the world could end and we wouldn't have known. But then, the world *had* ended. Not just for my mother. But for me, for Jake. Especially for Jake. Older and wiser Jake. He went foetal on me. Wouldn't let me put my arm around his shoulder, wouldn't let me whisper jokes into his ear like we had done on cold winter nights when body heat was the only heat and our breath hung in the air. Clouds of spoken words shimmering into whispers in our tiny room . . . shimmering into whispers . . .

Let me tell you a joke, he would say in happier times, let me tell you a whopper. But you must promise to laugh. I laughed and kept the promise before the joke had even started. He told me this one, doctor, maybe you will laugh. There was this man in a swimming pool, going through the water with no trunks or bathing costume on. Another man came along and stared at him, looking at his thing dangling in the water as he swam along. He had the biggest thing this man had ever seen; it went out from his legs and just kept on going to the other side of the pool. Oh my God, the man said, pointing at his thing and the man in the water stopped swimming and said, 'What's the matter, doesn't yours shrink in water?'

He'd laugh before the joke was over, the words barely out of his mouth before he spluttered into the pillow, trying to keep the noise down from our parents sleeping a few feet away. And Jake was funny when he laughed. Funnier than the joke. Funnier than what I didn't understand anyway. His whole body would rattle, his arms cover his head and he'd try to cram his fingers between his teeth. He didn't just laugh with his mouth, he'd laugh with his whole body. Then he'd stop, look at me with those deep sunken eyes of his. A master of the unspoken word too.

'Is yours like that?'

And I didn't know what to say.

In the car there was nothing to say. For me, pressed against the seat, my hands over my ears, for Jake balled up and frozen, for our father speeding along the road. Speeding, until he found a phone box and I watched him go out and phone, while all the time, doctor, all the time he was checking on us to see what we were doing.

I tried to be there with Jake, wherever that was. Too close to really see, too distant to touch; tried to prise his arms away from his face and got soaked in the process; soaked by his tears, by his snot, by speckles of blood that he etched out of his forehead.

'Don't Jake, please don't . . .'

'It was him,' he said, 'it was him,' he shouted, bursting out of his foetal position and making a grab for the door. He was uncontrollable. A rage in him that had got him smack after smack in the country, under the car . . . I went for his arms but he was away, oiled with fever, an anger slicked with grease, and he was out the door and running for my father. I watched from behind the window screen, watched just watched. Oh God, all I did was watch, all I could *do* was watch. He ran at my father who was still shouting into the phone, sweating and erupting everywhere, and he jumped. My father used the phone. Not just to call for help for our mother lying back there at the top of the slope but to put Jake's head back down on the ground. Like a fly, swatted and dropped to earth. He hung up the phone, picked up Jake, and soon Jake was back in the car; back in the foetal, back to tears and blood.

'Stupid boy, what were you trying to do?' He looked at me, did our father, looked at me and warned me without a word, threatened me without a sound. But I wasn't going anywhere and neither were any of us.

In our room he said, full of pride, 'I'll show you mine then.'

But I couldn't see, it was too dark in our room, the windows covered over with layer upon layer of thick cotton. Too dark not just to see, sometimes it was too dark to think, to imagine there was anything beyond the drapes.

'Can you see?' he asked, and I nodded, but I couldn't really. I saw a shape between his legs, I saw his skin change and go even darker if that was possible, and I suppose it was, anything was possible in that room, in that bed with the two of us.

The police came and my father talked to them like they were old pals. All the time one or other of them would come up and peer in the car and ask us if we were all right.

'Yes, sir.' I would say.

'No, sir,' Jake would reply and then they would just go as though we had been ghosts, unseen and unheard. All Jake would say that day and for days and days after was. 'It was him, he did it.'

'How do you know?' I would ask but, of course, I didn't need to ask. I knew as well as him.

TAPE 1 SECTION G

'In you come, in you come,' the strange voice had said.

I had been told that behind the curtain was strictly out of bounds.

'Don't ever, ever go in there,' my father had said. And we never did. At least not more than once. Jake had been once and look what had happened to him; had the sun taken out of his heart; had the joy taken out of his laugh. And now me, I had done it once, gone beyond the flower curtain and into a forbidden land.

He went mad when we got back from the country. Our father. He cursed the spot where our mother had fallen. We watched the ambulance men lift her body up, still loose, not rigid. Flexible when I thought it would break. Jake looked, then didn't. He watched and then hid his eyes with his hands. I tried the same but when I covered my eyes with my hands the fingers just fell apart. I saw scissors cutting a view of a terrible thing into my head. Relentless. It was all so relentless. I couldn't stop seeing. My father, his grief, his tears, being moved from one policeman to another, a shoulder to lean on, a sympathetic pat on the back while they lifted her body into the ambulance and slammed the doors.

It was all we could talk about, all we could think about.

'It was him, it was him,' Jake said, as tense as tense could be.

'I know, I know,' I said but I didn't. I believed Jake but I didn't know. We had been playing, she had died, my father had cried and we were taken back to the house to our room to start a new life. Straight away, my father changed everything we had previously known. We moved into one room in the house while strangers filled up the rest of the building, with new noises, creaks, groans all day and night. He put bolts on the door, extra strong shutters on the windows and a curtain rail down the middle of the room.

'Never step across when I'm not here,' but he was always there, doctor, never a moment when he wasn't, never a moment when we weren't close to the front line.

'This is our home and we shall have to make the best of it.'

'What about the rest of it?' Jake asked.

'That's not ours any more. Things will be different now that your mother's not with us.'

And they were, they were very different.

We got dressed up. In black, from head to foot. Jake soiled his face with earth from the cemetery gardens, darkened his face like a combat-hardened veteran going to war. Camouflaged.

'I have to do this,' Jake said.

My father said, 'Wash your face.'

'No,' Jake said. Standing his ground, standing on the ground, a few feet away from the coffin making its way to the hole in the ground.

'Wash your face or I'll wash it for you.'

The people there, distant relatives never seen before, watched and stayed silent.

'We're being left alone,' I said to them inside.

'We're being left alone with him,' I kept on chanting as Jake and my father began to tussle at the graveside.

'Is that a good idea?' I asked.

'No,' Jake said to my father and bent down and scooped soil into his hand, soil that other hands had already used to throw at my mother. He scooped the soil, cupped it in his hands and smeared it on his face. My father spat on his palms and spread his saliva onto Jake's face turning soil to mud, turning Jake's rage to dirty tears. He tried to push my father's hands away but he was too strong, always too strong, and soon he gave up and stood staring ahead, his arms by his side. I looked down at my black trousers, white shirt, black tie. Looked at my father cleaning his own hands with yet more saliva. And I scooped my own soil, a mere thimbleful, and traced two fingers one either side of the tie down my shirt. My father didn't see. But Jake did and smiled. Solidarity, I thought.

'Too late,' Jake said.

'In you come,' the voice said. Then the hands of the voice pushed me to the ground. I was between the voice and my father in a darkened room. Somewhere, somehow I knew it was a beautiful day outside. I kept thinking I should have stayed the other side of the curtain. The hands of the voice held me tight, too tight I thought, and squirmed to be free.

'Don't move.' The voice was stern, the pressure hard until I could feel the jagged edge of his nails digging into me.

'Take your pyjamas off,' my father said without moving.

'Take your pyjamas off,' the voice whispered into my ear. I could feel spit on my neck. Hate that, doctor, hate it hate it hate it. The smell of someone else's spit. A terrible thing. A terrible smell. But not someone else's, not everybody else's either, I suppose. Not my mother. But then she kissed without saliva, pecked us all over our bodies with dry lips, no moisture seeping out of her. But the hands with a voice dribbled onto me as he pulled my pyjama top off.

'No,' I said.

'Do as you are told,' my father said. He walked forward out of the shadows into the light of the oil lamp. He was naked.

Jake said to me once, 'Show me yours.'

My father showed me his. It was too dark for me to see

Jake. I didn't understand. I knelt between the voice and my father. I could see everything.

'And the trousers,' the voice said.

'No,' I said.

'Do as you're told,' the voice said.

'What's wrong, Jake, what's wrong?' I said to him when he woke me up some night. He was trembling, bones rattling, teeth chattering. Everything moving.

'Can't say, won't say,' he told me, pushing himself to the edge of the bed, squeezing the wall.

'Where've you been?' He wouldn't say. I crept under the bed clothes and pecked his legs, his arms, his fingers and pushed myself between the wall and him until I was face to face, eye to eye, blinking with him as he frightened the life out of me.

'Where've you been?'

'I've been . . .' he said, his voice a harsh whisper . . . 'I've been . . . There,' and folded and bent into the rhythms of grief. A terrible thing, doctor, a wretched, awful thing to see my brother Jake heaving with grief, his cage rattling in time with the springs that warped the mattress.

'I see,' I said.

But I didn't.

'Come in here, come in here. Quickly, quickly, quickly,' she spoke in hushed tones, words dampened by fear, her arms around my shoulders, gently but firmly ushering me into her room.

I asked, 'Where's Dad?' but she put her hand over my mouth and put her lips to my forehead.

'Ssssh. I have something to tell you,' she said.

Her voice sounded far away, her body shimmering.

'I have something to tell you, Jake.' I pushed and pulled him as he slept under the covers. Solid as a rock, tight behind sleep's lock. When sleep came. And it was never easy, always a rough, shattering ride but when it came, everything closed down and he would be a log to lie against, while I tossed and turned with questions that Jake had no need to answer when he was dead to this world. When the world was dead to him.

But I kept trying.

'What . . . what . . .' he gurgled into the pillow. His eyes, deep piercing holes, glass hollowed out from more than skin and bone, eyes that have taken in everything that they have seen and more that they have not.

'Jake, you must wake up, you must.' He turned onto his back and pulled the sheet down from across his face and squinted at my shadow hanging over him.

'I have something to tell you.'

Jake followed me into our mother's sanctuary.

'What is it, what is it?' Jake bounded into my mother's room, leapt onto her bed and started wrestling with her clothes, throwing scarves and jumpers in the air. He looked so happy. We both thought that. My mother and me. We paused to take the moment in, then to let it go. A loose grip, doctor, a loose fragile grip for a fleeting moment. A life made up of moments. Jake caught the scarves and the jumpers which came raining down on his head. I laughed at Jake and so did my mother but it was more an intake of air with her, more a backward sigh. And backward sighs were still new to me.

She led me to the bed and settled me on its softness beside the wild Jake. It was her room, doctor, although she shared everything with my father. But it was still her room. Everything that met the eyes was hers, or old and distant family's. A living breathing history. Old things that coated me with dust, that cooled me down, that unnerved me slightly. But not Jake. He was in his element. On the bed, a trampoline of one's own, alone in his enjoyment, alone without my father. She sat down while I caught Jake's arms and pulled to him to rest. He squirmed for a while, not wanting to be told to settle or be still and still she waited, her body still, as patient as ever while he calmed himself down, watching me as I held him.

Jake shut his eyes and said, 'Is it a present?'

And she crumbled, the vision of our mother shimmered

again, fading from view. She smiled at Jake, then buried her head in her hands while I did the same. Jake stopped mid-jump and let his body fold and fall to the mattress. I looked at him, then my mother and wondered what had just happened. Jake did not see what was in my eyes but he felt it, and for both of us it was a last chance to see our mother before she had kissed the earth on that country slope. She faded still further when I heard the front door close when I hadn't heard it open. Jake jumped off the bed and rushed to hide behind a curtain while my mother sat up straight on the bed, rearranged her hair and looked at the doorway. No one looked at me. In a moment the weather changed, doctor, from calm to storm.

My father stormed into the room.

'Well, what are you two doing in here then?'

And my mother faded from my sight. Without a whisper of goodbye.

TAPE 2 SECTION A

'You've been in there, haven't you?'

I hadn't said a word. I had just wakened him and he had looked up and into my eyes. He knew before I told him. But what else was there to know? He had been there, after all. He had been in my shaking legs and arms, he had been there in my urgent stammer, he'd been in there where a sense of your own smell just left with the wind.

'Why?' He was angry. Not angry at my father, but angry at me, a different look, a different point. He didn't strangle me but shook me; he didn't hit me but dug his fingers into my arms and said, 'Didn't I tell, didn't I tell you?'

'Yes you did,' I replied.

He threw me against the wall and turned his back to me and I found I had no balance left. I fell off the bed and thumped onto the floor.

'Keep it quiet in there,' my father said.

'I wish you were dead,' my brother replied under his breath.

And I lay on the thin carpet inspecting the thin line of marks made by Jake's fingernails side by side with wounds fresh from the other side of the curtain.

I had let Jake down.

And he rushed in, dived into the room and grabbed us, a shoulder under each arm, a head on each breast.

'No one should be indoors on day like this,' he said. He stamped the ground in excitement. A bull excited, a bull grabbed by the horn.

'Get your clothes on,' he shouted, 'We are going in five minutes.'

'How long, Jake?'

'How long what?' he shouted, Jake shouted. Bad temper, and lashings of fists. Half at me, half at the world. Angry young man I guess you would say but maybe angry young boy would be better. A teen rage. A childhood pique. Oh God, doctor, he was in a rage all right and the world should have been warned. When my mother had whispered into my ear on our last day in the country, on her last day when we were in the country. She had said, warned me in fact, 'He's a wonderful, beautiful boy, your brother, love him always, respect and care for him always. But he has a temper. A terrible mood. Like your father, like everyone's father, for all I know.'

'How long were you next door?' I said again.

'You shouldn't have gone,' Jake said without fists.

I could only shake my head.

'And what did they touch . . .'

Jake didn't want to talk. He raised his hand in the air, pushed his chin against his chest.

And I had thought and I had thought that he had calmed down, that the rage was gone. But it wasn't. Transmuted, transfigured. It was still there, hiding, undercover then leaping out. His rage jumped onto my stomach, his rage crashed into my face, spit and words falling into my mouth.

'I can't remember. Do you understand, I can't remember.'

I didn't then but I do now, doctor. You can see something in your head time and time again, night after night, year after year – as I did, as Jake did – and it can make no sense whatsoever.

'It's time to go. Cars up and running; hop along and jump in.'

'I'm sorry,' Jake said, 'I'm sorry for shouting at you.'

Of course, he was. So was I. Everybody was sorry, the people in black at my mother's grave, the policemen with their arms around my father's shoulder. But then the stairs joined us, reunited us if you like. Our mutual understanding that the stairs were the badlands, our mutual memory of our rooms, our mother's inner sanctum. Maybe a month, maybe a year had gone by. Maybe the last time we had visited the country.

TAPE 2 SECTION B

Where we had lived strangers sang and screamed and cried, and laughed.

My father said, 'Come on, quickly down the stairs. I don't want to have to see or talk to anyone.'

'Tap that door,' Jake whispered into my ear as my father encouraged us with his hands to move faster. I could hear his laugh even if my father couldn't. It was better than his rage; and his hand, his spare hand, tickled my side.

'That one,' I said.

'Come on, come on,' my father said. 'The day's going to be over before we even get to the car.'

The door flew open and we all jumped. My father the highest, then Jake, then me. We were all good at jumping. Then the whole house jumped. My father flew over the top of us into the man's arms. But not a hug, not a kiss. A hit. The man fell down, head onto the top stair, a sickening crack. My father stood behind him and then rolled him down the stair. One step at a time. And we followed.

'Come on, come on.' The man next door was on the step ahead of us.

'Jake,' I said, 'I can hear a joke.'

'So can I,' Jake replied.

'That man, boys,' my father laughed, all three of us skipping over our neighbour, 'was one step ahead of us.'

We laughed because it was funny. Jake in his throat, me in my chest. My father everywhere. We toppled with hilarity into the car, fell horizontal into the car while we caught our breaths. Other neighbours looked down at us and saw a happy family on their way to a trip in the country.

'Lovely day for it,' someone shouted to my father. He leant out the window, rolled up his sleeves and shouted back. 'Lovely day for it.'

Up, up and away. We flew, at least my father did. Forgot he was in the car, forgot we were in the car. And whistled. Whistled as though he was happy, with me wishing that Jake was happy. Jake, poor, older, wiser Jake, slumped in the back seat of the car with my arm around his shoulder. I could feel his bones grinding against each other, his limbs conspiring to spasm, his words tightly coherent.

'I'm going to do something,' he said.

'What you going to do, Jake?' putting my head next to his mouth, hot breath and hot words filling me with fear.

'I haven't decided . . . yet.'

I had heard this before.

My father said, 'I don't want to hear any whispering back there.'

Jake could scheme. He could churn his mind over and over again, simmering, sometimes boiling. There was an edge to his voice, a tone I had heard before, a few times before Mother died, countless times after she went under the ground. My mother would try to lift him up even though at nearly thirteen he was almost too much for her to gather into her arms.

'I'm defusing the bomb,' she would say to me as Jake

struggled in her arms, as she gathered his legs and lifted him half off the ground before he got the better of her and ran to a corner.

'He's not as bad as you think,' was her phrase, her stock answer to all Jake's wild plans, to all of his scheming revenge. She eased my fear for him, for myself. All the time. A drip-feed of reassurance, doctor.

She said. 'Try to love him, Jake, will you do that for me?' Jake howled into the mattress, kicked pillows across the room, dug splinters out of the wall with his nails, then my father came into the room demanding silence and he spat at him, the gob of spit landing on his shoe and the last I heard, the only thing I heard, before I buried my head in one of the pillows that had landed beside my mother was, 'You'll regret that, boy.' He didn't, but I did. And Mother, who got under the pillow with me, shook with me under the thick cotton, joined her tears to mine in salty union, certainly agreed.

Poor, brave Jake.

'Where are we going?' I asked my father.

'Don't ask.'

I heard Jake say, 'Who cares?'

'Don't ask, you'll be told when we get there,' my father replied.

I can remember the country, I can remember but it surprises me. There's not much I can remember outside our home, a few of the journeys but not all of them and the ones I do happened mostly after Mother died.

'I want to go back to the woods,' Jake shouted out suddenly.

'What woods?' my father replied.

'The woods, you know . . . the woods. Where we went with Mother.'

'We're not going back there.' Terse, terse, terse.

'Leave it, Jake, let it lie.' I pulled his head down onto my shoulder, tried to cram my finger into his mouth but he bit and bit hard and I yelped mournfully to the other side of the car . . . Oh Jake . . .

'I want to go there or I am not going anywhere,' Jake shouted, too near to my father. He stopped, an emergency stop in a clear road on an early spring day, no flowers but some temperature. Beautiful, in other words, a beautiful day in the country.

My father managed a two-handed slap into Jake's face, both hands off the steering wheel, sandwiched together for extra impact and Jake went slam into the back seat.

'We are never going back there, understand?'

Jake said nothing and all I wanted to do was to look at the tall sycamores in an unkempt wood by the roadside, not the same wood, though. Of course, I mean.

'Understand?' my father said and pulled Jake's legs forward, the gear stick pressed between his legs.

'If I change gear maybe you'll be the son I want,' my father said, ignoring the horn of a passing car and pressing, always pressing his face close to Jake's face.

He smiled, 'Good joke,' he said.

'Bad joke,' muttered Jake stupidly, always stupid with the replies, never knowing when to keep his mouth shut. His strength. His weakness.

'Sometimes you just have to know when to stay silent,' my mother had said.

'No, good joke,' my father replied and slammed the gear stick into reverse.

TAPE 2 SECTION C

'You're dreaming, you're dreaming,' Jake said. 'I know, I know, I said. Then I woke up. Then he woke up.

'Are you awake?' he asked.

'I am now,' I replied. 'I was dreaming.'

'I know. So was I.'

My father stormed into the room, biffing the curtain, the flowers in full swell.

'Who was making that damned noise?'

'We were dreaming,' I said.

He looked at me. Vicious curl of the lips.

'What do you have to dream about?'

I looked at Jake, who looked at me while he edged himself backwards. 'Come closer,' he whispered . . .

'A lot of things,' I answered, trying to edge myself away from my father.

Jake whispered. 'Don't talk to him . . .'

My father said, 'Useless. Useless, useless, useless,' and I felt my head hit the floor, the red and brown flowers looming large, blooming in my face. I felt my legs go under the curtain, its ticklish swipe on my bare midriff then my head, cocked backwards by the drag, catching sight of Jake, dear once brave Jake holding onto the thinnest of layers of wallpaper shouting, 'Dreams are better than this . . .'

'Write that down, Jochim, the boy might have something there.' He laughed, I didn't, and Jake cried.

My father drew the curtains closed and I could no longer hear Jake's voice.

At night sometimes my mother crept into our room when it was just our room, no curtain, no brown cotton flowers hanging limp and stale in the air. Everything in its first bloom. She crept and lay at the bottom of our bed, resting beside the soles of our feet, breathing through her mouth, wrestling with her hair which she drew in bunches over and over again until her face was hidden.

'What's wrong?' Jake would ask when Jake would talk.

'Go to sleep, boys, go to sleep.'

'But what's wrong?'

She didn't answer, never would answer, never would put her troubles onto us. Kept them tight inside, locked but not hidden, each terrible secret dripping off her face onto our bare legs.

'Nothing's wrong. It's a wild night outside.'

There was barely a breath of air coming through the half open window.

'This little piggy . . .'

She had grabbed Jake's big toe. He screamed.

Then I screamed.

'And then this little piggy.'

She had changed the mood, changed *her* mood and within minutes of her stealth into our room with the world on her shoulders, she had Jake and me writhing in our twisted bed sheets, thumping the mattress begging her to stop, tears brimming and flowing down our cheeks, our arms unable to reach her as she slid off the bed out of reach.

'And this little piggy never went home.'

A voice called out, 'And what have we here?'

'Jochim,' my father said in a deep serious voice, 'I'm not sure.'

'We will have to see, won't we?'

'My thoughts exactly.'

'Leave him alone,' Jake shouted through the curtain. A new bravery, Jake of old, rekindling his heart for my sake. It made me smile. Even lying on the floor with a stranger, a man my father called Jochim standing astride of me, it made me smile, made me laugh, in fact. A quiver then a belly laugh that shook me from head to toe.

'What are you laughing about?' Jochim leant down, his big nose, big lips bulging with blood.

'What are you saying?' my father said to Jake, billowing the curtain with his fist.

They saw laughter and were suspicious. It was that sort of world.

I looked at Jochim and felt nothing.

'I'm not laughing about anything,' I said.

And Jake said, 'I wasn't saying anything.'

And we were both silent.

Jochim undid the belt of his trousers and they fell down into a heap around his ankles. Could have been funny, doctor, in another time, another place. Maybe he could have started to run, side by side with my father with his trousers down around his ankles and they could have raced, and fallen, and I could have laughed.

As it was, with Jochim leaning over me, I was left low and wet, pinned to the floorboards with the weight of a different generation.

Ha ha.

He came and went in the middle of the night. Jake was asleep. I was awake.

There were muffled voices from behind the flower curtain. Then it moved. Then Jake moved, turned over in his sleep and put a bony arm across my chest. I was tense, he was loose. Usually, always, it was the other way around. Our mother whisked him out of bed once, when she had kissed us both good night, me on the ankle, Jake on his chest.

She said, 'You're as stiff as a board.'

Jake just smiled and let my mother massage his shoulders, his back, his head.

My father said, 'Ssssh.'

Then there was silence. The flowered curtain moved with a breeze I didn't feel.

Hadn't felt a breeze since the last time in the country.

'Let the wind blow those cobwebs away, boys,' my father said.

But neither Jake nor I could find any cobwebs.

We drove for hours. I was cold, Jake was out cold, head on my shoulders, hands tight between his thighs. He was mumbling in his sleep, gurgling and hanging a thin line of saliva out to dry between his lips. He was gone and I wish I had gone with him. *I come from outer space.* I tried to hear the sounds that tumbled out of his mouth, I tried to decipher the tones above the drone of the car.

'Never . . .' I heard, the line of saliva broken.

'Never what Jake?' I whispered into his ear.

'Never . . .'

'Go back? Go in? Go there? What is it Jake?'

And my father said, 'We're nearly there.'

'Where's that?'

'You'll see. Somewhere you've never been before.'

'Never . . .' Jake said lifting his head in sleep, the jolt of the car shifting his weight from one side to another.

'. . . go there,' he said.

We went to the city. We had thought and Jake had even hoped it would be the country to find our mother.

'She was never buried. There was nothing in that coffin that went into the ground ashes to ashes and dust to dust,' he said.

'She's still there, in the country, in the wood. Still there. Waiting for us.'

Jake was gone but not asleep. Jake was somewhere but not in the car, not the room which was our home.

If we had started out in the afternoon, we had arrived at night. The car halted and my father sat with an air of satisfaction behind the wheel.

'Where are we?' Jake asked.

'Where are we?' I said to my father.

'This,' he said turning around with a gleam in his eye, a seam of a smile splitting his lips, 'This is the site of an adventure still to come.'

He jumped out the car, slammed its door and breathed in the night air, his chest heaving in then out, breath after breath clouding the air in front of us.

'Get out the car boys.'

Jake was half asleep but, fully rebellious, slurred his orders to me, touted his next act of rebellion to me.

'Just say nothing. Silence will be our defence. Silence before our attack.'

'We can't . . .'

And then Jake, quiet, angry, violent, loving Jake pulled me closer to him, put his arm around my shoulder, his hand across my mouth.

'Silence.'

My father was too busy with the air, playing with clouds in the beams of the car light – at first. At first he seemed to be lost in something, like when Jake would go off into the stars, like when we giggled ourselves into hysteria when our mother tickled out feet. At first. But silence could never be on our terms. Always on his. Jake was breaking a rule but upholding it.

'Get out the car . . . boys,' my father said, blowing his air towards us.

I squirmed and Jake held me tighter than tight, clutching me ever closer to his wiry body. Bone against bone.

Then he came to get us.

'I'll get you out.'

And he did, true to his word, to his bond, to his everlasting promise of moving us from one location to another without consent but with resent. *Meant to be, meant to be,* I heard myself saying despite Jake's fleshy gag.

'Out, out, out,' my father said.

We were like protesters, resisting our father's force. First my legs, then my head crashing onto the ground then Jake, his hand torn away from my mouth, landed beside me, our heads clashing, our limbs cushioning, then worsening our fall, with jutting angles.

'Do as you are told and you will enjoy yourself. Believe me, you will.'

'I will not believe you, about anything,' Jake said breaking his rules and spitting earth out of his mouth onto the ground.

My father laughed. I didn't.

'You said silence was our best defence.'

'Before we attacked,' he reminded me.

He was older and wiser. And he had been behind the curtain before me.

Another car arrived, parked behind us, headlights still full on.

Jochim stood in front of us. Jake shuddered. I stared. Jochim smiled. My father licked his lips.

Something happened without words being spoken. In the beams of the car headlights, my father and Jochim were shadows. Moving shadows. Like the dark figure of my father tiptoeing through the room in the middle of the night; like the dark figure of my mother sitting beside the window. So many shadows, doctor. Jake too, covered in sheets and darkness and hair that fell around his face. Too many shadows.

They just stood and talked. I could see Jochim's big, bulbous nose. It caught the darkness. His profile made me shudder, made me want to hold onto Jake as tight as I could. And he let me, Jake did, let me hold on as tight as I wanted and I loved him for that. When it mattered, when it came down to it, doctor, he was there, right there beside me, for me. And then he wasn't.

My father came away from Jochim, took the light with him and then I could see his face, sweating even though it was cold, smiling even though I could see nothing funny about the situation. With two arms he wrenched Jake to his feet.

'No,' Jake said, letting his weight stay on the ground.

'Yes,' my father, said pulling his weight off the ground again.

'No,' I said and tried to get off the ground.

'Ha,' Jochim said and pressed my chest back into the tarmac with his foot.

Jake was in shadow, so I couldn't see his face. That bothered me the most. For a last memory should have something more than darkness, should have a smile, a tear, should have something. I had my mother's smile still in my head, had her lips still somewhere on my body. But Jake was pulled off into the darkness out of reach of the headlights and then I heard a car door slam. My father's car.

All the time Jochim kept his boot on my chest while I writhed and struggled to break free.

'You'll waste your energy, and you'll need it. It's a long walk to anywhere,' Jochim said.

But the energy was not wasted. Jochim didn't understand that. My father didn't understand that. But Jake did. And the last sound of dear brother Jake was the familiar sound of his feet hammering against the car door, trying to break the locks, trying to get out, to get away, to be back beside me on the

tarmac, back in our shared bed, back with our mother at the
the top of the slope.

The car sped off, skidded, then righted itself and hummed
into the distance. Jochim without moving his boot from my chest
leant over, so I could see nothing of the sky for his nose which
touched my cheek. I felt his sandpaper tongue on my lips wiping
away the spit before I had a chance to launch it into his face.
'It's goodbye time, kid. Have a nice life.'
The last thing I felt was his hand across my face. The last
thing I thought of was Jake in my father's car battering the
door to get out. The last thing I saw was my mother lying at
the top of the slope. Cold and stiff in the deep mid-winter.

TAPE 3 SECTION A

And Jake is not here. And . . . Jake . . . is . . . not . . .
here. Say the words, weave a meaning. Wave goodbye on a
road with nothing but dust. Dust to dust with my father and
brother Jake, ashes to ashes with my mother. It's the way it all
goes, doctor, the way it has always gone. Left to lurch home
along a road I didn't know. Left to devices which must be my
own. Not anyone's any more. Left in a house full of strangers
with not a sigh from Jake, not a tickle from my mother's lips,
not a hit or a ruffle of the flowered curtain. Left.
Jochim had left his smile on my lips. Swiped it from his
face and slapped it onto mine while my father took Jake under
his wing, pushed him into the car and sped off with the dust, a
cloud I couldn't see through. Still can't. Some clouds are for
rain, doctor, some clouds are for not seeing the sky. Know the
difference? I did and do. Walked all the way home with
Jochim's smile on my lips, wandering through places where
no one smiled back, walked along roads my father had sped
along with me and brother Jake and our trips to the country
with my father and his belt and his shining red face huffing and
puffing. Walked into a wood I thought I knew, where I
thought I would see our mother lying so still and silent at the

top of a wooded slope. Wandered but didn't find; looked but couldn't see anything but trees. I listened for Jake, waiting for his shout, a shout for joy but more likely a cry of pain, but listened nevertheless, but never the more urgently, for something. Even the sight of my father full of anger and toil and sweat. But I didn't see him. I saw no one but had the feeling, had the gut and the ears that someone was watching me. Get out and get away, doctor, that's what was in my head, get out and get away until I could find our home, till I could find our room where Jake would be lying smiling and waiting.

I sensed only shadows around me. I fell on the bed, closed my eyes and waited for their touch. perhaps it would be my mother, claiming a patch of skin on my arm or leg all for her own, a good night kiss that clamped itself to me . . . but then it was Jake rolling over in restless sleep, an arm folding over then under mine, arm locking us into mattress, secured for safety from my father's touch. But then it was my father's touch in the middle of the night with no other shadows about, the restless noises of the house gone. He was waking me up, taking Jake's arms from under my shoulders and lifting me up. Being carried by my father in his arms was different from being carried by my mother in hers. Different, doctor, different enough to make me cry. Sometimes, mother would wake us both from sleep, Jake and me, wake us and lift us to the windows and show us rooftops and night skies.

'Look up to the stars, boys, look up to the stars.' And Jake and me hardly could respond, drugged by sleep, half-open, half-shut eyes blinking at the night sky while our mother held us close to her, one brother for each arm, one love for two hearts.

Then my father used my head to part the flowered curtains, used my head to ram the cotton flowers. The softer the touch the more unbearable the pain. Nonsense, doctor, complete and utter nonsense. But there you have it. To feel pain from the soft curtain was unremarkable to me; to feel warmth in the cold room in my mother's arms brushed by the draught of a gusting wind was nothing short of miraculous. It came down to touch.

The touch of my mother, the touch of my father, the touch of brother Jake. And now the touch of shadows.

In the empty room, my body was being rolled from one side of the bed to the other, pushed and pulled, rolled and rocked by shadows, which crept into my head even with my eyes screwed tight shut. I lay until the shadows chased me into sleep, followed me, then cornered me until I could do nothing but wait for nothing, nothing in my head.

TAPE 3 SECTION B

Time went out the window. If it could have, it would have. If time could have got past the shutters my father had shut once my mother had died, bolted and nailed, then it would have. I would have joined it too, if I knew where it would take me. As it was, as it is, I was stuck where I was and now where I am. Stuck without Jake to hold onto, stuck with nothing but the memory of dry kisses between my toes, quick pecks on my chest, left with my red weals and healing scars from my father's belt. Left.

I did things. Time was spent.

I spread myself out on the bed, stretching my legs from one side to the other, wrapping myself in the sheets, rolling over and over until I grew dizzy and fell on the floor. I picked up the game we had all played, even my father when the mood took him; I picked up the sticks and dropped them onto the floor and spent hours trying to be as good as Jake had been. I took turns for him, tried extra-hard for him, to mimic his play; I took turn for my mother giggling at every mistake, laughing at my shaking hand. Just as she did, just as he did. I even stormed into the room and kicked the pile when I had had enough, shouting at the empty room.

It fell short of everything. I ran out of things that kept my mind from wandering back to the road in the city where Jochim had whisked away Jake, where I coughed and sput-tered with fumes of my father's car. I kept going back, kept getting taken back. And if I wasn't there I was in the woods, racing back up the hill, charging through the undergrowth with Jake, rushing to save our mother. Too late. Too late then, too late now. Nothing to do but climb the walls, with my nails hooking into the plaster. Nothing to do but look behind the flowered curtain.

I put my hand through the gap and saw it disappear. There was no light. When Jake had scolded me, throttled me for going behind the curtain, he said there was never any light from there but candles. Beeswax candles, Jake said. The worst kind. And Jake was right. There was a smell in the room that hit me as if my father had launched his belt at my face. I went from one room to the other, went from one world to the other, doctor, and Jake said to me, without being there, without being a hundred miles near probably, 'Don't go in, you might never come back.' But it was all of them that had never come back. My mother was still in the woods, my father was on the road somewhere and Jake, God only knows where Jake was. By my side, was what I thought in the end, by my side, taking the risk with me.

I saw shadows from the visit there. I saw Jochim leering at me through the glow of candles; I saw my father lying flat out on the ground, a smile on his face, a hand outstretched. Then Jochim faded into the walls and my father into the ground and all went black again. But I had seen enough in a few seconds. I saw the belongings of a lifetime, my father's, my mother's, even Jake's toys all piled high in a corner of a room, squashed and pressed together so tightly I didn't dare move in case they fell and I would be found by Jake returning to rescue me under a pile of my father's belts. A fate worse than the breath of Jochim bending over my chest; a touch worse than my father's liquid splashing across my face.

In the dark I found the candles left to burn to their wick, splashes of wax on the wooden floor. I sat in the middle where my father had lain and looked back into the room. All around me were the sounds of the strangers in the house; the floor-boards above me creaked under someone's weight, the walls shook with someone's laughter and I sat cross-legged waiting for Jake to come running and pull me away from the room. I waited for my mother to sing something, anything, into my ear and to take us both back to the world we had known before that visit to the country, before the flowered curtain had been parted.

SAD

I had my first taste of the psychiatrist's chair when I was five years old. And I mean taste.

They took me, my concerned, professional parents on the recommendation of a host of third parties. The friend of a friend had been told by a friend of a friend whose daughter worked at the nursery I attended that I was behaving strangely and might benefit from early intervention.

It might be nothing but . . .

I know what they had seen, I *remember* what they had seen because I remember what I did. I was the perfect subject for such early psychological evaluation since, because I was so young, memories hadn't had the opportunity for covert, behind the scenes activity – there was no need to recover them, they were there dripping off me, waiting to be mopped up. Or rather the young girl with curly long hair was mopped up, ushered away by shocked and disgusted staff into another room, changed and dried while I was pressed firmly into a plastic chair to await collection by my parents.

I know young boys can do strange things but . . .

The big chair tasted stale, the leather tough and resistant to my young teeth but I gnawed contentedly all the same, playing up for the moment, feeling and enjoying the ex-hilaration of attention while my parents stood nervously in front of the psychologist's huge desk as though waiting to be reprimanded for bringing *this* into the world.

He's never so much as said boo to a goose before . . .

The psychologist nodded, resting his arms on the desk, looking at me, assessing the possibility for extended sessions, calculating how much milk could be drawn out of me and my situation. I looked back at him, constantly, kept my brown eyes on him, never wavering, holding steady to his eyes until he dropped his gaze by pretending that he *had* to look somewhere else or shuffle a paper or two. I remember the game as it was played then just as it is played now. You look away, you lose. That's how it went, that's how it goes.

No, no, no, never . . .

My parents were issuing excuses for my behaviour, refusing to sit down, unable or unwilling to be calmed. They were there out of duty, a manufactured sense of expected behaviour.

If you receive faulty goods you should take them back for repair or replacement.

Then there were the psychiatrist's textbook questions, delivered in a slow, reassuring manner, aimed, no doubt, to lull me into his confidence. I knew the tricks even before I had signed the subscription for *Therapist's Weekly*. I was a natural as far as I was concerned and if he didn't understand what had happened and needed to know from me the psychological nitty-gritty, then he was no natural, he was no expert and in no position to give me advice on what or what not to do.

A lesson was learnt in that padded room lined with the certificates and receipts of learning.

The first rule of psychotherapy is that the patient already knows what's wrong.

Let me see . . . the fat man was pretending to be pondering my silence, affecting for my parents' sake a position of consideration. *You were in the nursery and you were being allowed to choose, free play at the end of the day, right?*

Silence.

Uh huh, then you started to play with the little girl whose name . . . is . . . Chloe. Yes? Do you like playing with Chloe, do you always play with her, is she your friend?

Too many questions, I thought, who could be bothered answering them. He was falling into the staccato trap, the joy of thinking of questions to ask, overwhelming their coherence. A basic mistake. An academic error.

Now, on this day you were playing with the water, weren't you, all the usual fun and games, spilling it, floating things in it, just

*messing about, that sort of thing, eh? When you were playing at the
water, Curtis, did you feel you needed to go to the bathroom?*

Silence.

*Playing with water quite often makes us need to go to the
bathroom, did you know that?*

I tried to imagine the psychologist lying flat in the Mickey
Mouse, ten centimetre tub, a steady stream of urine escaping
from between his legs.

Was it easier just to go there and then, is that it?

He was giving me the chance to redeem myself, recoup
my parents' hope with the notion of irrepressible biological
need. When you need to go, you need to go.

*But why, Curtis, did you go in the tub, why, as we adults
say, urinate, pee, if you like in the tub? Did it seem the right thing
to do . . .*

I remember wanting him to hurry up or at least to give me
something else to sink my teeth into.

*. . . and was Chloe annoying you in some way, did she do
something wrong to you, say something bad?*

Motive equals tangible justification.

*Why, Curtis, did you put her head in the tub and hold it down?
Why did you do that? Can you tell me?*

Undoubtedly, but he wasn't getting squat from me. Not
all questions deserve answers would have been the response if
the vocabulary had been there and not all psychologists, if any,
know what they are looking for when they ask questions, is
what I would say if my intuition had gained voice. As it was, I
just sat there and said nothing, staring at the wall, looking
enviously at the fat man's big green chair and knowing that he
had nothing on me, knew nothing about me and was in no
way able to help me. That is, if I needed to be helped.

I could have given him some responses he might have
been able to cling onto.

1. I just felt like it, I don't know why I did it.
2. I hated her, she was just a girl.
3. Genitals look funny under water.
4. My parents made me do it.

Plenty of meat on those possible explanations, all of which would have given that backstreet psychohack loads of sessions to seek out the reasons behind the action and ultimately give help to bandage such terrible psychological sores opened up early in one so young . . .

But he got nothing, so he *took* something. He told my parents that children often exhibit a random sense of amorality which can be illustrated by an act of violence or occasionally self-mutilation. This is, he said, *'merely part of the evolving personality, the nascent and developing ethical self . . .'*

And this reassured them, my quiet loving parents, who wouldn't say boo to a goose. Being medical professionals themselves they warmed to his jargon. For me that was the scariest thing he said . . .

*

Josie is between my legs. And it's just where I want her to be.

Her hair is short, shaven to the bone, a velvet rub on my thighs. Sometimes she has long flowing locks, Hollywood brat type of thing; sometimes a carefully balanced bob is trimmed before my eyes but tonight she took out the clippers, put the number one guard on the blades and turned on. *Turned on.* The Josie of old, the cherubic face, pink cheeks, pink dresses, has gone.

She puts the clippers down, surrounded by her own hair, clumps of it sticking to her bare shoulders, a few locks tucking themselves between her breasts. She walks from the bathroom, shaking off stray hair and comes to the foot of my double futon, in my single flat with one purpose in mind. *What can I do for you?* she asks me giving me a piercing look between my legs. But I don't like it, too sluttish, too faraway from the sister I knew and loved. I tell her that the body should be mutable, the personality durable. And I make her both pert and alert to my pearls of wisdom.

It's been a long time. That's better, I think, and let her go on. *But I've come back to you now.* She clambers onto the bed the same way the skinny, goldilocked, annoying little sister did years ago, and there it is, there's the memory, plucked from the debris in my mind. But maybe it's a little fuzzy. Got to remember that the memory plays tricks, puts you on swings, pushes you around roundabouts, takes you up to the top of the rollercoaster then lets go . . . And got to remember too, that she's a lot bigger now, grown out and up a long time since we trampolined together on her bed. She's got curves where she had only kinks before. A quick check of a family snap held dutifully in a gold frame and I'm up and running.

Do you remember that time . . . I get her to say but cut her off before she says another word, before she helps me trawl another memory. I don't want her going back to gather memories, such a depleted crop surviving somehow on barren land – the head was shaved for a reason I remind myself. Tonight, she's all grown up – well mostly – and I want her in the here and now. Work is about memories, this is recreation and the best r 'n' r for a psychohack is the here and now. Besides tonight is designated a Grade 3 night – medium erotic images – and if she's going to start taking me back to when there were more kinks than curves I would have to upgrade it to Grade 2 and I didn't want to waste such lip-smacking images for a humdrum Monday, after a humdrum day at the psycho clinic.

The spivs at Breathhouse would be appalled by my attitude, my lack of jargon, even my lack of judgment. *Is this personal research, Mr Sad?*

She clambers onto the bed and works her way up each leg with a quick moving tongue. I just love the feel of her head on my skin and I start to tug. But then she takes too long, spends a little too much effort on my thighs. Monday is not a night for lingering so I move her up, speed up the fantasy so her tits are banging into my face – speed it up girl, I tell her, don't hold back on me now . . . *My time is yours,* she says to me, and I like the way that sounds, so I get her to say it more slowly this time, *My . . . time . . . is . . . yours . . .* the words are chewed by her thumb stuck in her mouth, a sudden and unrequested image of her rocking back and forwards, back and forwards in my mother's chair waiting as she always did for her to come home from work or parties or both. Not that, I tell her, tell myself, shaking her, shaking the image out of my head until she is back the way I want her, all shorn and lean. I smile. I can see clearly now, I sing to my Breathhouse colleagues, singing at the top of my voice as Josie swaps her thumb for my cock.

*

If it's Tuesday it must be porn night – or, to use some jargon, *video-based psychosexual research*, rather than the home movies of Josie and me playing about on some godforsaken beach at a time laughingly called summer; Josie and me on a swing in some shitty play park; Josie and me at bath time, playing with ducks, skooshing water on each other, aiming for the flat brown discs on our chests. All carefully edited, of course, the intrusive appearance by a smiling and proud parent cut out, their starring roles abruptly cropped. I saved and savoured these videos for when I had the time to appreciate them, otherwise I had a love/hate relationship with my VCR – not so much turned on as bored stiff.

A friend at a clinic in New York, the Manhattan Psychosexual Institute, sent some tapes to Breathhouse, or rather, the Unit I was in the process of setting up to *explore the psychosexual paradoxes inherent in inter-family relationships*. Word travels quickly in research circles, communication often fuelled by either paranoia or jealousy, often both, but I sensed that Peterson was different, not so much a competitor but a kindred spirit.

The tapes were strictly legit, of course, official seals and the like kept the customs hands well off. One of the many strands of the Institute's work was looking at the effect and purpose of non-specific pornographic material, ie not your average top-shelf bums-and-tits number, but the illicit use of what would normally be considered innocuous footage. It's well documented that sexual deviants of whatever hue or persuasion will gather whatever visual stimulus they can, whether it is cuttings from clothing catalogues or nudist brochures, edited highlights of children's TV or sports coverage of young gymnasts. Most of the videos contain little of interest, the kind of material that would appear strange but meaningless until it finds a context – a sign of perpetual lowbrowism maybe, a taste deviation perhaps, but not a criminal one. However, once John Doe is picked up for some inappropriate act, the police sift through the video collections and scrapbooks looking for evidence of intent, visual proof of the deviant thoughts that led to the deviant act.

One of the tapes is shit hot though. Sent to me, no doubt because of its family-orientated context. It contained twenty minutes of through-the-keyhole footage from some guy in Montana banged up for five years minimum for filming his sisters, cousins, nieces in the bathroom of his home. It seems Uncle Bob, a forty-year-old mechanic, had a big family who spilled into his home around Thanksgiving and Christmas. Then, once his charges, ranging in age from ten to twenty, decided to ablute, wash, shower or shit then he would get his camcorder and stick it into a suitably gouged hole in the wall disguised by some floral arrangement and film the girls in various states – undressing, shitting, preening and very occasionally masturbating.

Of course, Uncle Bob, being of limited IQ, took his work away from his home, into the public arena, into a public swimming pool, to be accurate, and his observational skills and expertise with the zoom counted only for the number of days he would waste away inside.

At least his work wasn't wasted, however – even if the poor schmuck wouldn't be treated, he would researched, case studied and so, like Peterson, I dimmed the lights and entered Uncle Bob's world. What the video lacked in fluidity – it chopped and changed nearly every few minutes in a typical homemade cut and paste fashion – it made up for it with zeal and a real feel for his subject.

I wasn't interested in any of the girls and young women he visited, most of them were bucktoothed or had backsides that could be barely framed by the camera. But I didn't need to see them, Josie just sprang up in front of the screen and took me into her toilet world just like she did years ago at home on holiday, just like she used to do before she caught me at the keyhole and bunged a Tampax into the lock. Now as the girls in Uncle Bob's video put theirs in, I took Josie's out, following her hand with my eyes while bucktoothed hicks dissolved from view. Just me and her. Then and now.

Peterson had added some notes at the end of the more formal report. Uncle Bob had undergone psychiatric tests, as the phrase goes, which is de rigueur for this kind of crime in most states, bar a few, where the only analysis is on how best to hang, draw and quarter the abominable sinner. These tests were of the usual variety. It's not therapy, at least not by the lay person's idea of therapy – a cosy chat in an armchair or on a couch with plenty of safety devices if one or two tears are shed in the moment. Hardly. What goes on in these tests is far removed from that, far removed from any notion of helping the patient; rather it's diagnosing the disease that's important.

The psychology versus therapy, treatment versus help argument starts right here.

A kind of mental ECT is employed. Show the prisoner some erotic images akin to the crime he is accused of – young girl gymnast in the changing room or boy swimmers fighting with towels, for example, and get reaction, monitor and record the reaction, use the reaction as evidence in court. Change the images again with the emphasis away from eroticising of the innocent to the eroticising of the *pain* of the innocent – footage of a young girl being penetrated by first one finger, then two, then three, and so on, or clips from XXX 1970s videos of a young boy being severely whipped with close-ups etc of his crying face. Again reactions are noted, recorded and used as evidence. Then there are background reports, testimonies from neighbours who would usually say that he was a quiet type or kept himself to himself, never harmed anyone – the sort of thing that gets you on an FBI list, fitting a deviant psychosexual profile, the encapsulated life of a potential psychopath.

One of the conclusions drawn from such evidence, and this is evidence that Peterson at the Institute says he uses to scrape faeces from his arse, is that Uncle Bob getting aroused by the more innocent shots is likely to be an *opportunistic latent*, meaning that while his paedophile tendencies exist, they are only likely to surface on certain occasions, and with certain children. In other words, don't let the guy work with children or have children. If, however, Uncle Bob gets a raging hard-on at the sight of the physical cruelty videos, then he is an *overt psychopath* meaning that he inhabits a world of harmful fantasy which is very likely to be then transferred into his way of life. In other words, lock the guy up and throw away the key.

What do you think, Sad? Would you undergo such tests and be happy with the conclusions? Why do you think these so-called psychiatric tests are used for the state prosecutors? You look for something bad, you'll find something dirtier than a hole full of shit. You catch my drift. Give'em enough rope sort of thing.

When the videos reach their end, the television turned off, the lights dimmed, Josie is waiting for me on my futon, slightly younger than yesterday, the adolescent pout just a little softened. I want her to say something nice, something comforting, to take us both away from Uncle Bob's seedy, pathetic world but she blurts something out that I couldn't stop.

Am I like those girls in the video?

I guess sometimes even semi-experienced psychohacks can't always keep control and I didn't want the question but I found myself compelled to answer it, moved by the look of concern on her sweet face. I put my hand on her head, the hair grown from skin to crew cut.

'Of course not,' I tell her. 'You are special to me. You're my sister and we love each other.' I squeeze the bridge of her nose with my fingers just like I used to do when we played in the garden at home. And, of course, I realise why the question came out. The doubt she had elucidated simply made us closer. The question was answered by our continued intimacy.

It's all worked out.

*

Wednesday is the night for dynamic research, which is to say, where the researcher, unlike those tired old fucks up the road, doesn't simply reread some Freud, scoff at Sacks or pour out some Gin and Jung, but actively seeks new material via whatever interaction is necessary – from mail order *Personality Restoration Packs* available from a P.O. box in Wales to the latest cutting edge soundbites from Psychology websites like *Psychnet*. Dynamic research is my home-life along with Josie, of course, and while the two balance precariously with each sometimes merging, sometimes conflicting, anything else domestic or mundane, is kept to a minimum.

In a minimal flat:

Corner 1: Research Material – magazines, journals, reports, video and audio recordings accumulated over the past six years.

Corner 2: Workout equipment – weights, dumbbells and a cycling machine.

I'm not setting myself up as some hormone freak, the kind of guy that walks into Breathhouse every other day, swaggering under the weight of his bulk, frothing at the mouth, armed to the teeth with every weapon under the sun saying *I am the angel of death, I have transcended earthly evil*. There's many a burly psycho that has passed through this system, derailed by steroids, unplacated by Prozac but for me the weights are to stretch my sinew not my sanity.

The second rule of psychotherapy is a healthy body doesn't necessarily mean a healthy mind.

Corner 3 : VCR, TV, Hi-fi

Corner 4: Futon

Sitting in my functional flat, I squeeze myself between shelves and explore the dysfunctional family stories that are my bread and butter – 57% of families of whatever hue or make-up have reported mental health problems. Love it.

Case studies prove to be the most useful. The *Journal of Reactive Psychology* has always been one of my favourites since my student days, when I would hole myself up in the library and look for the far-out, the freakish, the downright perverse. In many ways it was this journal, along with a handful of others, that steered me clear of educational and clinical colleagues and into research and, in particular, the monitoring of inter-family sexuality behaviour patterns. In the current month's issue of *Reactive Psychology*, Peterson had followed through on a case study, a study which he and other psy-chosexual researchers call an x4 – in other words a situation where four generations of abuse – grandson, son, father and grandfather – have been identified. Peterson was given the case after the grandson was referred by social workers to the Institute. Given the case because other third-rate, triple-rate-per-hour therapists couldn't handle it. Sheep in lambswool sweaters, the lot of them.

The situation had first been picked up at school where the grandson freaked his teacher out by drawing an anatomically correct, anatomically erect man fucking a young boy. Apparently the boy had a prodigious talent for drawing and had managed to represent both his own face and that of his father's with unnerving accuracy. The boy was whisked away by the authorities as was the father who, under questioning, revealed a classic abusive history.

Peterson then very diligently records the systematic ques-tioning of the father and the equally systematic therapy given to the boy. I kind of skim-read this part – the psychother-apeutic tactics of comforting and revealing are all too well known to me and many's the time I have been lectured by learned colleagues at Breathhouse as to the value of such therapy while always at the back of their mind, sotto voce, beneath their words, is the implication that research such as mine has little or none of this quality.

Tangible work, Sad, begets tangible results.

Fuck 'em. They put a Band-Aid on a gaping wound and sit around catching the blood as it leaks out. They're so certain that it will work that they never think to change the dressing . . .

Anyway, Peterson goes on to discover that the father had been physically abused by his own father − kept in sheds overnight, locked in cupboards, starved for days on end − that sort of thing − and had only managed to put an end to the abuse by running away − and, get this, by running away with the circus! And the reason why I like Peterson's work is that he doesn't overlook this detail, or rather, he doesn't allow it to become a non-relevance, citing it as merely being a route of escape. It's more than that, much more than that. The guy ends up flagellating elephants, wanking stallions and fucking zebras. And while third-rate researchers would have over-looked the circus connection, Peterson explored it fully − interviewing circus performers, taking a gander at the big top − and discovered that what had been thus far labelled an x3 became an x4 when Peterson discovered that this man who had bullied his son, who in turn has interfered with the boy artist, had in fact killed his own father in a brutal showdown, blood apparently covering a large portion of the house they lived in. The reason. The circus lover had confronted his own father about some incidents that were coming back into his memory about dodgy camping holidays where his father had shown him more than the ropes.

And this was one article in one magazine with piles more to wade through, all waiting in the corner of the room and all with the promise that after my hard night's work, I always, always had the prospect of Josie lying in wait for me in Corner four, for a night of variable activities, eternal intimacy; to fall between her thighs and breathe in her scent after an evening spent with the fucked-up and the freaked-out was such rich reward.

*

Thursday is, has been for the past six months, at any rate, my late night at work. Encounter group with Dr. Curtis Sad, Breathhouse, 1st Floor, Room 4, says the notice board at the outpatient department. Kind of strange, really. I've never wanted to set myself up as a therapist and I guess some would say I'm even vaguely critical of the whole growing phenomenon of preventative therapy – treatment based on the likelihood of deviation, getting to the stable door and choking the horse's head in it, sort of thing. But the bigwigs at Breathhouse, each a paid up member of the big names in Psychologists' social clubs – The Shrine, The Dome, The Citadel – were all for it and all junior staff such as myself had to not only volunteer for such duty but create a programme of active therapy . . . *of relevance to the community, Sad* . . . which, in my case was a group therapy session for potential deviants or rather a wide range of Joe and Josefina Public who were concerned not only about memories and experiences surfacing now they were adults, but about the effect this would have on their otherwise normal family lives.

I expected about one tragic bastard to turn up with a shifty look on his face, but at the first session there were eight people there and eventually the numbers on occasion went up to eleven or twelve, but always with the same half dozen or so as the group's hard core. So to speak.

Another sad encounter . . . how do you feel, Sad . . . were just some of the inane wisecracks I got from losers in the admin block where the sessions took place. Researchers were persona non grata – fully fledged clinical psychologists, who strode around Breathhouse's Victorian corridors, clicking their heels, shunned us as academic upstarts, and nervous psychotherapists seemed to cling to the walls whispering to each other *this island's mine . . .* But I was above and past all of that before they had the chance for poor jokes. I'd heard them all before and besides they were jealous, jealous of the fact that when I went into that room with my group milling about with poly cups of scalding coffee glued to their hands and equally, an sheepish look stuck to their faces, I had their full attention and at least 75% of their awe. The penpushers, terminal jumpers, couldn't match any of that.

The set-up was more or less the same each week. Any new members of the group had to introduce themselves. With my benign encouragement they would stand up and tell the group why they were here. Bog standard group stuff really, practised the length and breadth of the country from Al-Anon to groups for the relatives of car crash victims. *Hello, my name is Sooz and I believe I was abused.* It was usually very moving stuff and once the new member had sat down to have their hand held or shoulder squeezed by one of the hard-core six, gentle questions were asked, never about the authenticity of their stories, God forbid, but always about how they felt now, how they felt then. Then, once this had been done, conversation was always triggered and under my guidance the group discussed topics for the evening such as *Mothers and Daughters; Fathers and Sons: How to Deal with Recurring Memories; Is it better to forgive or reveal? Living with the Legacy of Abuse* and, of course, the recurring favourite, *Am I One Too?*

It was always curious to see how people dealt with being at the group. And even curiouser to see how some secreted their visit behind dark glasses, pulled-up collars and nervous looks back into the corridor. It was clear that many had forced themselves to come and saw the sessions as akin to a visit to the dentist – a painful but necessary thing – while others no doubt saw Sad's Thursday evening encounter group session as the highlight of their week. Let me give you two examples.

Around the third week, with numbers teetering around the five or six mark with only two having been at all the sessions, one man, Brent, arrived. He was a bundle of nervous energy from start to finish – a scar-faced whirling dervish who strode into the room and rankled the others by refusing to sit down. While the others clasped their coffee timidly, Brent downed his in one go, black, three sugars of scalding coffee, and announced to the usual hush in the room, 'I was in Al-Anon for three years but I'm still drinking.'

There was another new member in the group, a middle-aged woman, dark looks and a brow that was constantly furrowed. She refused coffee and sat on the chair furthest from mine. It was clear once everybody settled down that Brent would have to speak first. His edgy vertical position was devastating the calm of the room, his lack of reticence about wanting to tell his story was a kind of violence that battered the sensitive egos of the group.

'Funnily enough my Dad ended up in *Gamblers* Anon. He'd bet on anything that moved all his life – dogs, horses, boxing – Christ, if it had a chance of winning he'd place a fiver, a tenner on it and sit back in the bookies, in his armchair and watch some loser waste his money. He said he needed practice. I was a kid of about twelve say, just starting up at the big school and I was impressed by the wad of £1 notes shoved in my hands. He taught me the ways and means of poker, five card stud, five card brag, all the games where the cards were wild and tame. At the end of each hand he'd say to me, 'The loser has to take off something.' Strip poker, in other words, I suppose you'd call it, very fucking one-sided though. He taught me the game but he had years of experience under his belt, as well as about three layers of clothing, and so he never lost. While I ended up in the scud every time. T-shirt, jeans, socks ('counts as one') and then I was left in my pants, sitting in front of him, him with enough clothing to survive in the Arctic, never mind the pokey den he brought me up in. If I won a hand I could put something back on but it never got too far. Sometimes I got the trousers back on, only to lose them in the next hand. I learnt that it was easier just to put the socks on. There was no, what d'you call it, modesty left anyhow.'

Since the group had only just started, most of the people there had no way of relating the story to others except their own and I sat in my padded chair looking at their faces, knowing that their stories were going to be full of tears, dusted down memories that tore and stretched the mind to breaking point. There would be painful images shaped and moulded into something real but while they wrestled with demons known and unknown, Brent took off his shoes, and revealed his bare feet, wiggling his toes with remarkable agility . . .

'And I never could wear socks again,' he added, giggling relentlessly, collapsing into a chair, smothering his mouth with his jacket.

'And our other new visitor tonight is . . . ?' I gestured towards the middle-aged woman sliding down her chair at the back. Eventually, under the supportive smiles of the others around her, she stood up, her back hunched, her hands clasped, looking both terrified and disapproving of Brent, who quietened down to pick at the hard skin under his toes.

'My name is Sofia and I was abused.'

Now in other groups this kind of statement brought rapturous applause from others, who believed that simply stating the problem out loud was half the battle, whereas of course it was merely a skirmish. Here, in Sad's encounter group, I actively discouraged congratulations on admission.

The third rule of psychotherapy is never trust what the patient says.

'Both my mother and father hit me. As a child, if I did anything wrong they would take turns in meting out the punishment and they both had their own ways and their own scales by which they worked out the most suitable punishment. My mother would grab both my arms and twist my wrists, burning my skin, and sometimes she would just simply hit me in the face with the palm of her hand, not a slap, but a flat-handed punch. My father threw things at me and then if I refused to cry or show remorse for something that I hadn't done he would run over to me – and he was a big man, well over six feet – and twist my arms up my back, pushing me against a wall. Sometimes repeatedly. Now I want to ask you, Dr. Sad, and any of you here with children of your own. What if I do this to them? I love them dearly and I would never touch a hair on their heads, but sometimes I remember the rage, the overwhelming anger of my parents, and I think to myself – will it visit me, will I blank out and next thing I know see my children in a pool of blood?'

Half the group was listening to her, nodding their heads in understanding while the other half was torn between sympathy and fascination as they watched Brent, blowing between his toes, saying out loud just after Sofia's speech, 'Don't you just hate the pieces of fluff that get between your toes? Where the fuck do they come from?'

I bunched up my notes, tapped them on my clipboard like a newsreader and said, 'Well, we certainly have quite a bit to respond to tonight, who would like to start . . .'

I loved the Thursday night sessions in the end, hated them at first. They seemed too much of a humdrum chore, irrelevant to ambition, but there was always something to liven up the session. Best thing about it was that the staff car park at Breathhouse was literally two doors away out a fire exit and while at the end of the session the quiet ones who rarely said anything beyond their piece and then never came back would lie in wait for me near the exit, hoping for a free and more private consult, I could nip out the fire door and be away before they had a chance to utter the dread fuelling line *'I didn't want to say this in front of the group but . . .'*

*

Fridays are heaven-sent. Just me and Josie. No Breathhouse, no fuck-ups, no intrusions. I come in after work and kick the evening off with a joint – home grown from behind outhouse number one in the expansive and mostly overgrown grounds of Breathhouse. The grower, a staff nurse, supplies most of the hospital. Long-term residents as well as about half the psychohacks benefit from his green fingers.

Best time of the day, watching the clouds of smoke rise above me while Josie descends. Her hair has grown back in remarkably quickly since the last time we were together and some of the longer strands tickle my chest as she unbuttons my shirt, easing her soft hands down the side of my body. Friday is a grade two night, set to warm myself up for Saturday when all hell in its sweetest form breaks loose. She's a teenager, slinking into adulthood with sullen intensity. *I hate you, loathe and detest you*, she says to me, her lips pouting, her hands impatiently tugging the shirt away from my back. I let her carry on, the body mutable, the personality ringing in my ears as true to life as ever; besides, there is no reason to stop her, this our own private Idaho and back in the old house I couldn't stop her anyway. She'd run away from me as I tried to catch her leg, and I'd grab hold of her ankles, or maybe her calves sliding her towards me with a big smile on my face. *Caught.*

And in the here and now – if there needs to be such a distinction – she's chasing me, off the bed onto the floor, dragging me by my belt until my shoulders touch the floor-boards. I want her to turn nasty, this being Friday night. I want to up the contact, reduce her age and bang us into grade two. She's always had jagged nails. My mother tried to show her the finer points of manicure and the art of nail polish but Josie would have none of it. She liked to fight too much, like to use her hands to scratch and slap her brother when he got too mouthy, which was, believe me, all the time. We fought like cat and dog, typical brother and sister scenario. Now she was getting her own back. *Go right ahead.*

I felt the edge of her nails drag across my bare chest and I made sure the neighbours could hear what a good time we were having. *Make them jealous*, I tell her and immediately she clambers on top of me, her thighs pressing hard against me and she rides and moans. *Louder*, I tell her, not wanting the neighbours to have to rush to get a glass against the wall. And louder she goes. And we have music, sweet fucking incredible Friday night music. I try to sit up, my hands going for her short skirt, to lift it, to see what was underneath, this being Friday, but she takes my hands and throws them behind me as she moves up to sit on my face.

Everything is there to smell and feel, her sweat, the tights, the lingering odour of her. Unmistakable.

*

When she was 14, I took her tights from her room and sneaked around to the bathroom, where I could hear her talking to herself, lost in the vapours of bath oil and some memory. With no lock on the door, it was easy for me to crawl along on my belly, sliding into the bathroom, the mist above me blocking out the ceiling and steaming up the mirror. With the tights in my hand, I drew close to the edge of the bath, her body facing away from me, drops of water splashing onto my face. When she hummed some tune, I knew it was the right moment and I jumped up and drew the tights around her mouth, stopping the hum in mid-flow as she bit into the nylon. Her body writhed in the water and I took it all in. The long legs, the islands of bubbles drifting across and snagging on her pubic hair; her breasts poking out the water, shaking as she fought against my grip.

'Get out,' she managed to scream through the gag.

*

She got off my face and turned me onto my back and took the rest of my clothes off. Then she used the belt to strap up my hands tightly behind my back. I could see nothing except the loose splinters of unvarnished wood on the floorboards, before I closed my eyes and felt her index finger worm its way into my arse. First joint, second joint, to the knuckle. Then bliss.

*

Saturday afternoon. Josie's running from one corner to the next and so on around. She's small and thin enough, at about age ten, to slide under the weights bench and pause for a moment, a wild look in her big brown eyes, the rings and curls of her hair blowing haphazardly in the gusts of her breath. Then she's off again, up and over the TV and video in corner three until she finally comes to rest, a sliding tackle under my futon and she is still.

I'm in the opposite corner of the room, pretending to look through some papers, filing with one eye on the folder balancing on my lap, the other on her legs disappearing under the futon. She was always good at chases, loved it in fact, her whoops and yells echoed round the rambling house of my parents, secluded as it was from the sounds of distant neighbours. And that's what I'd tell her. *No one can hear you scream,* using my best horror voice, and she'd shriek and dash under the stairs. Just like she raced to hide under the futon, the loose sheet slightly parted so that she could witness my approach.

Oh yes, I'm coming, I tell her putting the folder to one side, kicking off my shoes so she won't hear me as I quickly dart to the door, a blind spot from her gaze. I can feel the blood beginning to rush in my body, the adrenalin kick only Josie can install.

In my parents' house she dived into the cellar, locking the door behind her. I could hear her taunt *you can't catch me*'s but the chant soon faded when she realised I had the keys, both the mortise and the Yale. I poured myself a glass of milk, stuffed my face with a jam sandwich and turned on the TV. I knew what she would be doing. She'd be edging closer and closer to the door, pushing her ear against the wood, listening to hear what I was doing, wondering if she could come out yet. I'd let the keys jangle in my hand, loud enough for her to hear.

In my room, I can hear her giggle from under the futon as she peers out, trying to calculate where I am, but before she can see me standing by the door, my hand gently rubbing my half filled cock, I run onto the mattress, thumping it as I land. I can hear her laughter, the nervous gasp and then nothing but silence in the room. The neighbours somewhere are playing music, but we are lost to our game.

I tap the sheet one side then the other, first left then right, to keep her guessing and under me I can hear her little legs scramble from one side to the other. *What you doing up there?* she asks me. I tell her to rephrase the question. *What are you going to do?* which I like the sound of more. Wait and see is what I tell her, hitting, not tapping, the sheet. This is Saturday night, after all, grade one activity, where bounds are temporarily forgotten, the censor, the PC patroller, the professional etiquette moderator shunted to one side in the name of pleasure and relaxation. As it should be.

I made my way slowly to the cellar door, pencil torch in hand, and put my ear to the wood, trying to work out where exactly she was. I decided she was not on the stairs any more but, fed up with the wait, she had gone down into the cavernous cellar, piled high as it is with years of junk, unwanted, unusable or unsuitable to my parent's fickle decorative tastes. I put the key in the lock making as little noise as possible. It would be nice to surprise her, even better if she thought she was being rescued by her parents.

It was a classic cellar, all darkness and creaking floorboards, but I did my best to descend slowly, taking each step carefully, bending over to peer into the gloom. At the bottom of the stairs I flicked on the torch and pointed it towards the darkness. The junk was unbelievable: piles and piles of magazines, machines and domestic mayhem, all of it discarded to the cellar's dust and cold, damp feel. There were so many places to hide, even more for a young girl of ten, as thin as a rake, capable of hiding between, as well as behind, any of the dozens of tea chests stacked from floor to ceiling.

Before I moved any further, I shifted an old wardrobe in front of the bottom stair, blocking any quick exit Josie might attempt. I could see her running to the bottom of the stairs, full of laughter, thinking she had managed to double back on me, only to find the hulking piece of mahogany blocking her way. I could see myself standing behind her, laughing too, watching her thin arms struggle with the thick wood.

I lower myself over the edge of the futon, enjoying the feeling of yet more blood rushing to my head, enjoying the feeling too of my cock pressed against the mattress. When I lift up the other side of the bed just as she is about to scatter out from under to another corner of the room to start the chase again, I decide enough is enough and grab her leg just as she makes a break for it. Say it again, I instruct her.

What you gonna do, Curt, what you gonna do?

I know exactly what I'm going to do. Without letting go of her leg, I slide myself off the futon and in a swift movement I am on the floor, my head just poking into the darkness, a darkness lit by two eyes. Josie tries to keep her other leg out of reach but sooner rather than later I grab hold of it, the thin ankle easily slipping into my firm grasp. There are still giggles coming from her but her laboured breath interrupts their flow. For a moment, a long moment, my eyes meet hers in the tense duality of our play. She is wearing a simple dress, plain green cotton, a cereal pack charm round her neck, an old bracelet of my mother's ridiculous on her thin wrist. We hold the moment do Josie and I, hold and savour the moment.

The pencil torch soon picked her out, her green dress suddenly lit up against the dark stains on the dusty walls. I moved the thin beam of light slowly from her legs to her heaving chest to her face, framed by an old wheel from my father's car where she sat, her arms holding onto the rubber rim, a grip I could see from five metres away that was as tight as tight could be. She didn't make a sound. She didn't giggle or yell or shout. Nothing from her.

I walked towards her and she sank further into the tyre. I

could hear her say something but her voice was so soft, so quiet that I couldn't make it out until I was standing at her feet.

'Mum and Dad will be back soon,' she told me.

'I know,' I told her.

It's been a hard week at Breathhouse, new crazies arriving all the time, more paperwork, more couch work, I guess, but I can feel the stress easing out of me, the joint, the moment, Josie, all of it helping me to unwind. But I can't wait any longer, patience is not a part of relaxation, and I pull her towards me, so that her legs bend around my waist. She is so beautiful, her smile as she gazes up at me so inviting, so warm, so . . . revitalising, are the words but the actions mean more, much more. I bend over her and put my lips to hers, tracing my tongue across the chapped and bitten skin, then I let my nose trail its way down the thin cotton dress until I reach her crotch. I close my eyes and then open them again, switching from one shadow to another, from one sense to another. With my lips so close to her skin I tell her to whisper to me. She responds, *Oh, Curtis . . .* in a voice I don't like. Too much like a whore, but I urge her to continue.

Curtis, this is so special.

And I smile at that. What a nice thing to say.

She knew what to do, she always knew what to do because she lost all the time. *To the victor the spoils . . .* She took off the green dress slowly and as it bunched around her ankles she pulled off her vest and held it in her hand, uncertain what to do with it. I took it from her with my teeth. I stripped off my own clothes, letting each item hit the floor with a muffled thud but we both jumped when the buckle from my belt clanged on the concrete, quickly followed by the revving engine of my father's car above us. Josie looked alarmed but I knew their habits, knew their form, knew the routine and rituals they followed. They wouldn't come down into the cellar. And the only sound I heard after the slam of doors was the sound of my own voice saying, 'You do it like this . . .'

*

Wednesday night. Received a fax from Wayne Peterson at the Manhattan Institute. Peterson's excited, as only Peterson can be. Seems he's found himself an interesting case study – lucky bastard, I always think when he regularly faxes and enthuses about some find, some discovery he's made. Cutting edge psychology. All I get at Breathhouse is some freak whose fed his budgie his toenail clippings for the past fifteen years until it got all choked up and now he's full of pathological guilt. *I need, doctor, I need to do an autopsy for my own peace of mind* . . . Still, on a maudlin Wednesday night it beats listening to the neighbours fuck upstairs.

She's squealing like a pig, I say to Josie. *I don't do that, do I?* I get her to say to me. I know, I reply. Then she laughs, covering her mouth coyly with the back of her hand. I love it when she does that.

It seems Peterson's excited because he's found some poor guy who shows an extreme form of intrusive memory. Now, this sort of memory can be dull, stale stuff in the wrong hands, which are the usual hands – psychohacks gleaning the mundane from their clients as they all tread wearily on the memory mill, from A to B, from associative to behavioural, and back again.

Peterson's speciality isn't usually memory research – God knows what his speciality actually is, but weird ideas and fucked-up interest in the fucked-up community has certainly got him and the Institute a shit load of grants. Anyway, seems that this guy, a twenty-six year old banker has been undergoing therapy for depression. This, of course, isn't that unusual, half his office is probably on the couch, but it was a classic case of the therapist getting much more than he bargained for, a classic case of opening a can of worms.

During therapy, as most people get more and more distressed, they get the occasional intrusive memory, with the phrase 'it just popped into my head' usually leapt on and pummelled by the hack therapist, bludgeoning the imagery out of some inconsequential tittle-tattle until all meaning is eroded and, more importantly, all opportunity wasted. However this banker, Richard Wattle, didn't just get the occasional intrusive memory, he had what started out as a trickle, then a stream, then a complete flood. The therapist got on the hotline to the Institute and got Peterson to sit in on the session and what Peterson described was amazing.

Richard would start the session normally enough. The therapist asking him innocuous questions, enquiring about how he was feeling, what he had done, what he had thought about, what he had dreamt about. The usual. The kind of conversational reassurance that's run of the mill up and down the country. Then his facial expression would change, a kind of twisting grimace that replaced the nervous smile dramatically. Of course, the therapist would ask him what he was thinking about, but the memories flashing into Wattle's mind would have been best served by the question *what are you seeing?*

Wattle would describe the image of his father stretching a rope from one wall of their family living room to the other, making it taut about three metres off the ground. He would order the young Wattle to lie underneath the rope and then he would clamber up onto a chair and walk along the rope. Wattle described himself lying down on the floor watching his father traverse the room, his arms outstretched for balance, convinced that his father would fall, fall just at the point he was directly over him.

Then Wattle's face would change and he would return to his description about feeling unhappy at work and unlucky with any of the women in his life. Am I gay? he asked the therapist who simply fielded the question with another question, *Do you think you are?* Typical therapy tennis, the sort of game that I've never wanted to play.

Peterson, in the margin of his notes, comments, *Jesus, the guy's just described a fairly bizarre memory unrelated to the subject of his depression and the therapist has hooked onto his concern about his sexual orientation!*

And then just as the therapist is about to launch into another question about Wattle's current state of nervous upheaval and, it must be said fairly mild depression, another memory interrupts his halting flow. Again the face changes and again the therapist asks him what he is feeling.

This time he describes his father lifting him up off the floor when he was maybe ten years old. In one swift movement he is raised and placed carefully on top of the kitchen units. Wattle describes this with horror, his hands covering his face, his legs pushing away from the couch as though he is trying to get grip enough to escape. His face is only about thirty centimetres from the ceiling, its old plaster coated with grease. On his bare legs he can feel the decaying lumps of spattered food, the oily texture of dust and grease which coat that never dusted area of a kitchen. He describes moving his head to one side to look at his father and all he can see are rows and rows of the decaying corpses of bugs and mosquitoes snared and starved in the sticky mess centimetres away from his face. He can see his father who stands and watches his son lying on top of the units. And he does nothing.

After this the memories take over the session, intrude until the original point of the therapy is lost. They come tumbling in, Wattle's face contorting with pain, fear and horror. His father lays him down in a bunker on a golf course and practises his short game using Wattle as the marker for his inevitable bogey shots . . .and so on. Wattle at the end of this is a gibbering mess and yet somehow finds the means to dismiss these memories, explaining away these intense life markers as weird daydreams, as teases with horror that crop up because of the therapy and are really not that important. The therapist, all at sea with such a tumultuous set of psychoses and reasoning, is unable to say much, apart from, *Perhaps we should talk about your father at the next session.* Of course, Peterson is having none of it and he makes sure that Wattle's next session will be in the Institute.

He invites me over to the States to witness this session. As he always does. Increasingly, as we have discovered our ideas have more and more in common, we have both been threatening to visit each other, and I relish the invitations via email, fax or phone. *Come on over, we'll have a ball, grab a few beers and talk about the wonders of the human mind.*

The thing I like about Peterson is his sense of irony.

*

Sunday night. And Josie is so young. Young enough to play doctors and patients, young enough for the green dress that would fit her so well in a year or two's time to look big and baggy on her. I can't remember well enough. A floral dress hangs on her for a while but I don't like its cut, the way it makes her legs look short and stubby. It has to be the green dress. *When the patient is out of synch with his memory it can be necessary and legitimate to improvise.* But there she is anyway lying on the futon giggling, shrinking from the cold touch of the stethoscope. I don't know what is wrong with her. It hasn't been decided.

In my parents' house I took my father's medical bag and searched for Josie. She was injured, terribly hurt in some crash or accident; badly enough so that she couldn't be moved, had to be found. I was the practitioner with my father's stethoscope proudly around my neck, his white coat, ridiculous and oversized, covering me from head to toe. I made the sound of an ambulance ee-awing my way through the house. *I've come to help you, make a sound to let me know where you are.* I heard a faint cry from the kitchen and walked briskly through with a grim and efficient air.

'Where does it hurt?' I said to Josie, looking down at her, lying spreadeagled on the kitchen vinyl.

'Everywhere,' she replied, and I bent over her broken body with a grim look on my face.

There were scars and red marks on her legs from earlier play; a bruise on her right arm stood out against her pale skin; a scratch from the cat on her neck, her skin raised into a thin red ridge. There seemed to be little wrong until I tried to move her leg. She squealed in pain.

'Does that hurt?'

'Yes,' she replied breathlessly.

I examined the thin, bony leg, while watching her face for signs of pain.

'I think it's broken. I'll have to set the leg.' I told her. 'Be brave.'

My father had at some point set my mother's foot after she had broken it in a fall and I tended Josie in the same way. I raised the leg, letting her bare foot rest on my knee.

'I need something to keep the leg still,' I said to her.

I took off my shirt, my skin goosepimpling with the sudden exposure and drew her dress up past her thighs. I tightened the shirt and bound it round her leg just above the knee.

'There's some blood, so this will help.'

Having bound her leg, I wasn't sure what to do next. I asked her if she thought she could put weight on it. She said she would try. With difficulty and with the help of my arm she stood up and we both looked down at the blood-soaked shirt. I could feel her arm around the bare skin of my waist and its touch reminded me of my responsibilities.

'Let me listen to your heart.'

I turned her round so that she faced me, her face close enough for me to feel her light, rapid breaths.

'Lift your T-shirt up.'

I pressed the cold metal of the stethoscope to her chest and she breathed in quickly. I remember the moment, the sense of being caught in time, just Josie and me, with me to the rescue and her hands around my waist and her heart in my ears.

On my futon, she's still in pain, her head burrowing into the covers.

'Are you in pain?' I ask her.

'No,' she replies.

'Then, you soon will be,' I joke.

'In pain there is pleasure,' she says but then I get her to change it to a giggle. Josie was never that philosophical.

I touch every part of her body, watching her face as I press and prod. Her body contracts as my hands slide between her thighs.

'What about here?'

'Especially there.' She smiles up at me but again I don't like what she says, something about the words, the tone that seems . . . unsuitable. It's got to be right.

'Don't talk. When you're this ill, it's never good to talk.'

In case she doesn't understand I press down on her, pushing my weight against her. My body, my mouth on hers.

'The kiss of life,' I allow myself to say.

*

Thursday night. The Sad encounter group meets again. Same faces as there have been for a while, including the two newcomers from last week, Brent and Sofia. Both of them, it seems, have made an effort to be different this week. Sofia is brimming with confidence, beaming in a purple dress, full of smiles towards the others in the group and, more worryingly, particularly fond of flashing her grey teeth in my direction at every opportunity as I shuffle my papers. Worrying, because it's inevitable that one of these fuck-ups will fall head over heels for me. Now I know that sounds arrogant but there has been plenty of work done on the relationship between the therapist and patient, the artificial intimacy that this can cause. Not that it is always artificial of course. One young therapist at Breathhouse fell for a schizo with delusions of grandeur and was caught fucking her royal tush in the bare and bleak consulting rooms. It seems his colleagues were alerted and concerned when they heard her crying out, 'I command you, my loyal servant, to do this for me . . .' Such stories are always in the air at Breathhouse.

I can understand. Nature calls and you just have to go. But there is little chance of me seeing anyone at these sessions whom I'm likely to want to bed. Only room for Josie and me on that futon and neither of us likes to share our space, our bodies with anyone else. We are faithful to each other.

Brent is sitting tight on his chair, coffee untouched in his clasped hands. The picture of calmness, the illusion of serenity. The erratic and adrenalin-fuelled behaviour of last week seems a long way off – his coil has been wound up again, getting tighter and tighter, as he sits there staring into space.

When there are newcomers to the group the emphasis is always put on them for the first few weeks, although, of course, everybody gets the chance to talk and continue their discussion of themselves. I ask Sofia if there has been a situation in her own family that mirrored her upbringing and thus brought out rage that was visited on her by both of her parents.

'Yes, there has.' Her confidence looks suddenly as though it is going to crumble.

'It's not easy to admit, but my previous therapist said that I should start with honesty where my parents lies' left off.'

Jesus that's just kind of moronic psychobite that you would expect from a high street therapist sitting in their rooms with a crystal ball and a copy of the book of dreams.

'Honesty being the best policy . . .' I say to wind her up, all the time watching Brent who has begun to roll his head from side to side as though stretching a stiff neck.

'Of course, of course,' Sofia agrees, flashing me a smile. Get on with it.

'Well, James is my youngest and he ruined one of my antique cremation urns by opening up the bottom and scattering the ashes into his older brother's milk while he wasn't looking.'

'You have cremation urns?' I ask her.

'That's right. When my father and mother died they both

indicated that they wanted to be cremated and even chose the urns where their ashes could be put.'

'And you kept them, despite all they had done to you.'

'My other therapist said I should keep them when I mentioned I was going to throw them out at the time when all these memories started coming back. He said that looking at the urns each day would make me stronger, more able to face their abuse and give me a direction for my anger.'

Typical. Coming up against this was a good reminder why I hadn't gone into the high-street business. This woman was looking for psychoses in the wrong place. And that half-wit of a psychohack was pushing her further over the edge. If I cared I would get her to change tactics and give James a big smacker for doing the right thing.

'I so much wanted to hit him, he looked up at me with a smile on his face and I thought, you did that on purpose, you know how much those ashes meant to me, and you still went ahead and did it . . . I wanted to hurt *him* in return.'

'And did you, Sofia?' I ask in my deepest, most meaning-laden voice.

'Oh no, I would never do that.'

I had to turn my attention elsewhere, otherwise I felt I was going to be the one doing the hitting.

'So, Brent, you're quiet tonight.'

Wrong thing to say. Reminds me that I am after all still learning the game.

Brent leapt to his feet and pointed a shaking finger at me.

'I told you, I'm not going to play. I don't want to play and I won't.'

Brent's voice had gone up an octave and he was rubbing his leg as though some terrible itch had just overwhelmed him.

'Well, Brent . . .'

'I said, I won't and you can't make me.'

He made a lunge for me, both arms outstretched with my neck as their destination.

I saw it coming but remembering the old psycho school adage - *regression is often followed by aggression* - wasn't enough and I only just had time to hit the red button under my desk before he was on me, his warm saliva spraying onto my face, his hands maniacally gripped to mine as I protected my neck.

As in a bar room brawl, everybody fled to the corners of the room and I could see Sofia out of the corner of my eyes, her hands covering her eyes, her head shaking. The red button had been fitted into all seminar rooms a few years back after a spate of attacks on staff. It was a good idea but security seemed to take a long time and Brent's crazy grip was not getting any looser. Strangely, although Brent posed a definite physical threat to me, I got sidetracked into thoughts of yesteryear and, as I felt his grip shifting itself on my skin, I found myself watching Josie watching television, one hand in her mouth, the other idly tickling her clit, and the tingling in my limbs was the sweetest feeling, which was suddenly and abruptly terminated by Brent's hands being wrenched from my neck by two burly orderlies, who carried him kicking and screaming out of the room.

'Take him to the doctor on duty,' I shouted after them.

The others gradually came away from the corners of the room to sit back nervously in their chairs. Sofia was sobbing, the only sound amidst a terrible hush in the room. I needed to get back in control or no one would be returning the following week and some nice overtime would go down the pan.

'I'm okay, and Brent will be okay. It's happened before and it will happen again but you must try to forget about it and concentrate on why you are here for yourselves. If you let what happened put you off then you will suffer more than Brent is suffering. Sometimes tension and repressed feelings can come out in no other way than violence and, if we recognise that, then we allow for the possibility of violence in all of us. Allow yourself that anger just as you must allow Brent his and we will carry on.'

I loved the sound of my own words, just like I loved the words of nearly every sycophantic essay I ever wrote to get qualified.

The fourth rule of psychotherapy is that the end always justifies the means.

I've gone way beyond worrying about appearing a hypocrite in my job here at Breathhouse. In many ways it is a prerequisite for the job. And, no, I'm not just spitting out a cheap putdown. It's just how it is. I faced that a long time ago and the only sleepless nights I have are usually because of Josie.

'So, would anyone like to restart tonight's session? Adam, how is the aggravated impotence coming along . . . ?'

*

Tuesday. The first part of the week is now devoted to research. In this job, if you really care, I've been told, you are expected to blur the boundary between work and home.

The fifth rule of psychotherapy is that a good and dedicated researcher shouldn't know how to relax.

Josie isn't happy, though, she had got used to routine attention. She's stomping around my room with a mixture of anger and sorrow. Anger in her thumping steps, sorrow in her eyes. It can't be helped, I tell her, work is work is work. *Just like Dad.* I get her to snap at me with a furious look on her face. I like it when she takes us back home.

Actually, no, it isn't, I tell her and make a grab for her. She struggles but I've got her tight around her tiny waist. He was, I tell her, a high-paid, underworked GP who tossed a few prescriptions into the air and watched his rich junkie housewives dive for them, Valium in their eyes. A charlatan with impeccable manners, the Raffles of the GP circuit, knew fuck all but was raking it in.

Not like you, Josie corrects herself.

Not like me, I tell her again, and push her gently away so that I can return to the video that came mysteriously through the post without request or even an identifiable label. All that is inside is a 60 minute tape and a note from a place called **The Psychosexual Caucus** in Ontario, Canada with *we think this will be of use to you*, written in a barely legible hand.

The fact that I haven't heard of this organisation only slightly surprises me. Psychosexual research is a growth industry – a whole gamut of shit pours through my door unannounced and often unwanted material from such illustrious organs as the **Christian Research Unit**, dedicated to finding cures for a whole range of psychosexual illnesses ends up brimming in my bin. It seems nearly every major university has a research programme lurking in some subterranean office or lab with a whole host of experts feeding the constant demand from film, chat shows, journalists and the like for expert voices to wax lyrical or at least blind with science. But psychosexual research, like any parent that has a prodigious amount of children, has been unable to control the even more substantial growth of its offspring, psychosexual therapy.

The videotape turns out to be an amateurish 60 minutes of closed circuit television footage, *Inside the Therapist's Office?* Some squinty graphics at the beginning of the tape declare it to be the first example of CCTV porn – which I find difficult to believe anyway – but the location it shows catches my attention. Unbeknownst to its therapist, a whole series of therapy sessions have been taped. That in itself is not that unusual, since many therapists now seem to be videoing their appointments, usually with, but occasionally without, the patients' consent. The idea touted is that such sessions are used in teaching technique for up and coming therapists – posture, physical attitude even decor are analysed and dissected in detail. *A potted plant placed to the right of the patient will encourage positivity.* If the patient has allowed audio recording then the transcripts are pored over, for their qualities and failures. *Hesitation in recitation of a life story often denotes sincerity and not falsehoods, as commonly thought.* This video, however, hardly seems official when in the spartan room with dishevelled armchairs a camcorder can easily be seen in the corner. It seems to be a case where the watchers don't know they are being watched. Classic CCTV, the tape announces . . .

What really goes on in a therapist's office? Have you thought about going to a therapist to talk over your problems, with your marriage, your state of mind, those hidden things you don't want anyone to know about, apart from a total stranger? Then watch this video. It may change your mind.

The video then shows a motley procession of both therapists and patients sitting in front of each other and, there being no sound, we can only see their mouths move from a distance, their legs cross and uncross, their hands clasped on their laps. The interaction is positively desultory, a numbing tedium which drags on and on. But it seems this is just to set a false pace, to lure the viewer into excitement by contrasting the first ten minutes with the frenetic editing of the remaining fifty. At this point the video concentrates not so much on the session between therapist and patient but what the therapist does while the patient either isn't looking, or is awaiting his or her arrival. One bespectacled hack is seen thoroughly picking his nose, flicking crusty snot under his chair, while a young woman cries in front of him with her head in her hands, the burrowing stopping abruptly when she pulls herself together enough to look at him. With a different therapist, an older, Freudsimile type, the video begins to live up to its hype. He is seen to show a young man to the door at the end of their session, they shake hands and wave goodbye. The moment the patient is out the room, the therapist starts to rub his groin, slowly at first, but then frantically, while the other hand pushes under his shirt to tweak his nipples. His eyes scan the notes in front of him, devouring his patient's words. After a minute or so his trousers are around his ankles and with his back to the unseen camera he proceeds to masturbate, his body shaking as he quickly orgasms. The CCTV camera just catches a thin jet of sperm fly into the air onto the patient's chair. Hurriedly – well, at least, the film gives that impression – he rushes to wipe the cum off the chair with his foot before hopping to the door, pulling up his trousers and opening the door to some dishevelled old man who hobbles to the chair while the therapist returns to his.

The video – in true porn fashion – quickly cuts between scenes building the 'action' up – leading the viewer through a sorry and often hilarious parade of wanking, scratching, vomiting, gesticulating therapists, all against the backdrop of this bare, hospital-like room. The final scene has a female therapist walking over to her male patient, unzipping his trousers and sitting on him and while the man's face remains relatively obscured the therapist shakes and rolls about as she pulls her skirt up and tights down and proceeds to ride her patient into normality.

Breathhouse was never like this.

At the end of the video, the same shaky graphics offer us another opportunity to watch a similarly thematic selection of CCTV highlights, this time from a GP's consulting room. **The Hidden Surgery**: *Why you really have to wait so long in the waiting room.*

I make a double mental note. To tell Peterson at the Manhattan Institute to get a hold of a copy of *Inside the Therapist's Office* and to write to the Canadian Caucus to make sure they send the GP video. Research has never been so entertaining.

*

It wouldn't have surprised me if the child psychologist my parents took me to when I was twelve had been a candidate for the video. And I mean that in a nice way. He was very different from the one I visited after the nursery urine incident. That one had been as stale as the air in his padded office, as flushed as the plush decor, as soft and yielding as his big swivel armchair . . . Ki Wo was a different kettle of fish altogether.

We have to take you to see someone about this, Curtis, we hope you understand that.

The problem wasn't my understanding, everything was as clear to me as it needed to be, it was their confusion they were trying to comprehend.

Ki Wo welcomed us into his brightly lit office, tastefully decorated with minimal Bauhaus furniture and colourful silk flowers in strangely curved vases. He didn't take long to catch on. Whereas the previous hack had danced around the subject of inappropriate urination, equivocating with platitudes and generalisation, Ki Wo obviously enjoyed cutting to the quick.

You might prefer to wait outside, Mr. and Mrs. Sad?

They weren't keen. My GP father was not impressed with either Ki Wo's office decor or his manner. Or even his apparent youthfulness. He was far too brash and straightforward. Ki Wo very quickly appeared to be the kind of child psychologist who called a spade a spade or identified a cigar simply as being a cigar. My parents wanted from him what they hadn't got from the other – reassurance that my activities were only a temporary aberration and a normal part of growing up that they had hitherto been unaware of.

We must have read the wrong books, my father laughed.

Ki Wo smiled politely and moved his small body onto the seat beside me, squeezing us both against the sides of the chair. My parents frowned but it made me laugh because he caught me by surprise, broke through before I had had time to work out what defence I would need against this latest action brought by my parents.

It's not right Curtis, it's not right at all. Josie and you have separate beds, there is no need for you to sleep in the same bed, no need at all.

Ki Wo asked me, flashing his perfectly white teeth and winking his left eye at me while holding his right arm out to distract me from the imminence of question. He was good, I later realised, very good.

'What do you think about when you sleep with your sister?'

My parents looked horrified and probably began to wish they had taken Ki Wo's advice and stood outside, trembling beside the coffee machine. It was a good question, both perceptive and tricksy at the same time. It was designed not only to encourage me to reveal as much as I wanted to about the situation, but also allowed Ki Wo to assess the reasons and the manner by which I withheld information in my answer.

'She's my sister, I like being close to her.'

Ki Wo smiled, patted my thigh and got up to walk behind me. It was a good answer, both tricksy and accurate, with the added bonus that it made my parents out to be shallow and shortsighted thinking that I was acting out of some kind of innate malice. How wrong could they be?

'What about when you have a bath, do you feel the same then?'

'Yes.'

My parents were sinking further into their chairs, glancing at each other, looking for something to hold onto.

'Do you think you'll feel the same, say in five years, when you're seventeen and she's thirteen.'

'Sure.'

'Do you touch each other?'

Ki Wo's question was asked in combination with the friendly laying of hands on my shoulders, his head slightly bent over, his eyes looking into mine. My parents were not so calm and it seemed that someone had just slipped an eel down both of their necks.

I turned my head and looked him in the eyes.

'No.'

The sixth rule of psychotherapy is if the patient looks you in the eyes they are invariably lying.

'Ah, Curtis . . .'

Ki Wo seemed to accept the lie with a whimsical sigh, as though he was disappointed with his own expectation of the truth.

'Do you want to touch her, anywhere on her body? Does it mean something to you for that to happen?'

It was another good, if somewhat awkwardly phrased, question but I decided I had to put a stop to the line of questioning – it wasn't taking me anywhere and my parents were going a shade of purple I didn't think was possible.

'I like playing with Josie, we have good games, we play

rough with each other. She likes it, I like it. She can play like a boy and we touch each other all the time, we test each other all the time. It's a good game.'

Ki Wo smiles and sits back down on his own chair.

'I'm sure it is, Curtis, I'm sure it is . . .'

*

Friday night. Josie in the exercise corner, idly trying to lift a dumbbell from the floor to her chest, her thin twelve year old arms barely coping with the weight. I'm on the futon in a bad mood. It's all getting too much at Breath-house, papers and forms and requisitions for everything from Valium to toilet rolls piling high on my desk. It was not what I had signed up for. All around me is the paraphernalia of trivia I had sworn would not intrude on my life with Jose and yet here it is. Head-aching admin returns, instead of ground-breaking case studies.

After Ki Wo's unsuccessful intervention in my parents' ongoing battle for my psyche, they upped gear and took firmer action. They separated us and instructed us to spend less time with each other; they sought a pop star poster world for my sister and signed me up for at least two youth clubs. I could tell they were worried.

Usually there's secret delight when a parent discovers erotic material under the mattress in the son's bedroom, a public scolding mixed with private pride in their young man coming into manhood; the satisfactory melancholy of seeing the offspring transit from child to adulthood . . . But my parents were worried by what they found. It wasn't *Hustler, Mayfair* or *Playboy* under the mattress but C. I. Sandstrom, *From Childhood to Adolescence*; F. Barker, *The Normal Childhood* – study texts stuffed with photocopies from McKean's *Intro-duction to Biology*, with diagrams of female and male genitals, with graphs illustrating the range of ages and type of changes from puberty to adolescence.

They were concerned that pocket money wasn't being spent on sweets and comics, on going out to hang around a town square trying to procure cigarettes and alcohol. They were concerned that I was holing myself in my room alone, or worse, with the Josie of tender years, and reading these texts.

What on earth do you want to read these books for?

They didn't understand that I had a master plan already in operation, a veritable runaway train that could not be stopped. My first taste of research, and I liked it. At school I had ten fellow pupils under observation, five boys and five girls, their pubescent development being carefully monitored at every available opportunity. With the boys this was, of course, easier. At gym times I would surreptitiously observe the progress of each of my five male subjects. And over a relatively short period I was able to observe that James (A1) had developed underarm hair and that six months after the survey was started his voice was noticeably squeaky. On the other hand Philip (A3) had changed very little from the beginning of observations – he was still small and smooth with a high-pitched voice and virtually no hair on his upper lip. With the girls – since I was not privy to their changing room – it was more difficult to accrue evidence on sight rather it had to be via empirical suggestion. So, during cross-country runs or volleyball I mentally noted any further development of breasts or hips and in tight running shorts sometimes it was possible to discern the development of their pubic mound. Only the gym teacher noticed.

You've got an eye for the girls, Sad.

After each session of observation – and there was usually something to record each day – I would return home and chart these results in much the same way as I had read in Sandstrom's book – general charts with the average ages of pubescent children overlaid with my own small sample. I also wrote anecdotal notes, which I found invaluable when trying to recall the exact situations where observations had taken place. And this anecdotal recording of my observations, as well as the charts and diagrams, helped me assess my own progress along the pubescent time line.

On seeing Richard (A4)'s dangling genitals in the shower, I was able to compare and contrast his with mine and judge what was happening to me. With Jane (B1) I saw the least amount of development among the five girls in the sample and she seemed to be the closest in physical type to Josie – small, very slim, with just the faintest hint of breasts, a bump in the straight line of her hips.

All of this disturbed my parents no end. Maybe they read more into what most high street hacks would suggest was simply a phase, unusual and possibly anal in its manifestation, but perhaps not unlikely since I was the product of two professionals working in medical areas – my mother was a hospital administrator. Or maybe they were concerned not so much that I could be wanking over some cold diagrams of hair growth and voice breaking, but that this was the first and irretrievable step towards a career in psychology – not an area they held in any esteem whatsoever

As a result I wasn't so much grounded but evicted. Evicted from my bedroom, from Josie's bedroom, from the house itself, told to go out and see something of the world. I was told to go to the cinema, to the local cafe, to hang out with my school friends. *Just once in a while, Curtis, I would like to see you with boys your own age.* But if they had understood and not just been bound up in their parochial world of ruined livers and sick lines for the lazy, they would have known that such pressure from people of a different generation would have the opposite effect. I did go out more but not for the reasons they wanted me to. I went out and observed my two different groups in a variety of settings, thus, as far as I was concerned, adding weight and the strength of diversity to my observations.

On the bus on the way to school I noted B1 becoming uncomfortable as talk amongst the other girls turned to French kissing and lovebites. At a teen party I saw A2's erection straining against his jeans as he made out with B2. Eleven

centimetres duly noted in my head then transferred to note-
books hidden since the discovery of their existence by my
parents, not in my room, but in Josie's. They never thought of
looking there.

*

Monday night. Another parcel from Peterson arrived
today, a thick wad of paper with, unusually, no video or
audio material. Instead there was a confiding tone in a lengthy
letter. He seems to feel that, although we have never met, our
mutual interest in psychosexual research and inter-family
sexuality, our disdain at conventional research techniques
and disgust at conventional wisdom based on these conventional techniques has brought us close together.

*I reckon you're an FPP, Sad. I get this picture, a scene in my
head man that we're on a psychosexual website, inter-family
sexuality on the Internet, surfing the scum water making sure we
avoid the fall, that big fucking wave that shuts us down. You can't
do that, you can't say that. You know what I'm saying. You and
me Sad, we're two of a kind. Jacobi in Chicago for sure, Petit in
Paris maybe, all of us make up this group that no one can stand.
They think of me as a pariah over here, all of us at the Institute are
fucking pariahs with every chance that ain't no one going to give us
no money this time next year. You believe that? If we were fucking
pariahs they wouldn't waste their fucking money on us, man, we're
piranhas more like, waiting to bite those leather couches with their big
fucking paychecks. This ain't the X Files, this is the Sex files. And
no one wants to believe either of them.*
*I've enclosed some notes for you man, some words on the latest
bunch of freakouts to walk through our swing doors – no Psychosexual
Institute of good repute would have two doors marked Entrance and
Exit. Swing doors are where it's at. R. D. Laing's alive and well and
living in Manhattan. But here's a thought, let's get something going
together, man, some dual research. I'll show you mine, if you'll show
me yours. You know what I'm talking about, some transatlantic study*

that cuts through the shit, man, with not a couch in sight. Think about it. Therapists are like tattooists, Sad, we all get a kick from working on each other and you're next, boy. Take it easy.

Peterson's notes were based on a series of interviews with FPPs – fantasy prone personalities – who had been going from couch to couch finally ending up at the Institute. *Dereistic thinkers* he called them, where John or Josefina Doe had an increasingly strong potential for a fantasy life that blurred the edges with reality. Of course, this can be humdrum stuff in the hands of most therapists, where some pseudo freak walks into his therapist's office for a cheap rate reduction session and wanks on about how he dreams of fucking his girlfriend's sister and how when he's making love he can't get her face, even her tush, out of his mind. Ten a penny would be my response to that kind of thing, but Peterson being Peterson didn't entertain the mundane when it came down to it, he was an expert ambulance chaser. He found the best case studies and made them all his own. A researcher's researcher. The people that he spoke to were making some gross distortions of reality, warping it more than a ten hour acid trip, and weaving into their personalities the kind of avoidance manoeuvres that make daydreaming look like a day in the park.

One example, satisfying the criteria of the Mental Health Inventory, was of a high-achieving lawyer who arrived home from work in a highly derealised state, agitated and sweating profusely. He told his wife who had seen him leave for work that morning that he had been to a brothel in Paris, France and had been unfaithful to her not just once but four times with four different women. The man was broken up in the extreme and his wife shrewdly deciding that he wasn't really the philandering type and was especially unlikely or unable to take a round trip to Paris for a four-time shag, got on the phone to the therapist's hotline that they both subscribed to, who put them on to some college locum ill equipped to deal with such an extreme dissociative experience, but who luckily had heard of Peterson at the Institute.

When Peterson met the man, he not only, as is normal methodology, got the man to account for his missing time and to recognise at what point he relaxed his reality monitoring devices, but he also encouraged him to describe his time in the brothel in Paris – something which some psychohacks would not want to touch in case they got their manicure bitten. *They took me into a huge room and hung me up. Put my wrists into handcuffs, put the handcuffs onto a hook hanging from the ceiling and they let me dangle. I don't know how long I was there, but I was there long enough for four women, each one with a different hair colour, to come into the room, sit down at the table in front of me and eat. They sat and talked to each other, broke long baguettes with their hands, drank wine from tall crystal glasses but all the time ignored me. Then, for some reason, they all stopped eating at once and one by one came over to me. Their heads were at the same height as my genitals and in turn they blew hot breath over my skin . . .*

Peterson wasn't that interested in the exact details but apparently the man gave a very detailed account of the progression of activities – from four-way oral sex, to four way rimming, with each allowed slightly varying techniques while all the time the lawyer hung by his hands.

Peterson tried to get the man to find the point when and how he reinstalled his reality monitoring devices and, as far as he could gather, it was on the journey back from work.

Along with the notes on FPPs, Peterson had also included in his package a host of commentary on memory retrieval/recovered memory therapy or, as Peterson puts it in his own hick meets prof way, *'that all-purpose, fuel guzzling pick-up truck that drives by itself once the wheels have been set in motion'*. From previous correspondence I knew that Peterson was somewhat disdainful of the whole recovered memory movement. *Maybe it's because my talk show appearances are drying up right now, but it seems to me that no one wants to know about the intricacies of experience, the spectrum of reaction that memory can serve up to us in so many ways. Right now, all people want to hear is the shock horror revelation from some office worker who suddenly realises that her father touching her cunt in the bath when she was six is the reason why she can't let a man near her at thirty-six. Or some mountaineering schmuck can't get it up over six thousand feet because he suddenly puts two and two together and realises that his father carried him on his shoulders at the fun fair when he was thirteen . . . thus warping his sense of height, encouraging latent vertigo! Jesus, Sad, I can't tell when the movement started and the backlash stopped but the participants in this debate, the endless prattlings by those for and against Recovered Memory, are missing the point if not their paychecks. The fucks who winge away to their therapist for months on end, for X dollars per session, are small fry, goldfish in an ocean, spiritless idiots who have swapped fundamentalism for therapy. If a memory has got any value, any reality, any heart-rending, stomach churning, head-fucking quality, then there ain't no recovery involved. It's there in everything they do, say or think. They're the ones you've got to get hold of, Sad, they're the ones where the real stories are at.*

Peterson, I realised, as I'm sure he intended, had planted the seed of something in my head. From my own correspondence he would have gathered that I was tired of the seemingly endless procession of trivial psychotics stopping off in my waiting room on their way to community care. I felt that my role as psychosexual researcher was being debased each day, each day I felt like a GP dealing with aches and sprains when really I wanted surgery. *Mind surgery.* Peterson screamed at me in his scrawling handwritten notes, *some ground-breaking, breath-taking work is what the therapy world needs . . .*

The thought of collaborating, of pooling together research from either side of the Atlantic, research risky enough to jeopardise both our funding sources, filled me with excitement, especially since I'd heard through the Breathhouse grapevine that there were two new arrivals, supposedly mute and with a fucked-up history to die for, but as yet untouched by the psychohacks. With some wangling I knew I could put on hold the day to day humdrums that were sent to me and begin some research. In fact, Peterson couldn't have timed his suggestion better – a quiet spell at the clinic and suddenly two institutionalised wrecks filled to the gills with a history no one had bothered to listen to *and* not a caring relative in sight. And so it was with self-conscious irony that I knew Peterson would appreciate that I rushed home to plan my experiment and tell Josie the exciting news, while I waited for her to put on that pretty green frock that fell over her straight barely kinked hips. When things are going good, you just have to make them better. Yes.

PREPARATION

The set-up was simple, or at least minimal. The unit was the last in a row of five annexed buildings or outhouses as they were called; its square-shaped, flat roof appearance offered the same contrast as the other outhouses to the fading grandeur of Breathhouse Psychiatric Hospital itself, lying half a mile back towards the main road. It surprised no one, especially not me, that the unit occupied such an isolated position. Its physical location represented perfectly its status or at least the status of psychosexual research. *You're moving into the Wild West, Sad, no one comes outta there alive . . .* Or so I was told by the laddish interns and brutal orderlies at the Admin block on day one of my tenure as researcher.

Even amongst the five outhouses there was a pecking order. The long thin building devoted to anorexia and bulimia research was both cable ready and had its own homepage, devoted to the latest findings. Next door two smaller, but in mint condition, outhouses housed two researchers devoting their last few years before premature retirement to the study of SIDS, or Sudden Infant Death Syndrome. The two balding, childless doctors spent much of their time poring over newspaper reports, confused GP statements and hospital documentation on infant deaths, either that or they were on the phone to some poor parent grief-stricken and devastated while Pelly and Fale scribbled down their circumstantial evidence in the hope of finding some correlation, some shred of directional evidence. There were rumours, even though they were both married, that they were gay and that the reason that they hadn't got too far with their research after years in outhouses two and three was that they were too busy fucking each other. Someone up at Breathhouse sent them an Xmas present of a baby doll in small coffin-shaped cardboard box. Pull the cord on the dolls back and it would say, 'Time for me to go to sleep.' Gallows humour of course. Just another day at Breatt-house.

Outhouse four was much the same as two and three, both in better nick and more expensively furnished than mine, but it was rarely used. It was set aside for potential use as a halfway house for any patient on his way out of Breathhouse into the community. As my time wore on at Breathhouse, however, the facility was used less and less, the preference being for patients to bypass this stage and be *immersed* in the outside world straight after treatment.

It seems to me that when it came to the last of the outhouses they simply ran out of money and had nothing left to cover its flaking walls, detiled floors, or even to heat the hall that took up much of the space. In winter I don't think I've known a colder place. It was a joke, of course. When I parked my car and jogged down to the unit, orderlies would shout out, *Hey Sad, do you want to borrow my hair dryer, get some heat into that shithouse of yours . . .?*

They didn't understand but Josie did. At home she listened to my moans and groans with a caring smile and a gentle touch. If I needed a pillow she would rush and get me one; if I needed a drink she would pour some amber liquid and lift it to my lips. I counted myself as both lucky and contented. Some of the corduroy cocoons who called them-selves psychologists avoided their homes, their wives, instead opting to spend their time debating with colleagues in Thai restaurants the finer points of egotic theory or autoplasty or speculating about the effects of aversion therapy on their spouses. So much for them. Josie skipped down the corridor behind me on the first day after my lengthy conversation with Peterson and I didn't have to debate anything with Josie. What was in my head was in hers and vice versa.

This was not the first time Josie had been in the unit. Six months ago, she had suddenly appeared in my office at the end of a long and tiresome day. It was a Friday so she was young, at the long curly hair and pretty floral dress stage, and she just opened the door and smiled. I wanted her to say something that would ease my stress, that would take me away from the slagheaps of paperwork threatening to fall from my desk.

Shall I lock the door behind me?

I liked the way she said that, loved the way she managed to squeeze through the smallest gap in the doorway. She closed, then locked, the door, putting her fingers to her lips and stood stock still, listening.

*

When she was twelve she put her fingers to my lips and told me with her eyes and a shake of the head to be quiet. We listened at my parents' door, waiting to hear the tell-tale signs of my father's snore, the click of the light on my mother's side of the bed. When we heard the reassuring sounds, we trod carefully downstairs, opened the back door and went out into the moonlight. A perfect summer's night. There was a shed at the end of the garden my father used to stockpile an array of garden tools and machines, barely touched, some still in their boxes waiting for the moment of retirement when my parents' garden dreams would be fulfilled.

She said she had something to show me and led me by the hand into the dark hut which smelt of burnt wood and spilt petrol.

Have you got your notepad? She had heard the trouble I had been in, had heard the argument between my parents and me about my lack of extrovert sociable behaviour, my tendency to note down the pubescent process of my peers at school. *You can read too much into things.* I had shown Josie my research and she was fascinated by the diagrams and tables which charted the arrival of adult features. She asked me if I had done the same tests on myself and I said yes; she asked me if I would do the same for her and I said of course.

She had on her nightie and she sat up on the workbench pushing aside cans of oil, tins of paint. She lowered her nightie past her shoulders to reveal the beginnings of her breasts, the swollen appearance of her nipples. I wrote furiously. She laughed at my scribbling hand.

I think she said, 'That's not all.' Maybe she didn't. But the gist is what matters.

And the gist was this. She lifted up the hem of her nightie past the top of her thighs to her waist and bunched it there. I saw that her crack was no longer hairless, that a veritable jungle had appeared since our last encounter in the basement of the house. I was breathless while she was proud. I could tell. Even in the darkness I knew she was beaming with pride. I reached out and touched, expecting to feel the hair wiry and dry but it was soft, the beginnings of curls ready to cover her skin.

I think she said, 'Does yours feel like that?'

I lied and mumbled something like 'I don't know' but I was unconvincing and she jumped down and put her hands down the front of my pyjamas. 'It is, isn't it?'

All the time I managed to keep writing, the pad up in the air above her head filling three pages with description and two drawings – one a side profile of her body, the other a sketch of between her legs.

*

In my office it looked to me as though she had just stepped out of the gardening shed and onto my padded couch. I loved that couch – to me it symbolised everything that was hackneyed and clichéd about psychotherapy and it was something to be embraced, a remembrance of flat-footed, dangerously chaotic, *seriously* diagnostic times of yesteryear when the science was in its infancy and no one really knew what they were playing with; when research was truly experimental. Nowadays, of course, most of the fully fledged psychohacks up at the main building of Breathhouse shunned the couch, believing it to give the wrong impression to the *client*, believing it to create a predestined notion of what the relationship between patient and doctor should be. Knowledge versus ignorance; control versus chaos. Instead they talked to them while swimming believing that aerobic activity stimulated memory retrieval or they walked with them for hours on end, working their legs as well their patient psychoses, hoping to get fit while justifying the activity with some facile idea that physical activity facilitates the body's production of serotonin. *Walking a mile makes you smile . . .* Tell that to the poor fuck of a therapist who was beaten to death by the oars of a rowing machine he had encouraged his delusional patient to try out . . . *You'll feel great . . .*

They were paying lip-service to the politically correct; secretly relishing the return of locked wards and chained patients . . .

When Josie lay on the couch, the floral dress riding up her thin delicate thighs, I got out from behind the desk, double checked the door and lay down beside her, breathing in her scent, putting my fingers to her lips and saying, just as I, just as we both used to say, 'not a word, not a word to anyone . . .'

*

The unit is dominated by one room, or maybe hall or disused gymnasium would be a better description. There was some debate as to what this, the oldest and most far flung of all the outhouses, had been used for originally. Speculation abounded but as few people stayed longer than two or three years at Breathhouse, apart from a few venerable dinosaurs who could barely remember their own name, never mind the intricacies of others' split personalities, there was little consistency of opinion and so there was little confirmation of its former use before being adopted as the new and exciting home for research into inter-family sexuality. One of the less plausible explanations, but more entertaining, was the idea that this big hall, with its varnished floorboards stretching 50 metres long and 25 across, had been used as an indoor exercise area for long-term patients at Breathhouse. Here in the depths of winter, orderlies and psychohacks could guard and watch in a secure and confined space the activities of their charges. *Patients would shout out their number while we took bets on who would do the most laps . . .*

Although there were long windows running the length of the hall, they faced north and were blocked by trees growing close to the glass, and there is no doubt that the huge overhead lights would have been clicked into action, spotlighting the aching limbs and torn minds limping their way round the hall while the hacks sat back and the orderlies acted as though they were at the bookies – all this while twenty or so diehard fruit baskets spun and collided with demons and Gods . . . inner demons and outer Gods.

On first sight, some were reminded of uncomfortable school days with benches to sit on and broth to be eaten, while others shivered and shuddered at its austere and disturbing history, but to me, when I took charge of the unit and all its rundown sundries, I was inspired and awed by it and spewed forth ridiculous superlatives that had the hall set up as a cross between a *Diva* flat, with *Gitanes* jigsaws confounding stubbled aesthetes and the barest and biggest of sterile laboratories, that essential bare canvas for my complex visitors. In this hall, I thought, mental gymnastics shall know no bounds . . .

If I was overawed by the hall, the rest of the facility was considerably less grandiose. All effort and design by some pre-modernist schmuck of an architect had gone into the hall and when budget and imagination had run out, he had added a small room to be used by the resident psychohack, myself in this case, and an even smaller, cupboard-like room to be used by my part-time secretary, engaged to process the words of my patients, to doctor my ramblings into some kind of administrative order.

Beth was a perfect secretary for me. Reliable and silent; thick-skinned to the point of being remarkably in control or repressed, depending on your school of thought. She had seen sights in the unit since it first opened that would have sent many a PA running for that safe temping job in the city.

Within the first week she was typing out the confession of a Falklands War veteran, once stable factory worker turned combat fatigue casualty, a manic hunk of a man running up and down the short corridor of the unit, defining the symptoms of post-traumatic stress disorder. One moment he was calm, debating with me ethical dilemmas posed by blowing up Argies at Port Stanley, and the next he was racing out the room to Beth's desk and launching her pen holder as though it was a grenade proclaiming that *they* were everywhere and Port Stanley must be liberated. *They are hiding, always hiding.*

The following few weeks in that first period at the unit, while both she and I were finding our feet, Beth got her eyes opened to the best and worst of human frailties, a supermarket of off the shelf and off the wall neuroses and psychoses. After one particularly heavy day that saw at least three visits by hospital security and gruff orderlies to remove patients sent down for research analysis from Breathhouse, she sat back in the swivel chair and said dryly, *This is some way to earn a living.* The irony was of course that most people in this job were brain dead, paralysed into inaction by knowledge. Living rarely came into it.

She came to understand my irreverence, my lack of respect for protocol and while she may have found it difficult, she kept her mouth shut and diligently processed the words of a hundred crazies. She wasn't a machine, however, and she did get upset when hearing the tapes of a child killer, oozing and waxing lyrical about his crimes, or the sad, sad tale of a woman who had lost everything through a series of tragic accidents in one day, a kind of nightmarish twenty-four hours no one would have believed on film let alone real life. There was nothing to do when she slumped over the computer, tears in her eyes, her hands shaking. Even a rock can crumble, I would say to her, there's nothing wrong with getting upset by what you see and hear and read in this place. 'The unit is a melting pot of frustrations and mental disease,' I told her. 'Once you've been in the job a while, once you can sleep at night without a thought to what you have seen during the day, then you'll know you're okay. Until then, you are welcome to climb the walls, if you can find a space.'

I think she understood my humour. I was evangelical about the need for it. Still am.

The seventh rule of psychotherapy is never lose your sense of the absurd.

The hall provided me with a sense of opportunity. It initially rejuvenated a lacklustre existence in the years after qualifying where I found myself far from ideals, sorting out the heads of trauma victims and deranged grief-stricken family mobs. But the rejuvenation had been temporary and, while I awaited replies to my applications for research grants, my valuable time was taken up with short-term psychos waiting their turn in the dock as I reeled out some truism which Beth typed and delivered. Process equals death. There had been little opportunity for one of my psychoanalytical pets, *milieu therapy* - an old-fangled idea that the socio-environment during therapy is of the greatest importance. Shit. The first and possibly last time I put pen to paper for one of the more august psychology journals was to expound on the idea that environment is everything when it comes to not just treating patients but researching their stories, and hence their lives, and hence their psychoses, but I guess I went too far for those dried and shrivelled editors, guess they couldn't understand the logical extension to the theory – the more extreme or deeply buried the story the more intense and viable the environment should be. That part was cut.

Do you mean, Sad, that the house of a serial killer should be recreated in all its shocking realism and the murderer treated on the premises? It would never work and, what's more, it would never be allowed.

Sheep being shepherded into a pen and left to rot; academics finding their niche and sticking with it. Same thing; same old story.

Down the centre of the hall were two thick tarpaulin curtains, difficult to draw open or closed because of their weight, and which divided the hall into two spaces or, if my ideals ever took shape, two worlds. But although they were heavy and could not be ruffled like stage curtains or parted simply with bare hands – at the side there was an ancient mechanism that whirred and purred them across the wooden floor – they were movable – an important factor in my plans. Once I had served my time as psychohack dogsbody and terminated the daily queue of flotsam from the main building at Breathhouse, I hoped to get the opportunity to draw the curtain and let world meet world, like meet like, even . . . Best of all, there was a third world created, a narrow corridor in between the two curtains, wide enough for me to walk the breadth of the hall in white shoes, unseen by the hall's occupants, and yet with a few strategically placed viewing points, or rather, clear plastic, sewn into the tarpaulin's heavy duty material. I could enter and leave the two worlds as much as I wanted – essential for the non-interactive strategy used at the earlier stages of research, when observation is everything; where observation leads to a more accurate environment creation.

But this world of extreme milieu therapy would have had my colleagues agog with the waste of space and resources – *there's a queue around the block and back again, Sad, and yet you only want to take on what? Two cases? Get real!* but I paid no heed to them. My patients would need time to feel at home or rather *feel at home* in the unit and I needed time to create the environment that came from the stories of their lives. It was so simple it hurt.

In the midst of preparations Peterson faxed.

Hey, Sad, things are on the up and up. I've got myself a doozy of a patient and a new location.

Just been on an amazing walk, blew the cobwebs out and took half my mind with it. It's made me realise that I haven't been out the city in years, holed up in those whitewashed, institutional walls, banging my head against the tiles, watching others bang theirs. You forget how vicious that circle can get, eh? Even a psychiatrist can cry in the dim privacy of his own torment . . . shit, there I go. And yet, here I am; in fact, here we both are. The shrink and the patient; the therapist and the therapee. What a beautiful place for the fucked-up.

It's been kind of an ambition of mine to combine stimulants and therapy where some kind of psychoactive drug is used as part of the treatment of a patient. Of course drugs and therapy have the kind of history that no one would want to shout from a hilltop even in scenery as beautiful as this. As good as the idea is, I needed to separate it from the sterile, locked-door, ECT image of professional drug administration. Back at the Institute we have schizos aplenty, some quelled into near zombie-like status, others propelled into quasi-euphoria, as well as a whole range of detriments – people who for one reason or another have found their way into our consulting rooms – who have ingested enough pills to fill these mountains. But, as you well know, the image of drugs and therapy is not a good one and I have been kind of waiting for the opportunity to sidestep the expectations people have and maybe take some time to retrace the steps to a more authentic, more startling form of therapy. Location is everything in this little theory of mine. It's no good being holed up in some office and, to speak of transcending established protocols and processes of treatments, I need to be in a place like this – all huge trees, steep mountains and rapid white water – where backdrop could influence process and vice versa; where the line between patient and doctor becomes indistinguishable and less than important.

Cutting edge stuff in the Delong Mountains, Alaska.

Some time ago, the idea was planted in the heads of our funders that there was a great need for a halfway house between the two worlds we at the Institute are meant to traverse and, with the idea that real estate in this kind of location never really loses its value and can always be sold to some snow freak, they were sold on the idea. I guess everybody liked the idea that when the place wasn't being used to cure and comfort, it could always be used by employees at a knockdown rental. Everybody was happy.

I got to the cabin about eight hours ago with my mysterious stranger, my pale, waxy friend – darling to his parents, X21 to the files but Languid to you and me. Languid? It kind of suits him. And his problem? Well, he's an eighteen year old mute born to a family steeped in family traditions, big on the financial markets, and make the Amish look positively liberal. You hear what I'm saying, Sad, this family's got everything, money, connections and power but what they don't have is a son they can parade round at parties and say, 'Here's the next in line . . .' I'd be lying if I said that I was their first port of call; people like Languid's parents don't hang their dirty washing on the line, know what I mean? They came to me in my box-like office after having tried both the church and beatings by way of a cure and, while pushing Languid into a chair, they uttered for them what must have been a cry for help.

'Make him normal.'

'Normal?' I asked provocatively.

'Like us.'

This was a conventional family seeking solace in the unconventional.

Still, the timing was good because, as you know, not only do I have these theories roaming around my head but I have also managed to wangle a combined travel and research grant to bridge the gap between institution and environment, to take psychotherapy and psychological research on the road, a smart convoy of cutting edge technique.

Well, that's what the blurb said and here we are, a stopover between the insane and sane worlds, in a log cabin at the foot of the Delong Mountains. The picture is, as they say, complete. Don't breathe a word to a soul.

And, as for Languid, well you know me, Sad, I'll do the best I can, for him and the best for a new kind of psychological investigation. Between you and me, psychotherapy is dead. Long live psychotherapy!

I admired the world Peterson had created for himself. There was no room for self-doubt or, worse still, professional self-doubt. 'Don't be sorry, be certain' was the motto for a new breed of psychotherapy.

*

I watched him through the plastic viewing patch in the tarpaulin, pressing my face against the scratched plastic surface, trying to keep my restless feet still on the floor. It was around eleven o'clock at night. Beth had long since departed and Josie was asleep on the couch in my office. Neither of us had been home for days. Beth had brought in supplies, necessary food and drink, enough, it seemed, for us to hold out in case of siege, enough for me to be able to stay at the unit and concentrate on the work at hand.

If he heard me walk along the narrow corridor, he didn't react, nor did I expect him to. He wasn't catatonic; however he wasn't as stiff as some of the fuck-ups that had been through my hands here and elsewhere. Catatonic was a land where reaction was either muscular or non-existent, a place of refuge sought by the desperate or the unlucky. I had seen catatonic patients who were like kids with a new bike screaming round the block or the consulting room, full of excited agitation, except of course there wasn't usually a bike involved. Then there were the sculptors who assumed a form moulded by their psychoses – these patients of whom there had been a few up at Breathhouse – configured their pain into bizarre and strange postures, keeping them, holding onto them for hours. There would be sweepstakes amongst the healers, bets taken as to how long a certain posture, a particular limb, could be held in an impossible position. But Click – a name I quickly warmed to, eschewing the need for using the much hated official file names – didn't fit these categories and he came to me with his behavioural attitude classified as catatonic stupor, where there is a reduction in the patient's normal spontaneous movements, where there is a significant decrease in reaction to the outside world. Beyond his family no one had known Click in any other shape or form.

Above all he was silent. No one had heard anything from him since the day he was taken from his parents' caravan; through the variety of institutions that had housed him right up until the moment he now sat in his part of the hall edging closer with silent curiosity to the black-curtained corner where the equipment needed to develop photographs had been placed prior to his arrival.

No doubt my Breathhouse colleagues had a sweepstake going already, taking bets on how long it would be before he talked, and working against this was the underlying anger that given the opportunity they could have made him talk. Whether it would be sense or drugged up drivel wasn't important to them. '*Not talking, Sad, on the second day, Sad? Well, if you need some help from the boys and girls up at the big school let us know. We could have him talking within 36 hours with a few long lunch breaks in between.*

Of course, I knew what they would do. They would go softly softly first of all, marvel at his upbringing in the caravan, admire his maturity in the face of adversity and, of course, laud his skills with the camera. They would build him up, even in his silence, waiting for the moment to knock him down into verbal communication. Then they would enquire about his relationships with his mother and father, searching his face for weakness, dents in the psychological armour, that they would locate and pierce.

Target practice for the 90s. Psychotherapy, memory recovery as a form of lethal weapon.

If he was still unforthcoming they would fill him with drugs, not a part they would advertise to the general public, nor would they necessarily inform the student psychologists who toured the hospital from time to time. It wasn't something that the head honchos at Breathhouse wanted to be known. Patients like Click, suckled by institutions, filled to the gills with brain-spilling drugs . . . ? There was no glamour in his impossible recovery, no smiling recuperative photo for this year's year book. But it *was* economical – x number of hours to identify and cure patient z at the cost of y means saving of w. Cures per capita that's what counted.

But not for me and thus not for Click. We had all the time in the world.

The half of the hall occupied by Click was in its earliest stages of transformation. The trick with milieu therapy is not to impose a familiar environment too quickly. A lot of the patients had been away from the point or location of trauma or incident for some time, many had been institutionalised, like Click, and to suddenly recreate a familiar environment with a view to rendering them at ease and at home would have been unrealistic. Their sense of location, and consequently, the effectiveness of the therapy, of the research would have been dulled by years in a more sterile place.

To take a toy away from a child and return it years later will not bring back instantly the feelings and emotions the toy first engendered. Good research and, no doubt, good therapy takes time. As days wore on after his arrival, he got closer and closer to the darkened corner. On days one and two he sat on the mattress almost dead centre of his section of the hall, unmoving, everything unspoken. It was easy to see why he had been passed off as a non-speaker. Bound up with a verbal blockage brought on by trauma would have been the off the cuff diagnosis made by hacks in a hurry and there it would have remained, there *he* would have remained, shuffled from one institution to the other until the streets beckoned. On day three he discovered the set of light switches I had wired up for his use to dim the bright overhead lights and fade up the red bulb behind the curtain. I had left a trail of obvious breadcrumbs for his psyche to feed on, all leading to that one corner of the vast hall. Firstly, there were books on developing photographs, which he devoured with silent appetite, then came the switches which he played with until his part of the hall resembled a club, red and white lights bouncing off the walls, reflecting on the varnished floor. Eventually I knew he would go behind the curtain and the unseen secrets of his spools would find their way into the hall, into him and into my research.

This part of the hall had had only a few visitors in the past, brief patients on their way to somewhere else, patients designed to tide me over, justify the bills until longer-term studies such as Click were assigned to me. But it had already housed its share of damaged goods, of tentative preludes to the big experiment.

There had been a boy, younger than Click when he was

discovered in his caravan life, but as old as Josie ever got. The Jumper, Beth called him, not because he was a suicide risk with a history of tall buildings and hurried meetings with concrete. Nothing so simple as that. If it was that simple he'd still be up at the main building, having his ills analysed until there were a hundred reasons why he would want to take his own life but precious few for him not to. No, he was called the Jumper because unless he was strapped to a chair – or as was the case up at Breathhouse, where he was held fast on a hospital bed, big leather straps across his chest and legs – he would leap from one spot to another and then another circumventing whatever space he was in with these big leaps, giant steps landing first on the left then the right. Neil Armstrong was his other name. My colleagues had little time for him.

You have him, Sad, he's perfect material for research, damn all possibility for cure, that's for sure.

Of course they tried to delve into his mind, tried to excavate rhymes and reasons as to why he would want to invest his young life in such odd, anti-social behaviour. He had been shunted from one school to another as the behaviour worsened. The doctors had identified a gradual increase in not only the size of his steps as he grew older, but also in their frequency. So what at first had been a charming if eccentric way to behave in junior school became an alarming and annoying attention-seeking device in senior school. He was abused by teachers, beaten up by his peers and his neck wrung more than once by exasperated parents. His mother complained that there were constantly pools of urine in the bathroom to mop up as his aim skipped from one side of the bowl to the other. Worse still, according to her statements to the good doctors up at Breathhouse, were the splatterings of his shits, which would cover the bathroom floor. His father told of manic mealtimes, where, unless one of them held him into the chair while the other force-fed his food into his mouth, his agitated leaps would cause food to fly all over the place and induce a kind of motion sickness in both of his parents.

Normally orderlies had to carry or wheel in some of the more reluctant admissions to the unit. This boy was different. He leapt from the ambulance straight into the unit and, with a remarkably cool head, Beth pointed him the way and rushed ahead of him to open the door to the hall. I remember both of us watching him through the slit in the tarpaulin bouncing from one side of hall to the another, his poker face strangely at odds with his energetic movements.

'Strong legs,' Beth observed.

What the psychologists up at Breathhouse had failed to discover was the origin of these movements. They had asked all the usual questions about family, home and dreams; they had poked and prodded his history, his sexual desires, his parents, but this elicited nothing but the usual mediocre ultra-normal lifestyle that parents will often testify to in wayward offspring. *He was such a quiet boy, doctor.* But they had asked him the questions while they strapped him to the bed; they gave him reassuring and encouraging touches on the shoulder, ingratiating their way into his confidence, while he writhed and wriggled on the hard hospital mattress. They couldn't see the wood for the trees; they couldn't understand a sense of context for their ritualistic investigation.

It was a game and the whole lot of them at Breathhouse were too unfit or too fat or too stupid or all three to understand the route to understanding the reasons behind the boy's movements.

He was one of the shortest-stay visitors to the unit, not really ideal for the long-term inter-family sexuality experiment I had in mind for the unit but at least he would make use of the space and it served up a useful precedent for me, a *modus operandi* that would be the blueprint for all future experiments, culminating with the two present inhabitants of the unit. I created a tactile and realistic world for him within the hall and the jumper, Neil Armstrong, whatever his real name was, marked a crucial point for me. He encouraged me to think not only for the patient but also for myself; taking the pseudo-sincerity of the fly-by-night therapist and dumping it.

I created the environment for his treatment. I painted targets on the varnished floor, like targets for an arrow with a black inner circle worth ten points, a red circle worth five and an outer blue circle worth three. As he bounded about the hall in a random way, I began to leap from one circle to another, counting out loud my score, whether I hit the black circle or the blue. I could see the curiosity build in his eyes, I could see the desire to join in overwhelm him and temporarily upset his rhythm, but within minutes he was jumping in the circles following my steps, shouting out his score, and with his expert leaps it wasn't long before his strong legs outjumped mine. His score equalled, then surpassed my own, and the triumph on his face was clear for me to see.

And then and only then was the time for questions. A time for answers. An uncle had been a keen amateur long jumper, a fact that was neither unearthed by the shrinks up at Breathhouse nor divulged by the father himself - if indeed he knew, and no doubt there was an element of fear of recrimination if ever a connection was made. The uncle would take him for walks in the country but instead of what one might expect of an easygoing intergenerational relationship, the uncle had taken it upon himself to train the boy in the art of long jumping, not just with the usual track and field methods, but by bullying the boy into leaps with reasons. Sometimes, the boy later said, he had to jump over ten lit fires in a row, with each mistake causing blisters on his legs; then there were rows and rows of inter-locking streams where a mistake was punished with thick mud and cold water, but, most commonly, the boy had to run in circles around his uncle, with each jump that was either too weak or too inelegant punished by beatings with a stick. Apparently this went on for weeks until the boy snapped and didn't just run away from his uncle and his dreams of log jumping glory, but jumped all the way home and refused to stop. Of course, praise or a sense of achievement might have helped him at that crucial stage, but the uncle was too ambitious and too cruel to do that and the parents, along with everyone else involved with the boy, were too puzzled, confused and angry to comment on how well he jumped.

When the boy's score passed five hundred with mine still in the two hundreds, he stopped and said in a breathless voice.

'I won.'

*

Josie and I have argued. It was Saturday night, after all, supposed to be a grade one night when Josie and I immerse ourselves in each other, forgetting about the outside world. Getting it on. You could call it a habit, the shrinks up at Breathhouse would call it an aberration and just about everybody else would call it an abomination. To me, it's just how it is, you do what you feel, you act what you think. Josie is my milieu, my socio-environment, she is the cause and the reason. She is instant research, a long-term case study for inter-family sexuality. You could say we were close. Sibling rivalry, sibling intensity, sibling love. All of it. I come from the laissez-faire school of psychology and I was and still am a good student. But Josie, well, Josie felt, it being a Saturday night after all and the fact that we hadn't been home for at least a week since the two new patients to the unit had arrived didn't help.

I made her say, *We should spend some time together*. But I didn't like that, so I took it back. Maybe she would have said that on a grade three night, when she was all curves and grown up, with a mouth on her to tell me exactly where I could take a running jump. But this was a grade one night, Josie was all simper and curls, thin legs and flat chest, and she didn't have the words to lure me away from my work, which was becoming increasingly compelling. So instead, I made her say, *You said we would play, you said . . . YOU SAID!*

I just laughed and that made it worse. Back home, her curls and straight hips at their point of origin, she would have had a pillow fight with me as I snuck into her room to tease her mind and tickle her feet. She would have thrown as silently as possible the feather-filled pillows through the air hoping her poor aim would just once connect with me. She wasn't stupid, she could tell when someone was laughing at her, not with her, and this just made her madder still. In my office, in the unit, the same hushed tantrum filled the space. Beth had gone home but Josie didn't know that and I could see her simmer then boil over with rage when I patted her head and said I had to go and look in on my patients. She ran at me and started to beat my chest, her small hands curled into the cutest of fists. I grabbed her wrists and swung her above my head and cleverly she began to use her feet to try and make contact with my face. 'Hey, hey, hey baby . . . we'll have some time together, don't you worry . . .' She didn't like my tone and I let her say so. *You're just saying that, you don't care any more . . .* I love the sound of her voice and wanted to add still more to it, get the icing on that cherry cake, so to speak. *You don't love me any more . . .* I pulled her to me, wrapped her legs around my waist and put my hands on her milky white thighs. 'I never said that,' I told her. 'I would never say that.'

I locked the door to my office behind me.

I wanted to check on the other new arrival to the unit, who had arrived five days earlier, at the same time as Click.

The same procedure as I followed with Click applied to 'Fright' – the ability of the social workers to irreverently nickname their 'finds' was one of their few enduring abilities and certainly one of the very few that I had much time for – and although he had been in the unit for those five days I had not introduced myself directly to him. Beth, as with Click, had been my intermediary. She was to tell him where he was, that I was his doctor and that I was looking forward very much to hearing all about him. Nothing else, apart from giving him the tape recorder. The time allowed Fright to adjust to his new surroundings and his section of the hall started with the same bare mattress as far away from his personal history as possible.

It was Peterson who had advised me of this tactic which flew in the face of the more conventional wisdom of my colleagues up at Breathhouse. They would be appalled by the delay. *You've got to get stuck into a patient, Sad, any delay can build further neuroses and extend the time allowed for viable treatment.* Peterson, on the other hand, eschewed all such mundane necessities as time and accommodation requirements; he didn't live in such a practical world, and God love him for it. Peterson lived above all that in a world of research, of pure investigation, a destination not driven to by results panic.

Give them time to themselves, as much as you think is right – if they're suicidal then sure they should be monitored by whatever unobtrusive means necessary and, short of banging their head against a wall for six minutes, they ain't going to do anything – but monitoring them is the key to whether they are liable to harm themselves, to tear themselves mind from limb or not. There is silence and there is silence. And I have never known a patient to be truly, profoundly silent. Your humdrum professionals proclaim a state of mute, a verbal catatonia when there are no words but you and I both know, Sad, that there are myriad ways to get yourself heard, to get yourself understood, to express without words nearly anything under the sun. Like love. The academics spend too much time looking at the negative when it comes to understanding silence; but they don't look at love and, Christ, Sad, just look at love and the communication of emotions without words there. Also, in the Institute, a patient is never far away from a camera or recording device – they are never truly alone, it's just that you are not getting some ham-fisted, third-rate, psychobabbling moron in there with them after they've been in the place for five minutes saying, 'How does it make you feel?' Come up to speed, Lou Reed, you say to that man; you give one big fucking roundhouse punch to anyone that contemplates that garbage. The only saying that I think applies here, Sad, is an old favourite of mine – give 'em enough rope . . . Know what I mean?

I took Peterson's wild advice when Fright first arrived, staying behind the office doors. But I allowed myself a brief glimpse of Fright's broken and limp body being half carried, half dragged to the room assigned to him. In my hands was his recent history passed on to me by the social workers who found him. In Beth's hands, as she showed them where to take

Fright, was a tape recorder and a pile of audio tapes. This, as Peterson would no doubt say, was to be my suspect device, my way of introducing myself to Fright but, more importantly, Fright's way of introducing himself to me. Surprisingly, amazingly, in fact, no one had thought to allow him the luxury of a tape recorder. I guess no one had cared, his status being deemed somewhat below irredeemable, a low possibility of him being rejuvenated into a worthwhile member of society and, hence, a low priority for intensive treatment. A lost cause doesn't look good in the prospectus for our Trust state. If he had been found when he was younger it might have helped, he may have got more attention but, as it was, he was one step away from a cardboard home and the digestion of meths.

The recent history as supplied by the social workers was brief. Fright had been discovered living in a cesspit of a flat in a large Victorian house. It seems the neighbours were alerted by a sickly smell emanating from a room off the first floor landing. It was a transient household and no one when questioned later by social workers had any idea who lived behind the door. When the police eventually broke down the door they discovered Fright lying in his own filth in a bed with sheets as stiff as cardboard. At first the police thought he was dead and the smell was familiar to them as that of a body having lain rigid for some time. But, in fact, Fright was alive and the odour had been caused by a variety of substances slowly rotting over a number of years – from food to dead skin; from motheaten curtains to the half-eaten carcasses of mice and rats.

Fright could not be moved or communicated with. When police approached the bed to confirm his living status he did not react. One policeman reported his wide open eyes, the pupils obscured by several cataracts, just staring straight ahead, unfocused and unblinking. The other policeman commented on the clammy, limp feel to his body as though all the muscle tissue had been sucked out of his limbs, leaving nothing but sinew to allow the movement of his arms and legs. An ambulance was called and the paramedic needed only one arm to lift Fright out of the bed and onto the stretcher. In his report the paramedic noted with barely disguised horror that the only resistance he encountered when moving Fright was his adhesiveness to the excrement-stained bed sheets, the tacky quality of body fluids including sweat, urine and semen that had created a thin web which stretched as the paramedic pulled him from the bed . . . *Like the skin from boiled milk* . . .

The professionals in the room debated amongst themselves as to Fright's age. They reached for clues in the two rooms separated by a worn curtain fulls of holes and tears. In Fright's room it was difficult to make sense of the absolute mess. A social worker called upon to make a background report contributed the following notes.

> I have never seen a room like it and I have seen deprivation and neglect in a wide variety of locations. It was not the typical scene of neglect brought about by socio-economic factors; far from it. There were many things in the room from furniture to paintings; from once expensive clothes to precious objects that all pointed to a family with sophisticated and/or moneyed lineage. And although the floor could barely be seen for discarded containers of food, ripped clothes and piles of faeces, it was evident that at some point this room had been a cultivated home. According to housing records the flat belonged to a Philippe Resnau, a widower with two sons, but it was impossible to tell from the first room when they had left, why they were no longer around and for how long Resnau Jnr. had been alone.

Another social worker commented on the room adjacent to Fright's.

> In this room it is clear that some religious and/or ritualistic activity has gone on. There are seventeen

patches of wax on the floor and a pile of white sheeting close by. The room was obviously occupied by an adult with an extensive interest in clothes, since most of the furniture in the room was wardrobes filled with empty hangers and a huge selection of belts. Apart from a large double bed and the circle of candles in the middle of the room, the furniture was located in one corner of the room, and it was clear that this arrangement had been undertaken to allow more space in the rest of the room. One can only speculate that this was linked to the candles and further speculation leads to the conclusion that the young man was involved in some way in the alleged ritualistic practices. Certainly, evidence from previous case studies indicates that ritual/sexual abuse is often accompanied by physical neglect. And the young man, whatever the cause, is certainly the end product of an extended period of neglect. The young man could be anything in age from late teens to early twenties, although his face appears much older.

When I walked into the hall, crept down the narrow corridor, with Click to the left of me flashing between white and red light, I could hear Fright's voice, a breathless, disjointed whisper that raised, then lowered in tone and velocity. It was both hesitant and seamless, as though even the uhms and aahs, the rasping, whispered pauses between words were part of what he had to tell. Of course, there was no guarantee that he would have used the tape recorder supplied and, if he hadn't, then I would have had to conceive another strategy, but for me much of this job is done on intuition; no preprescribed training as the Breathhouse lot would have you believe. *Procedure is everything; it allows for consistent support to the patient and staves off law suits.* Goodbye to all that because *that's* all it is for them. For most of my fellow professionals tape recorders or other audio or visual recording devices are hi-tech tools to be treated with suspicion, the result of government imposition with, no doubt, the worthless fucks always fearing that such recordings could be and would be used against them in a court of law. They would have kittens if they ever heard of what Peterson was aiming for. From his description it seemed that the Manhattan Institute was a veritable multi-media production studio; the first such psychological organisation to have its own website.

Anyway, intuition told me that Fright would talk. He wasn't clinically catatonic, the spivs up at Breathhouse had ascertained that much before shunting him down to me. He showed no reluctance to move from his bed in the house and was compliant rather than rigid. The only difficulty arose in the fact that he seemed to be having to relearn, like a victim of temporary paralysis, how to use his limbs. It was true that physically he was a wreck – undernourished to a terrible extreme, his growth no doubt stunted; and his internal organs would take time to adapt to the nutrients pumped into him since he had been found. And there was silence. His vocal cords may not have been eaten away in the same way as his muscle tissue, but they were as inactive. His body had been given poor nourishment, morsels gleaned luckily from the hoarding tendencies of his father, as shown by the mountains of canned food found in the flat, but his mind had been fed only the traumas of his past, a truly appalling example of real repetitive stress injury, a mental, not a physical, problem that the memory left to its own devices without company or stimulus will cause. As his vocal cords grew weaker as time went on his story, his traumatic story, grew in repeated and recited detail, manifesting itself in a whispered flight of imagination and detail; a barely audible life coming out of his head into an empty room. And when he was taken from the house and treated for his physical injuries, no one could make head nor tail of these words, seemingly gargled and strangled into incoherence. Just like Click, if he had been a kid he might have been more than a red line through a speech therapist's form, he may have got the attention that would have brought his story out – for me it was lucky no one was so keen and all that happened was that the spivs were concerned that his persistent sub-vocalisations signified the presence of psychosis but, while they fretted around his bed, they were aware only of the sound of his whispered story, not the words. For me, when I heard that just prior to his acceptance to attend the unit, he seemed like a perfect candidate for tape.

Some do-gooders, of whom there are thankfully few in psychotherapy, might have considered the spartan location Fright found himself in cruel and unnecessary. But those and such as those didn't want to understand, let alone cure, Fright. They wanted, at best, to pad him with comfortable surrounding and expected him to swap a hard life for a quiet life; from a hard bed to one made of goose feather and love . . . I reasoned, with all the adaptability that the milieu therapy allows me, that since he had escaped an avalanche of objects, a flat so close knit with the possessions of everyone he had once known, now wasn't the time to impose yet more and, besides, as his story unfolded, I would get a clear picture about exactly what I would put in the room when the time was right. And the time, as they say, was nearly right.

At other times, just as with the part of the hall Click was using, Fright's half had seen different scenarios, a mutating sense of location. In particular, unlike the rigid walls of the Breathhouse consulting rooms, Fright's sparse space had been a prime example of an early tactic of mine, a forerunner to my current interest in milieu therapy – direct location technique, or DLT. While some psychotherapist at Breathhouse brought out the usual array of psychological techniques, that jaded arsenal that renews itself with each fad, with each new pedagogical Mexican wave – regression, visualisation, body work and the like – I was more interested in combining the patient's story with the location where the story had its main thrust. This, of course, depended on the patient. For one of the first, Mary, the hall became a kitchen, a fully working, well-appointed kitchen, which anyone into domestic harmony would have loved.

I had been given a few days with Mary, had her sent down to me as a favour from Nathan Rathbone, one of the less agoraphobic of the dinosaurs at the hospital. She wasn't our kind of patient really – she was on her way to Insention, the nearest hospital for the criminally insane. Mary had killed her husband and two children, a girl aged four and a boy aged two, on a Monday morning, when most other people were winding themselves up for work or boredom. The police found her, a screaming, bawling mess covered with the guts and blood of her family that was.

She was being held at Breathhouse for a few days before being moved on to Insention and no one had the slightest bit of interest in her. *Not our problem, Sad, now, is she? She's crossed over to the other side and that means we don't waste one precious injection on her.* But Rathbone knew that, in the early days of the unit, there had to be a certain number of patients through my books, a quota of research fodder to justify the grant. It was a favour to me, even though she certainly didn't fit the criteria of the unit either – more violence than sex in her family outline – but it served to reassure the accounts department. This was before the Jumper case and I needed to prove to myself that DLT was more than simply a half-cocked idealistic notion and was a genuine method of research.

So, knowing the history and without any luxury of time, I quickly transformed half the hall into a kitchen area complete with units, cooker, fridge, microwave and, this was an inspired afterthought, breakfast bar. The kitchen workers up at Breath-house were very indulgent and much more cooperative than my psychohack colleagues. *Hey, Sad, you should invite us down for some breakfast, start off the day with some scrambled eggs and toast at the unit for Inter-Family Sexuality!* But the aim wasn't to reconstruct the exact location of her crime, in many ways that would serve simply to aggravate regression and most possibly non-communication, unless you counted screaming until blood was spitting from her lips as communication. No, I wanted to give the feel of a kitchen, any kitchen, not necessarily hers, since I was convinced that even with only a cursory look at the background details that this location was important. According to many figures, 50% of domestic disputes take place in the kitchen, 29% of those involving a kitchen utensil.

The thing about Mary was that she had admitted what she'd done, even though it would have been impossible for her to have got away with it – according to the police report, she had severed the right hand of each of her children and put them in her apron pocket. Terrible. Obviously. But with Mary, it was why she had done it that was the hook. She wouldn't describe, only admit. *Yes, I did it. I killed them all. Now I'm going to be put away for the rest of my life. If there was a death penalty I would get that, wouldn't I?* It was unlikely anyone was going to bother to find out. The shrinks at Insention were the kind of end of the line product you wouldn't inflict on your senile grandmother; they weren't so much on the scrapheap of their professional career but heading towards the open doors of the incinerator. They weren't going to be finding out and for Mary this was her last chance to get it off her chest, her last chance to tell someone.

Whatever else was accomplished during her brief stay, I certainly ate well. She cooked for both me and Beth – a substantial cooked breakfast, just as the spivs had joked about, homemade soup for lunch and then some fine lasagnes, souffles, terrines – she piled on the five star cooking for us while all the time singing away to herself, busying herself with spices and herbs, compiling lists for the next day's food and generally creating an incredible atmosphere. On the last day I had been enjoying her company so much that I almost forgot the reasons for her stay. Out of the blue, when it was just me and her finishing breakfast, I asked her if she minded if I gave her a recipe I had. I wanted to know what it tasted like but had never had the opportunity or the skill to concoct it. She said she would be glad to make it, especially since she knew she was going off to Insention very soon. The recipe card read as follows

INGREDIENTS
one woman aged forty-one
one man aged thirty-nine
one girl aged four
one boy aged two

METHOD
First peel the man and then de-core. Chop the
girl finely, being careful to discard the skin and
then slice the boy into julienne strips. Mix together
and allow to set until rigid on a flat surface.

She just looked at me and a comment on one of the police reports came back to me. *One minute she was chatting about her husband and two children, her voice singing their praises as though they had just been out for a summer's walk, and the next she stopped and fixed me with a stare that sent shivers down my spine. I have been with plenty of murderers in my time but none could chill me like this woman.*

I knew what he meant. Her eyes didn't blink, her face didn't move and I felt I was being drilled, pummelled into the wall behind me. Before I had given her the card, I had been interested to see if this direct reference to her crime, given the recreated location, would spring forth some viable reasons for her senseless act. I was young and naive, I suppose, but there you go. Suddenly the stare stopped and the shrillest of laughs pierced the hall and nearly my eardrum. I got up from the chair slowly, hoping to back away to the gap in the tarpaulin, realising that I was underprepared for what might follow, that this was not the moment for pure research but the moment to get out, lock the door firmly behind me and get that key down the nearest drain. By the time I was on my feet a fish slice had sailed past my head; by the time I was fumbling like a comic with bad timing at the tarpaulin, the roasting fork had imbedded itself in my forearm; and by the time I was running back up the corridor, the third utensil, a rusty carving knife, whistled past me and stuck into the tarpaulin at exactly my head height.

Confidence at some point restored, I took this as proof that the DLT method could and would bring results, but I learnt that the results could be best studied when I was out of range. When I told Peterson the story, he chastised me. *What a schmuck you are, Sad. On the day in question, when you were giving her the recipe card, which was the right idea, you should have swapped the Sabatiers for plastic bladed imitations and then, when she tried to carve you and failed because of their ineffectiveness, there is a good chance she would have cracked, broken down and told all. Live and learn, eh, Sad, but I guess you're lucky that you lived to learn a next time.*

This time. With Click and with Fright. This time.

*

Josie was having none of it. I guess over the years she had grown tired of being under lock and key, whether it was in the basement of our parents' house, playing hide and seek – which Josie usually lost – doing a striptease and undergoing an inspection, or in the steamed up bathroom of that same home, the splash of water, the muffled cries of tentative joy, the locked door and the key hidden in some corner of the room, some hole in my body. *Which cheek is it inside Josie? Which?* She would shout at me that I had gone too far, that the game was over and that I never knew when to stop. Never knew when to stop. A doozy of a recollection for a psychosexual researcher to make, the kind of phrase uttered with honesty that would be held against me when my certificates were torn up and my credibility hung out to dry. An epitaph for the researcher who went too far, who took one too many liberties and found himself scarred by the cutting edge of psychosexual science.

In dark moments when not even Josie can reach me, when even her touch isn't enough for me to evade doubting demons, I think that I will never get funding again once it's discovered what I intend to do. But as Peterson says, *if you're going to get anywhere in psychosexual research you can't be scared of getting dirty. If you want to learn anything about yourself and other people then you've got to learn to cope with a little smegma.*

But with Josie banging at the door of my office, I'm getting distracted. I'm back in the bathroom again, for another bath where the last thing on our minds is getting clean. I wanted to see her and she wanted to see me. It was as simple as that. She knew I was keeping the chart under the mattress in her room, the chart my parents had forbidden me to keep. Although they didn't see the need to keep track of my peers' physical development, I did, and while they would have been horrified to hear of a parent withholding a violin from a gifted young musician, they couldn't correlate this with keeping my psychology paperbacks from me. Josie was my accomplice, my first assistant and the bathroom was our office.

She stood up in the bath and waited for instructions. I told her to raise her arms above her head and I looked closely at her armpits. I could see follicles but precious little hair. I told her to turn sideways and I could see the swell of her breasts, the small nipples poking out into the steam. I asked her to stand with her legs wide apart, reaching from one side of the bath to the other and I noted the further growth and pattern of her pubic hair, the pink lips hiding the strange sculpture of her clitoris. She was laughing at me, watching me write the results into the notepad, fighting against the humidity which threatened to blot out my crude drawings, my hurriedly written words. Then we swapped places.

She stood on the bath mat while I undressed and got into the bath. I could feel her eyes on me and while she wrote the date and time and subject under observation, as I had in-structed her needed to be done for any results to have scientific validity, my dick sprang up, gulping its way to erection. She giggled and I told her to write what she saw, to record the angle and the extent.

'How do I know what angle it is?'

'I brought a protractor with me, it's on the mat.'

'What's a protractor?' she asked me.

I was appalled by her lack of scientific knowledge, the lack of awareness about the tools of the trade.

'Look at it and find out.'

She put the pad down, groped in the deep shag of the mat and found it. She came over to me, wrapped in a pink towel that seemed to make the rest of her pale in comparison. She held it up to me and my cock twitched.

'Keep it still,' she giggled.

'Easier said than done,' I replied.

But she learnt quickly, I'll give her that. She rotated the clear plastic until she found the correct angle. She asked me to raise my arms and tried to count the tufts of hair in terms of individual strands.

'A rough estimate will do,' I told her. I didn't want to be there all night, our parents didn't want us to bath together – no matter what Ki Wo had said – and I didn't want to arouse unnecessary interest in what was going on while they were watching television downstairs in the lounge. She poked my nipples and measured their diameter with the straight edge of the protractor.

'Not very big,' she said with disappointment.

'They're not meant to be.'

'Who says?'

'I don't know, they just don't go very big.'

'How do you know that?'

I stepped out the bath and reached for a towel.

'Observation is the key, Josie. You watch and you find out.'

'At school, you mean.'

'Whenever you get the chance. A good scientist doesn't rely on the limits of location.'

The limits of location. I liked the phrase and found myself wondering about ways I could use the phrase in other aspects of my life, wondering, that is, until I felt Josie's hand on my cock.

'Is this big?' she asked me.

I looked at her through the bathroom mist, her fourteen
year old body reaching up to my shoulders.

'Observation has led me to believe that it is, yes.'

She laughed. 'Is that good?'

'It is for me.'

*

When I let her out of the office she came running up the
corridor after me. She was suddenly so young. With each step
as my bathroom memory faded out and my unit reality faded
in, she lost a year until she was barely up to my chest. I wanted
her to be angry, I wanted to stir up a commotion in the
corridor with the two crazies either side of me, the quietest,
most deliberate crazies the unit had ever seen.

'Why did you lock me in? Why, why why?'

'I've got work to do.'

'What work is that?' she asked, trying to stay angry.

'Let me show you.'

I held her up to the plastic slit. Red light seeped into the
dark corridor, a red band appeared on Josie's face. She gasped
as she looked in and tried to squeeze my gaze alongside hers. I
couldn't see him at first until my eyes adjusted to the strange
glow from the coloured bulb. It was washing day at the unit.
In the true spirit of milieu therapy, the patient contributes to
the construction of his environment, sometimes in an abstract
way, where the inner trauma makes a tangible mark on the
space where the patient is. That, of course, would stick in
many a psychohack's throat. *Where's the evidence, Sad, where's
the evidence?* But Click's adjustment to this new life was
physical enough for the psychohacks to have choked on their
preconceptions. Looking into the hall through the plastic slit, I
could see two distinct lines, each with a dozen or so photographs hanging from pegs at regularly spaced intervals, and in
between each image, a page of erratically written text.

It was difficult to believe that this had been the young man
bred into inactivity by the institutions he found himself in, led

into silence by the absence of anything he had known, the absence of any foreseeable future. If it hadn't been for the zealous orderly determined to relieve Click of his ageing and grubby teddy, then he may never have got to this point. Of course – when he had managed to wrestle the teddy away from the desperate arms of Click – something no one had apparently done, with either child psychologists or child counsellors gently placing it to one side, being careful not to hurt the bear in case this produced some violent and irreversible reaction in Click, which would be that last thing they'd want from their half-hour session – the orderly discovered, if only they had put a firm grip around the bear's body, then they would have discovered a cache of films.

'I can't see him,' she whispered.

'Neither can I,' I whispered back, and it was only after a few minutes staring into the murkiness of the hall that I saw him lying on his bed, his arms behind his head, his thin legs crossed at the ankles.

'He's sleeping,' I told Josie, but I wondered if he was. I briefly teased myself with the idea that he had eloped and was now halfway across the Breathhouse grounds; it would have been so easy for me to reach for my keys but I stopped myself. I knew I was looking for an excuse to open the door and rush in and look at the photos to piece together the puzzle I knew was being recreated in that room. But I stopped myself. Early intervention could spoil everything and that was the last thing I wanted to do.

I took Josie's warm hand and spun her round to look in the plastic slit opposite.

'What's that sound?' Josie asked. And I stopped and listened. I smiled and lifted her up to the slit in the tarpaulin. Fright was sitting cross-legged in the middle of the hall. In front of him was the tape recorder and a pile of unused tapes beside it. His body was stiff and unmoving. He slid left, then right with an almost hydraulic movement and in the harsh light of his half of the hall, it seemed to me that there was a good chance he could have seen Josie and me peering into his world and, not wanting to add any kind of zoo mentality to his institutionalised incarceration, I pulled back from the tarpaulin. I lowered Josie to the floor, bent down to her height, hugged her close to me and pressed the side of her head, her ear to the tarpaulin. Listening was enough.

'And there was nothing for me to do . . . nothing, nothing . . . nothing. I went under the covers and waited. Even there, even there, doctor, I could hear the sounds of strangers in rooms above and below me.

My father said,' It's just scum here now, no one I'd want to know, no one you'd want to know. Stay away, you hear, stay away.'

I didn't need to be told but I was told anyway. We didn't leave the room, Jake and me, we didn't leave the room with our father, one hand in each of his; one hand that gripped until all our knuckles went white, until our arms went numb. Number than numb. My mother said to me, before our last trip to the country, before her last trip to the country, 'There's no money any more, boys, it's all gone, I don't know where, I don't know how, but it's all gone. This house won't be ours for much longer.'

And she was right, it wasn't ours at all for much longer at all. When she went under ground, the noise and shouts and screams came rushing in, through the big front doors, up the stairs and into our lives. We stood there, my father, Jake and me; one night before a drive into the country, we stood there listening to the sounds around us and we all three of us shook our heads, all three of us united somehow.

My father said, 'We can't stay here.'

Jake said, 'I don't want to stay here.'

I said, 'Where else can we go?

No one answered. My father put on his brown

leather belt with the gold buckle and hit the flowered curtain out of his way. Jake looked at me, big eyes in a dark room, and I looked at him. In a moment we had dived onto the bed and burrowed our way under the covers.

Still there now, doctor, but not with Jake. I grab pillows and talk to them; I put my knees against my ears and shut everything else out; I take one of my father's belts and try it on for size. It's too big. It doesn't fit. Nothing fits any more. Nothing.

*

Sunday afternoon. A fax from Peterson:

Languid's parents had agreed with surprising ease, all papers signed to that effect, and Languid was handed over to my tender care and my undoubted expertise. Perfect man, just perfect. The parents, of course, just want to have a ball for a weekend, let their hair down and get horny in the pool without their morose child staring at them and not saying a word.

As far as they were concerned and, more importantly, their friends, Languid is away at a salubrious camp for the sons and daughters of the very rich, indulging in all kinds of aquatic and exotic sports with children of his age and peerage. In actual fact, Languid is sitting about five, ten metres away, across the other side of the main room of the cabin, staring out the window looking at the view. He hasn't said a word, of course, the whole trip up in the car, he sat like a rock in the car with me bantering away, tuning and retuning the radio, trying to pick up on some sounds that might lurch him into the here and now. Amateur stuff I know - he's no coma victim waiting on some star from stage and screen to record him a tape and jerk him out of his reverie with some homegrown glitz. I know he's not like that but, hey, it gives me an excuse to listen to some nasty music. I don't suppose his parents have tried rap as an alternative therapy. Put your motherfucking hands in the air . . .

He's transfixed but only by the scenery as far as I can see, and who wouldn't be? What a view, what a place this is, Sad. My amateur self says who the fuck could have a problem in a place like this, but I kind of realise it's best to keep those sort of thoughts to yourself, especially if you rely on your income for people being fucked up no matter where they are. But, seriously, being here is an extension of that homegrown philosophy that travel broadens the mind, that the self is replaced by some broader need for survival and location is, as they say, everything. If a patient lives in a world of silence, take him to where silence is supreme; if the patient does not speak, take him to a place where there are no words; if the patient has retreated into a world where he thinks he is the only person, then take him to a world where he is the only person.

I knew from that first meeting with him and his parents I was going to like the kid, felt as though I was going to be able to give and take with him. And I feel as though I'm doing him a favour - if nothing else occurs or works, at least I've taken him away from his filthy-rich parents, concerned about their lineage and their image. They told me before I left about some of the therapists they had taken him to. He's been through the lot, Sad, every third-rate charlatan in the city has seen a fat fee for trying to, as they see it, bring him out of his shell. Shit, Sad, the dollar signs must have been ringing in those fucks' eyes when this fur coat brigade walked in. Visualise this, regress to this, think about the first time you did that. He's been through it all, has Languid. If he wasn't fucked up before he went to these renegades of the rational, then he surely is now. An office full of hypnotherapy junkies waiting in line for their newest failing to be exorcised or covered up, a thin layer of gravel over their drive, man; a couple of handfuls of soil over the shit they have just laid for themselves in their lives. It wasn't that Languid's parents believed in all this shit, far from it, they were from the school of thought, that venerable and esteemed school that says smack some sense into the little runt; whack the neuro out of him and make him a real man. The father wanted to send him to the military school he'd attended as a boy with the hope that the drums, the drills, the fake camaraderie would instil some normality in him. Stupid idea, of course. The mother wanted to keep him at home and get tutors, personal physicians and all this shit to sort him out. Not much better, and in the end nothing had worked and the last guy they had been to had broken the straw on the camel's back. Or whatever it is.

I know the guy as well, Sad, tried to get a job in the Institute because he thought he was so fucking shit hot. He was on the crest of the recovered memory wave, surfing that fucking paddling pool of ideas. This was ages ago, when the recovered memory bandwagon was beginning to roll and this guy had written about two books in the space of six months, explaining the need for this kind of therapy and how analysis would never be the same. He credited himself with 'discovering' many different types of memory – body memory, imagistic memory –and, get this, feeling memory where he managed to diagnose 100% sexual abuse in all his patients when they described this gut feeling they had that someone had touched their dick or cunt when they were a kid. This is the memory of emotional response he went on and on about. So, of course, when confronted with Languid, a boy of 15 years, he tried this out on him. But, of course, it transpires that he can't get a word out of him to make his point, so he tries to get him to draw these memories of emotional response, asks him to delve back into earlier childhood and search for these memories. Without a response, rather than the fuck's ideas being undermined, he made it clear that denial was evidence of their existence. Jesus, Sad, any memories I might have of fisting sequentially my parents' 15 cats is just malicious gossip and I'll sue, okay? Anyway, the parents were pretty uneasy about all of this – they had a healthy conservative distrust of recovered memory therapy, viewed it as some bohemian replacement to religion, where there was no God and no moral structure. Kneejerk Oprah, how to fake with Rikki Lake . . .And when this guy tried to localise the cause of Languid's mute demeanour by suggesting with the deftness of a drunk ballerina that at some point something may have shocked him enough to stun him into silence, something, for instance, like an unexpected finger in an unexpected place . . . Even when Languid's parents were telling me this, they hit the roof, so God help the guy when they discovered he was trying to infer sexual abuse from his silence. They probably would have had a contract put out on him for even thinking it, never mind trying to pry it out of him with a few pencils and a piece of paper.

But you know me, Sad, I'd be the first to stand up at an international therapists' conference, my plastic ID badge swinging in an air thick with bullshit and say YES, sexual abuse does exist. Shit.

I'd do a stand-up, toe-tapping routine if that's what it takes, especially if the conference is held in Thailand or the Philippines. I'd be right up there or in there, even, but Languid's parents weren't abusers, at least not in the sexual sense. Any other sense probably, but they weren't into his adolescent lingerie, know what I'm saying, they just weren't the types.

Check that out, eh, Sad, setting myself up for a professional fall.

But this place, Sad, fills me with an attitude that oozes enthusiasm. Things were beginning to get a bit stale back at the Institute, if I'm honest with you, and I think, though we haven't met, we have that kind of relationship, don't we? Call it intuition, call it transatlantic frequencies at work, but I know you understand where I'm coming from and, more importantly, I know you know where I'm going to and this paradise is exactly it. At the Institute the jade was setting in, the weird and fucked-up was becoming too ho hum and I wanted a clean slate, a fresh problem that hasn't been half corrected, half worked out. And although Languid's been through the therapy mill more times than your average loaf, no one, but no one, has got to the root, the cause, the nub of Languid. I've got myself an opportunity to get my hands on and my mind in, to stretch the muscles of my technique and my philosophies, and I ain't about to lose that, I can tell you.

So, on that note, Sad, on that clarion call to the faithful, I'll hang up and get to work. Catch you later, and keep that fax machine on, there's gonna be some hot communication, baby, and let's hope it's both ways!

*

By Sunday night I was concerned that things were not moving fast enough. After Peterson's fax I was charged with an edgy enthusiasm and for most of the day, I patrolled from one end of the corridor with its shiny floors and off-white, thinly plastered walls to the other, debating with myself the pros and cons of intervention and introduction. I had dilemmas oozing out of me and Josie was frightened by my behaviour. By way of comfort, I wanted to hear her concern.

I don't like you when you're like this.

Like what, I asked her.

When you're so caught up in your work.

But I don't like that, it sounds too much like a nagging spouse, so I get her to change it, and she twirls about on her bare heels.

I mean when you're not with me . . .

But I don't like that either, too *Last Tango in Paris.*

In this tense state I can't cope with her and I leave her dramatically as though we've had another childhood argument, when we would go to either side of the house and try to kill each other with the power of thought. *I'm going to get you, get you, get you . . .* One moment she was standing in the corridor and the next I was swinging the bare light bulb, the shadow racing over the bare vinyl floor.

I had to do something about this nervous state. I could analyse it for sure, and say that Peterson's excitement about his experiment with Languid filled me with the feeling that I was standing still, whereas he was moving in the fast lane of research. *A little friendly rivalry never hurt anyone, Sad. What are you afraid of?* I didn't like that. But it sounded a plausible reason for my state of mind. *Confront ghosts, exorcise demons.* It could be, too, that I was aware of the two stories finding voice or form in both parts of the hall, words and images manifesting themselves with little orchestration by me. It seemed I wasn't involved and I felt suddenly angry at that. I was very much involved as far as Fright and Click were concerned. If it hadn't been for my intervention in their lives, my request for them to attend the unit, then they would still be labelled mute detriments and locked up in wards with crazies with no histories to tell, apart from those of chemical imbalances or bad genes. God, I was even beginning to question my non-intervention when they first arrived at the unit. Maybe I should have charged in, brought them together for a double headed session and got the dirty washing well and truly on the line.

Shit.

The eighth rule of psychotherapy is never ask questions about whether what you are doing is right.

A third reason for my hyper state could be the pressure, spoken and unspoken, from the psychohacks up at Breath-house just waiting for me to fail, just waiting for the whole unit to come tumbling around my ears so that I would be left in the rubble with two unsavable casualties of the war. And Click and Fright would have no hope of moving beyond the four mainstays that were the *modus operandi* of my colleagues up at Breathhouse.

Drugs.

Care in the community.

Incarceration.

Group therapy combined with the above three.

Excess energy ate away at my reasoning and ironically I calmed myself firstly by pacing the length of the thin corridor separating Fright's and Click's worlds, and secondly by assim-ilating all the reasons I had given myself for the way that I felt. Who can give therapy to the therapist, when he knows that every tactic, every manoeuvre is a potential fraud, based simply on descaling any harmful or violent or extreme down to a manageable and describable basis. Who puts the therapist back on track when his reasoning is derailed? Who stops him from drowning in the most mixed of metaphors?

It was simple in the end. Peterson was the key. It was likely that he would keep in touch frequently now that he was holed up with Languid near his beautiful lake and this should be the spur, the challenge to make sure that I was not lagging behind, to make sure that whatever ground breaking action he was taking, I was doing the same in this dingy godforsaken place. While he had all the glamour of a Hollywood film, Robert Redford tackling profound difficulties surrounded by conifers, *can you save me doctor,* I had *Britannia Hospital* falling around my ears. Still, we both knew what we wanted. We wanted an outcome not just for Fright, Click or Languid, but for ourselves, and while Peterson was setting this scene, I was doing nothing except pacing between the stories, afraid that what I would do with them wouldn't be enough.

I knew what to do, knew what I *had* to do. The therapy had to evolve, the milieu to be kickstarted and my teeth sunk into the worlds of Click and Fright. Click's images, Fright's voice and Josie's love.

Josie.

An insistent banging on the door. *I'm going to count to ten, then I'm going to kick the door down, Curtis. D'you hear me? One.*

*

Another thought that came from my pacing the sterile corridor, another self-doubt that piled on with the others was the fact that much was riding on the biographical details that my two patients were churning out seemingly constantly since they had arrived. I had passed beyond the initial relief that they were at least communicating and not remaining mute, as many of the Breathhouse cronies had speculated. No, the doubt was working itself deeper. There was no guarantee that their histories, their images and words would help me create a milieu for either treatment or, more importantly, worthwhile research. The length of time Click had been in the hall could have been spent writing repeatedly *I have five fingers on each hand, five toes on each foot,* as one sad case had up at Breathhouse for three months. Yes, I had heard Fright speaking in songs, waxing into the small hours his angst, his lonely desperation, his fretful anger . . . I had gleaned enough through the tarpaulin to understand that but, beyond his undoubted poetic delivery, was there sufficient ground for me to build an environment that would bring an uncontrollable maelstrom out of his head and give me enough research flesh to gnaw on for months to come? For, as with Click, I felt that anything short of that would be a failure. A bad therapist puts up signposts on the road to recovery and is happy to leave it at that.

Looking through the plastic window in the tarpaulin, peering into the gloom that was Click's developing world was reassurance to ease my self-doubt. There was already an ambience being created in that room, just as the stark, functional mountain of tapes surrounding Fright created their own strange feel. The social work, psychology and police reports on both Fright and Click were fine, the structure of a life story delineated in cold bureaucratic language, all the information but none of the feel. And feel in this kind of research is ultimately the greatest asset, the most powerful tool. And, what's more, any therapist worth his salt, and Peterson would be right up for this, understands that the patient/therapist relationship isn't simply one of treatment or cure, it is one of symbiotic involvement, a sophisticated and intricate version, *I'll scratch your back if you scratch mine*. Their unique psychosis is fuel to an engine that drives both Peterson and me to where we want to go.

Of course, I knew Click's biography, as compiled by the social workers who took him into care while simultaneously the father was whisked off to hospital, his life under threat, apparently from a huge growth on the back of his head.

But I didn't bog myself down in these details. Just like Peterson, I saw the value in discarding the paraphernalia accumulated by others, the bumph of evidence that served to incriminate the father and conveniently label the child as victim. Perhaps the mother might be worth interviewing if she would consent to talk to me, but the authorities had lost all contact with her and the original complaint that sent the social workers rushing in was the only interview conducted with her. Since then there had been no contact. But I was not convinced either of that. I didn't want her bitching, back-biting details; I didn't want her story − simply and perhaps arrogantly put. I know the machinery, the cogs and wheels of marriage fortune, the squalls and spits of hate and lust, it is all too familiar and, at best, she would provide fodder for the middle-of-the-road shrinks up at Breath-house. That wasn't for me. It was the mechanisms of Click, the whirr and pulse of his experience that was so perfect for the experiment.

*

Before dawn the next day I prepared two injections of elothinedrine. One for Click, one for Fright, to be administered while they slept soundly on their mattresses, Fright's snores, and Click's higher-pitched grunts echoing around the hall. With careful monitoring and administering, this newly hyped drug *ideal for the prolonged sedation of the deranged,* was designed to keep them under for more than twenty-four hours, and this would allow me time to merge a recreated world into the hall, just as had been done before with the mad woman cook, the Jumper and all the other short-stay patients who had visited the unit. The same but different, bigger. Anyone reading this account after the event may well see this as the point where Curtis Sad crossed the line between experimental but legitimate research and downright abuse of civil liberties and established protocols for the care of mentally disturbed people. Maybe, but then there is the reassuring toilet graffiti I once saw at an international conference, coincidentally echoing Peterson's reassuring maxim, *it's not the journey that counts, it's the destination.* The depth of his ironic skills made it difficult to work out the exact motivation for such a statement and I guess that ambivalence was his and my strength. By injecting Fright and Click with a sleep enhancing and prolonging drug without knowledge or consent from them, I was no doubt making myself as bad as the psychohacks I revile, but then, to paraphrase some psychedelic fuck-up from another time, *don't look at the drugs, look at the effect* . . . That's the way I see it and there are plenty of rationales available to those that need them. I don't need to prove to anyone that what I want, what I do, is different from other psychohacks, this is combined research and treatment. This is the unit for the study of inter-family sexuality. The way I see it and understand it, even doped up for a few hours, Click and Fright, scarred casualties from an unfair war, are better off where they are and I guess the difference between me and my hack colleagues up the road, patrolling the wards fortified with G and Ts, is that I want them to wake up, I want them to be conscious of everything and not be stupefied into smiles without humour.

Fax from Peterson:

I've just been reading through the background notes on Languid's life story to date, The worst thing a parent can do to a child is to have expectations. That's not exactly the nub of psychology but there's a certain lay truth in it. In their way Languid's parents had scaled down their expectations of what they themselves could get from their son. There was an ideal at the beginning that interaction was what they wanted from him but, as months turned into years without a peep from him, they reduced their expectation to simply getting a reaction from him. As I've told you, they were middle-of-the-road, tending to the right, sort of people, and not the sort to settle down to an evening of violent films, filling their quiet suburbia with Uzi ricochets, but that's exactly what they did, hoping that their popcorn-munching son would imitate the set pieces and start kicking shit out of the dog. At the very least they hoped that they might get some colourful expletives. But nothing. The father unbeknownst to his wife, even tried a few soft porn videos on the boy in the hope that curiosity or embarrassment might encourage speech of some sort. Nothing. The last thing they had tried themselves before moving into uncharted therapy waters was leaving him in the middle of a village square while holidaying in Provence. From their hotel bedroom they watched Languid saunter around looking for his parents, eating a few ice creams and staring a lot at the sky. It wasn't the reaction they had wanted. They had thought maybe he would freak and run to some hapless gendarme and cry for his mother and father, the fear of being left alone suddenly bursting his verbal dam. Nothing.

This was a boy who had decided not to talk. A dream boat of a case that had many of my fellow hacks falling over themselves to get a shot at him. Guess I'm the lucky one, eh, Sad?

But I'm getting edgy, Sad, getting to the point where I think I should kick things off and not hang around enjoying the view. People

back at the Institute think I'm on some kind of paid holiday – no one
but no one views this as work, but then no one knows exactly what I'm
going to do up here. I'm trying not to give in too much to results panic
but it ain't easy. Christ, even a minute ago there, I was thinking I'd
better get something conventional going here and start a little card game
– now, is that a vase or two people French-kissing . . . Save me from
that, save him from that ! I've got a cutting edge reputation to keep for
Christ's sake. Anyway, we strode out the cabin about eight hours ago
and just got back. Okay, it wasn't exactly into the heart of darkness,
nothing was defined or solved in those eight hours but, Sad, I've told
you countless times. Patience is what it's about and out here patience
comes naturally. We must have made quite a pair, if anyone had been
around to see us, we must have been quite a sight. Ageing thirty-
something losing his hair and gaining his waistline, with this thin as a
rake, insipid, blond mouse. I could see why the parents wanted him to
talk, to live their social life and dreams because in all other respects he
fitted the bill. He had that aristocratic look about him that would no
doubt win him plenty of attention from his Ivy League peers. I liked
him. I liked him enough to try and find a way of communicating with
him that didn't rely on words.

   I tried out a few clichés on him, not to insult his intelligence but to
eradicate the need for the clichés themselves. I joked for the the first
hour, played the fool and revisited my childhood just for him. I told
him about how I used to shin up trees with the greatest of ease, like a
hairless monkey. My parents would find me up some tree whenever we
went near more than a clump of them. I loved the challenge, the fear,
the excitement, and even when I got stuck, the desire to continue never
drained. I did it again just for him and maybe a bit for me. I clambered
up some average size tree with less athleticism but with no less
enjoyment than in earlier days, and I fooled about trying to get him to
join in. But he gave me that look that got him his name, he just smiled
and looked at the scenery as I huffed and puffed on some branch.

   Then, I took it a step further and suggested we cross the rapids
rather than walk for miles trying to find a bridge or a safer place to cross.
I could tell that he disagreed and that in itself was an accomplishment,
not because he knew there must be a less dangerous place to cross than
the place I was suggesting – any half-wit could see the white water was

no paddling pool, know what I'm saying, Sad, that isn't the point. The point is that I knew that he disagreed without a word being spoken, without an eyebrow being lifted. It was, as they say, Sad, in the eyes. But I went across anyway with him following me, both of us getting soaked in the cold water. I was holding my own okay and I could have made it across the stretch of water but I thought that would defeat the purpose, so I lost my footing, stumbled into the water and went under. At this point I had to focus my attention away from my cliché scheme of getting him to come to my rescue like a post-traumatic stress Lassie and suddenly he would emerge out of his shell with a new and whole purpose, and concentrate on not losing my footing for real. The pull was quite strong and the thought did cross my mind that if his parents were here and saw that if their son lost his footing he would certainly be in trouble, I would be in deep shit with a malpractice suit as high as the mountains slammed into my face. Anyhow, I went under a few times to add some drama to it, plus a bit of coughing and spluttering for sound effect, and each time I came up I watched for signs from him. But, Jesus, Sad, I swear if I'd let go of the rock in my hands and gone floating off downriver like a fucking log, he would have just stood there, that look, that indecipherable, impenetrable look on his face. Not that I hold it against him. He's been through enough therapists and psychs to know that we all play games in order to make people realise that they are playing games with themselves and so maybe he knew what it was all about. He could have seen through me. Or maybe he didn't care what happened to the fuck that had taken him out into the country away from his nice home. I don't know. Maybe it was an exercise in the fruitless, but, as you know, Sad, you've got to clean the wall before you paint it, you've got to get a hard on before you can fuck . . . catch the drift? It was worth getting wet just to eliminate the obvious.

*

I am in the caravan with Click. Somewhere between the living and the sleeping accommodation. I can see the grubby walls with no decorations or pictures, just simple functional amenities. I can feel the threadbare underlay with my hands and I can smell a cocktail of rotting refuse and stale cigarette smoke. I am where Click wanted me to be. This is his world as seen, as lived. Josie led me into her world once when we were both very young, when we both could fit under the blankets, creating a tentlike *milieu* full of our smells and sounds. *Shine the torch Curt, shine the torch at me . . .*

Two.

I walk across the room to the frozen forms of the parents, to their terrible expression caught and held still by Click's camera. I am in the middle of a fight; if I put my hand out I can feel the strands of the father's hair as taut as the strings on a guitar. If I put my head between their clenched expressions I can feel their spit on my cheeks. In one brief moment I get the picture, get Click's picture. When I burrowed to the bottom of Josie's bed I knew I would find her, out of all places in the whole house I only had to look in one. *Found you.* Intuition is all the sweeter when proved correct.

The ninth rule of psychotherapy is let everybody know when you are right and tell no one when you are wrong.

The caption for this photograph reads *Exit and Panic are having a fight.*

As Click lies flat out on the mattress, I am gettting to know the caravan, its shadowy corners, its oppressive, threadbare appearance. I get to know, too, the life outside the caravan and I spend a lot of time around the woodsman's hut at the bottom of some anonymous glade. At the same time I listen to Fright's jerky, hoarse and uncertain voice in my Walkman. The two worlds collided at first.

As I stepped over debris on the caravan floor, I lost my balance as the car driven by Fright's father hurled around some country corner. Outside Click's hut, the focus of the image is pressed against the glass while I listen to the sound of Fright's voice reliving the rush of racing to his mother. *Hurry, hurry, hurry. Jake pulled and tugged, wrenched and forced me up the slope to the top, the clearing, my father wailing into the summer air. A world at full sun.*

I am both voyeur and eavesdropper, two characteristics essential to the observant researcher. This, I tell myself, is the nub of why I am here, why I am risking everything with this experiment. Nothing could have been gained by following conventional techniques, I have convinced myself of that. I only have to look at the dark mouth of the tunnel Click's father has hidden himself in to see what I have to do; I only have to hear the sound of Jake through Fright's voice to know why I have to do it.

No amount of yes/no interview techniques would ever have worked with these two. I, like Peterson, believe the therapist has to agree to involve himself in his patient's world. This is the Stanislawski school of psychotherapy, the method approach that sees the therapist immersed in a world where loss of control is part and parcel of the eventual treament.

I have arrived. I kneel down beside the sleeping Click, his chest heaving in short shallow movements. I spread the last photographs he took of the bear where these images were secreted for so long, the terrified portrait of his father being whisked away by social workers . . . the invisible figure of his mother disappearing into the horizon on the last day he saw her . . . I kneel down and turn up the volume on the Walkman so that I am in Fright's world with no holds barred. His voice distorts as much as the blurred scenery from Panic's car. I can feel tears in my eyes as he pines and whines and cries for Jake at every cost to himself. The skin on my neck prickles with sweat and pain as blow after blow lands on Fright. I see the wedding knives on the caravan wall and I want to tear one down and plunge it into the heart of Fright's father . . .

It is a long time before I can leave the hall. I have to haul myself first out of Click's world, scooping up his life in my hands and sweeping the area clean of any debris. Clearing the scene, laying bare the canvas before anything can begin. I take Fright's voice from my ears and do the same to his part of the hall. I have maybe a day and a half to organise these two worlds and I feel confident I can do it. With a little help from the patients at Breathhouse.

*

Fax from Peterson:
This is what I have to tell you, and you might not jump over the moon about it, you might even reach for the phone or a gun. What can I say? Therapy, not just friendship, should dare to risk. I've left all my blunt devices back in the city, all those tired old theories about counselling him into speech, rooting out original causes for his silence. This is the Delong Mountains, Alaska, and I can't think of a better place for a cutting edge.

*I've brought some LSD with me. Medium strength acid, I've been told, on the best authority from some guy who knew a guy who got a lift from the late and eternally far out Timothy Leary. A recommendation at least twice removed but you've got to trust someone at least once. Medium strength acid being enough to hallucinate on, get some pretty tough visuals but not enough to put you into a tank and regress into some kind of proto-human shit, that's William Hurt, isn't it? Wrong film, wrong psychoactive reasoning, but then it's along the same lines, I guess. I suppose this is kind of radical – now, at any rate, especially in these stringent times when you have to keep aspirin under a double lock, but back in the heyday of experimental research when Leary was a whippersnapper, he was tugging on the coat-tails of a bunch of scientists dedicated to the idea that acid was the gateway, the cure, **the** way of seeing the world in all its abstract totality. The law clamped down on all the emerging ideas that LSD was a potential treatment for everything from depression to psychosis. But I tell you, it's still radical for me and I hope Languid realises that this is a big step I'm taking. And I'm not just talking about the risk to my career, my reputation – shit, one lawsuit from some freak-out that has decided you put a finger in the wrong place or a probe on the wrong body part and you're outta there anyway, if you know what I mean. No, I'm talking about my head here, the last time I took acid I was a freshman, green around the ears and already needing to kick against the pricks, to get*

underneath the skin of what was far too conformist a fraternity for me.
But the boredom that led me to acid never prepared me for the mind
expansion, the rush of fear and strangeness, the complete and utter
weirdness of it all . . . shit, Sad, I could pile your office high with
paper if I was to tell you about the life and times of Wayne Peterson on
acid. Enough to say that it changed my life, man . . . And I guess the
idea is that it will change Languid's.

And maybe you won't want to read the next bulletin, Sad, I
don't know, I really don't know. Will I have to explain the difference
between putting a tab in a stranger's drink in the local bar and then
watching him wrestle with pool sticks and ogle moose heads, and the
pale Languid, a world of voice sucked out of him by timidity and
control? If I have to explain it or if you are professionally revulsed,
then get the shredder ready is all I can say.

*

Blade, Dogger, Synth and Treats have arrived at the unit,
brought down from the main Breathhouse building in a white
van, which is turning greyer and more rust laden with every
passing day. The hacks up at Breathhouse, my immediate
peers and superiors, were all highly dubious of my intentions,
asking as many ridiculous questions as they could think of,
assuming I was no more aware of their processes than some
first-year psych student. *We've done a lot of work up here on these*
four, Sad, so don't you go round messing with their heads or we'll
mess with yours . . . This was no more than I had expected, of
course. There was never going to be a chorus of approval. On
the one hand, they would be highly sceptical of any theory
into action stuff that had not been bludgeoned to death on the
wards up at Breathhouse. *Good theories are not ones which work*
short-term, they are ones which are proven long-term was one of the
many sayings being poured into my ears but, of course, the
other side was simply that they were jealous, that my carte was
pretty blanched and, within the scope of this crumbling old
building and a pitiful grant, I was being allowed to develop
some, as Peterson would say, cutting-edge stuff.

There was certainly an element of revenge in the four patients sent to me, picked, no doubt, not for their practical skills and prime rehabilitation but for their ability to fuck up my head and derail the experiment. Blade had been a door to door salesman for a kitchen and household supplies company. The usual set-up – company car, personal discounts and a lot of commission to be earned had he been up to the grade. Unfortunately, he hadn't been. Seems he showed little flair for selling plungers and stoppers; dusters or whisks. He took no pride, according to his background report, in any aspect of his job except when it came to selling some housewife or husband a superlative range of Sabatiers. It was reported on several occasions by concerned householders that he appeared a dull and unconvincing salesman when he came to their door and, while they might have expressed an interest in buying some or other object or tool, they were given little chance. Out came the knives, from their wooden presentation box and up into the air went the blades as he demonstrated how to cut or slice or carve. He was a large man, well over six feet, and his enthusiastic pitch yielded not sales but concerned telephone calls to head office as householders complained about the dangerous and unnerving zeal he had displayed. No doubt tired of fielding such calls, it was easier to let him go than to get to the bottom of it.

He drifted, like so many do when abruptly fired, unable to hold down even the most casual of jobs, and he was seen several times in the local park holding onto a box of knives like the ones he used to sell, which had been presented to him as a parting gift by some wag and wit at the company. *Beats a carriage clock.* As far as is known, he never used the knives to slice so as much as a hair off his own head, let alone anybody else's, but someone talking to a set of knives as intently as a lover to his love isn't going to remain at large indefinitely.

If Blade had a potential edge to his behaviour . . . *just keep him away from anything sharp, Sad* . . . then Dogger was as potentially unreliable, but definitely more sedate. A walking coma was one unkind description of his near-catatonic state. It was a case of someone who had been unhappy in the outside world becoming clinically depressed in the inside one. Which came first or which is the valid diagnosis it was unlikely that those schmucks up at Breathhouse would be bothering to find out. His background reports stated that he had grown up in a household overrun by dogs of all shapes and sizes, breeds and crossbreeds. An only child, he was nevertheless starved of affection by parents more concerned with doting on their canine offspring than their own human flesh and blood. And, of course, when the parents eventually went to that great kennel in the sky, Dogger was left with a household of more than twenty dogs, belching and farting and barking their way round the tiny semi-detached home. There was no life for him, I suppose. When he wasn't walking the dogs – no more than four at a time on strict rotation – he was feeding them, clearing up after them to the point that energy and money must have run out. Efficiently and no doubt kindly, the dogs were put to sleep also in lots of four – so as to make his understandable distress less wholesale and more gradual. Ultimately it didn't matter. With his parents gone, the dogs gone, and an overwheleming sense of ineptitude, he was a natural voluntary admission to Breathhouse.

I didn't hold out too much hope for either of the other two but both had apparently shown some building skills in Breathhouse's workshop. Synth had been sectioned on many occasions, which was often appreciated by the staff and patients up at the hospital. She was the one out of the four I had met or at least seen already. During her stays at the hospital she always found her way to a piano and started battering out any tune that came into her head – usually semi-classical pieces or folk songs that sounded familiar but to which no one could ever quite put a name. No one was saying she was a musical genius, even the non-muscial could tell that she made too many mistakes, for a start, and it seemed sometimes she was more interested in the audience than in the musical score. And I guess it was this interest in an audience that had led her to Breathhouse. It seems, according to the reports, that she had a strong feeling for performance, however inappropriate the setting, and she was lifted on several occasions from her doorstep, desperately clinging to the last, loud chord of 'Merrily We Shall Play' as an audience of angry and bemused neighbours looked on. If not outside her home, it was the park where she set up with her small Casio and 25 watt combo and blasted the pigeons and seasoned benchhuggers with 'Tie a Yellow Ribbon'. She was a borderline case – I don't mean for sane/insane, nothing as in depth as that, more accurately she was on the cusp of acceptable/unacceptable social behaviour – for sometimes after impromptu performances she was simply banged up for a night in the local police station, providing entertainment/torture for the criminal fraternity, but more often than not her persistence got her the paperwork that sent her to Breathhouse.

And Treats . . . Treats. Can't say I was happy about his inclusion in the team at all. Another faceless paedophile, in Breathhouse for three months of de-sensitising treatment before being shunted off to Hard Hill Prison to serve his x years for molestation and indecency. His reports were succinct and without elaboration. A typical, mid-thirties, heterosexual under-ager who had pushed the boat out too far, too publicly and too unashamedly for anyone's liking, least of all the law's. But I was told he responded to authority within the hospital much in the same way as he hoped girls would to him. Give him a bar of chocolate and he would do anything.

*

For three days I kept Josie under lock and key. After my parents had discovered my deviant reading practices, my child and adolescent psychology books stuffed behind unread comics, I was watched like a hawk when in the house and given a free rein and positive encouragement beyond it. Out of sight was truly out of mind. This didn't last long, they didn't and no doubt wouldn't on principle curtail their social life and a month or so after all the rumpus they were back into their usual routine and the sense of authority expected of me in my middle teen years was reinstalled and we were left alone for much of the time. A holiday weekend provided us all with an opportunity to pursue our interests.

I had read about the deprivation experiments of Hugard in southern France in the early part of the twentieth century. It was a research gem hidden away among the tables of teething statistics and hair counts so often found in studies of emergent children. Francois Hugard, reviled and later imprisoned for his unlawful experiments, had been one of the country's foremost child psychologists with eminent papers on a whole range of subjects. He had wonderfully high ideals. Not for him the laborious reassurances and platitudes that dominated this field of research, not for him the apologetic statements that trickled from the country's universities. He was a pioneer of theory into action.

He was also a complete and utter ambulance chaser and I loved him for it. In the documented case, and in several others apparently, which the book only briefly mentioned, he had close contacts with police and hospital sources, all encouraged, usually with bribes or stipends, to notify him of any cases of abuse or neglect that occurred in the small provincial district. Soon after setting up shop in the district's main town, an informant at the hospital told him of two children who had been admitted suffering from various physical and mental injuries incurred as a result of neglect. It was a case that immediately caught his attention. They weren't the usual waifs or strays, turned out by adults with neither the money nor the inclination to support them, the cruelty did not seem to stem from sociological or environmental disadvantage. The children were from the home of a prominent, widowed, businessman.

Hugard was shocked by what he saw in the two children, a girl aged twelve and a boy aged thirteen, but in the book I read he didn't dwell too much on the children's no doubt distressing state. He was more interested in what they had to say about what had happened and he came to an arrangement with the authorities who gave their consent for Hugard to interview them, collate and present evidence on behalf of the state. It was a neat arrangement, since it gave Hugard access to valuable source material and allowed the authorities to deal with the scandal and its consequences in a suitably covert way.

When I read the passage in the book, most of it went over my head. I was an able reader but hardly in a position to work my way round the langauge and mental obstructions of academia. Hugard, like many other psychologists, was at his best when he told the stories of his subject.

Justine and Pierre were held in the cellar of the house for nearly a year; a small, low-ceilinged, damp place under the ostentatious house of the businessman. They were placed there one cold winter morning by their father, who had asked them to look for some tools he was missing and they were discovered the following autumn by a gardener raking up leaves who responded to their calls for help.

Like anyone incarcerated against their will, they were hyper-aware of routine and it became apparent that for the businessman it wasn't simply a case of neglect and that he couldn't be bothered looking after his kids, shunning responsibility in an unthinking and barbaric way. It was more than that. With undisguised zeal, Hugard related that the amount of food given to Pierre and Justine was carefully measured so as to give them enough sustenance but never at any point enough to make them feel anything more than hungry. In other words he kept them at the precipice of starvation. But still more than that, he played a cruel game with them. Pierrre told Hugard that he would come round the back of the house where there was a small barred window into the cellar, its only source of outside light, and check on them this way rather than ever entering the cellar itself. Perhaps he thought that they might attack him if he gave them half a chance. In any event, the only contact they had with him after he locked the door and threw away the key was through this grate. When it came to feeding, sometimes he would give them no food or water for several days and then, he would place a tray filled with succulent delicacies and purest fruit juices in front of the barred window. Just out of reach. Then a game would ensue that neither Pierre nor Justine enjoyed. The father would push the tray towards their outstretched hands and then pull it back just if as they had almost touched some ripe pear. This continued for days until, seeing that they were at a dangerous point of weakness, he would remove the tray of luxurious food and replace it with water and bread.

Some nights I slept with Hugard under my pillow and in my head, my dreams formed and shaped by esoteric visions. Still, so many pioneers, I later learnt, had been driven underground or into prison that it seemed all that was left for psychology now was a TV series and an empire of fatuous diagnosis fuelling temporary reassurance.

Three.
'When are you going to let me out of here?'
I lay against the door of Josie's bedroom reading my forbidden books.
'I need to go to the bathroom.'
I was prepared for this, I told myself. I had receptacles waiting.
I pushed the door open just enough to allow a lemonade bottle and a small ramekin to be pushed hurriedly into the room.
'I can't use these.' Josie complained.
But I knew she eventually would and after two days I had two ramekins and three small bottles filled with Josie's excretions. She kept asking me, pleading with me to let her know what I was doing. She knew about the forbidden books, she had been a party to their continued existence by secreting them under her mattress. She knew this was research but she was too strong-willed to simply bask in the reflected glory of ground-breaking activities. She would hammer at the door, shout abuse and threats at me if I did not let her go. She was not an easy subject but her strident reaction served only to remind me that I, like Peterson years later, was at the cutting

edge of research and nothing was ever meant to be easy at the cutting edge. I told her this, of course, let her know that her shit and urine would be a fundamental part of some new and exciting discovery.

'What, what, what?' she shouted over and over again.

And if truth be told, and I suppose there is no shame in admitting this, since I was but an apprentice to such areas of research, I had not the foggiest idea either what to do with the samples or what on earth they could be made to mean. But holding the samples in my hand, the latest of which was still warm from its recent departure from Josie's body, I knew that this was an exciting and amazing place to be and I cherished every moment of it. At least, until I heard my parents' car in the driveway and I rushed to hide the evidence and release Josie to be flattened to the floor by the whirlwind of her anger.

Four.

*

While Blade and Treats dragged the coils of wire through the narrow door Dogger and Synth marked out 15 square metres with silver gaffer tape in Fright's half of the hall. Dogger and Synth were under strict instructions to follow the lines I had marked carefully on the floor with white chalk. Dogger looked as despondent as he had done when he first walked through the door, two burly orderlies guiding him and the other three towards me for their 'briefing'; Synth's hands twitched as she started at the opposite corner to Dogger, her head nodding in time to some inaudible tune.

Curtis, when are you going to let me out?

Five.

Speaking to my construction crew, my voice was that of an ardent and together coordinator.

The tenth rule of psychotherapy is always sound as though you know what you are talking about.

'The plan is simple. We have less than 36 hours to construct two objects using the material you see around you. The two objects I want to build are a caravan and a car and the main construction material is this wire. Now, your doctors up at Breathhouse have agreed to your participation in this as part of your ongoing therapy and there will of course be a wage paid at the end of the work. No one is expecting you to work for nothing and no one is forcing you to do anything you don't want to do. But you must understand two things. The work you will do here can be seen not just as part of the treatment you are already receiving but as preparation for an ongoing life outside Breathhouse – something which must remain important to you all. Secondly, you are not to repeat or mention or describe anything you see or hear in this hall. Think of it this way, just as you value your privacy in regard, to why you are here, then so must you respect the wishes of these two men. While you are working they will be here and although they will be thoroughly sedated for the duration it is essential that we do nothing to disturb them. Is that under-stood?'

Blade glared, Dogger stared at the ground, Treats shrugged his shoulders and Synth tapped out a 4:4 beat on the wall. The orderlies from Breathhouse left me to it, giggling and joshing with each other while one flicked his chewing gum onto the wall. *Research, that, mate!*

*

Six

Josie, Josie, Josie . . . what's wrong?

'When are you going to let me out?'

I passed by the door to my office, arms full of milieu paraphernalia – hooks and curtain material temporarily bor-rowed from the main office at Breathhouse, a battered camcorder kicked by many a dissatisfied patient.

'Soon,' I told her through the door, 'Soon.'

'Thats not good enough,' I heard her say in her best

imitation of our mother's voice.

I loved it when she pretended to be grown up.

An older Josie, back in the house, days after I had locked her away in her bedroom, days after she had decided to be closed to my approaches, came into my bedroom long after my parents had gone to bed, slid under the sheets and broke her silence.

'They'll go apeshit if they see us,' I told her.

'They won't, they're sound asleep. I heard dad snoring.'

'What if they sleepwalk?'

'Then so do I.'

I smiled.

'You're clever.'

Josie looked up at me and said as seriously as she had ever said anything before, 'Don't do that again.'

'What?'

'You know.'

'The experiment's over anyway.'

'What's the result, doctor?'

'I don't know yet. Results take time to analyse.'

'When's the next one?'

'I don't know that either.'

'Why do you do it?'

'I love my job.'

'That's what Dad says.'

'I know, but I mean it.'

*

Blade was glaring at me from Click's side of the hall as he wrestled with the tape in his hand, irritated by it sticking first to the left, then the right. He cut it with his teeth and handed it to Treats. There was an air of intense dissatisfaction about his jerky, inflexible movements as though he knew the job would be better served by a knife. Treats eschewed nothing but compliancy and without a word or grimace he stuck the tape to the floor, completing the first side of the chalked area.

I sat in the middle of the hall with the tarpaulin drawn back, a foreman at the building site of psych treatment. In my ears Fright whispered as though directly to me, *What do you have to dream about?* and then fell silent, from words at least.

On each of Fright's cassettes, despite the length of tape, there were huge gaps, where I only heard his heavy, laboured breathing in my ears, the echoing sound of his feet shuffling on the floor as he struggled to communicate. Sometimes he had simply forgotten to turn the tape off and I would be left hanging on his words, a long, long pause between sentences. Click's notes were equally difficult to absorb sometimes, as a whole page could have been written to describe the setting for a particular photograph and then scored out and rewritten, the revised version squeezed onto the same page. But the images were crystal clear, with only a few too dark to make any detail out. I noticed that these few blackened prints had been set to one side with no accompanying notes. Three photographs, three blank pieces of paper, hung up on a separate line from the other images.

Somewhere in his silent world, the images of these photographs. Unexpressed, undeveloped, but there.

The eleventh rule of psychotherapy is that it is not a science but a sport.

And the engine, the engine was all I could hear . . . Fright's voice rasps into my ears as Dogger and Synth look at the crude drawing I have made of the car and begin to flex and twist the wire to form the base of Fright's terrible vehicle. On the other side of the hall I can see Blade and Treats stretching up to bind together the two longest lengths of wire that will form the outer skeleton of the caravan. I lean down and, without switching Fright off, I outline a circle with silver gaffer tape. *The control circle* they called it in distant lectures and books. *In action research, where the dynamics of a situation can change at a moment's notice and often without warning, it is essential that the therapist is prepared.* Inside the circle I gather together my equipment. Such equipment – dry ice machine, fax machine, oil can, tape recorder, Click's teddy bear, spare Walkman, malleable mannequin with moving joints aged 10–14 – was essential for milieu therapy, like the wire itself which could be utilised and made to create whatever structure had been delineated by the patients themselves. In this case it was a car and caravan, other milieu researchers had recreated a toilet, a classroom, even an airplane for one compulsive mile high clubber . . .

The control circle, as well as acting as a focus point for the mechanisms of the research, can also be seen as a neutral space, a location within the general environment for the researcher to retreat into if the need arises.

The Breathhouse patients stare at me as I work and I just smile and tap the watch on my wrist.

This is hands-on therapy in its purest form.

Seven.

THE EXPERIMENT

Eight
I can hear the office door splintering.
Let me out . . .
Fax from Peterson:
*Hey, Sad, this could be the last coherent fax you get for a while
but I wanted to tell you this, to see how it sits on your shoulders, how
our transatlantic friendship copes . . . I slipped Languid his acid tab
about fifteen minutes ago and right now he's building the fire, keeping
it piled high with thick logs that some kind soul has already chopped for
us. He looks the picture of contentment. As for me, I'm at my
graduation ball in flares wondering if anyone will dance with me, know
what I mean? I'm nervous, Sad. But not in doubt. Understand the
difference. I have intense belief in the ideology of what I am doing and
I know I'd rather be looking at snow caps than the usual screwed-up
couch potato but the nerves bring out fear of results. But I wanted to tell
you that while there's a whole tab swilling around in Languid's
stomach at this moment, there's only a half in mine. He's on a whole
trip for the first time in his life and me, the seasoned, bearded, ex–
hippie, ex every tepid rock band you can think of and ex-demonstrator
in Madison Square Gardens with a big cannabis leaf on my banner,
me, I'm on half strength. It's got to be like that, Sad. The LSD isn't
for me, it's for Languid. Think of it this way. Does the doctor
prescribing methadone for the heroin addict swallow a few just for good
measure? Nope. If it is to have value I have to bridge the gap between
patient and doctor, find a balance between the two extremes of
intervention and abstention. Taking half is the way forward. I will
be on his wavelength but not vibrating with the same frenzy; I will be
able to respond to the verbal communication I hope will surge in him. I
need to see his face, not shamanistic visions. Call me sentimental, call
me a workaholic, describe me as unable to relax, but I want to be there
for Languid once the LSD has kicked in. Guess you might even call it*

guilt for setting up this whole situation in the first place, but the kid
would have eventually been pumped full of some kind of prescriptive
drug anyway – his parents had threatened as much, having exhausted
most holistic and video-based approaches – and if he was going to take
something to take him out of himself, then it might as well be the
granddaddy of escapism.

Nine.

Josie tried to keep me in the bathroom once. Out of
revenge, out of justice, no doubt. The old chair-against-the-
handle trick. She had seen it in films, old black and whites our
parents chortled away at on Sunday afternoons. It didn't work.
Maybe it was the angle, maybe it was the wrong sort of chair.
One shove and I was out.

Ten.

Why did you do that? Josie starts shouting as soon as I
unlock the office door but it's too much noise in my head so I
make her whisper to me instead as I lead her out into the
corridor, her hand clamped to my palm.

I am disconcerted, though. When I had left her in the
office she had been at the pale green dress stage, long legs,
narrow hips, the face of an angry minx and yet now she was
the youngest I had ever seen her, could even remember her,
dressed in a soft pink jumper suit. She was four, maybe five,
but young enough to totter on her feet, threatening to fall
with each step. When I closed the office door and turned
round, she stood blinking in the red-lit corridor.

What have you done? I make her say again to return us to
firmer ground.

'This is the start of it.'

The start of what?

'The experiment.'

I led her along the corridor that had been transformed by
Dogger and Treats. Dogger had forlornly held the step ladders
while Synth covered the white strip lights with red gels from
one end of the corridor to the other. The stained walls, garish
at the best of times, suddenly gained a new and shadowy feel.

Exactly how I wanted it. If the experiment spilled out into the corridor all would not be lost, a manipulable sense of environment could be maintained. *Expect the unexpected in milieu therapy.* Click would think he was in a darkroom and Fright would feel he had entered his father's lair.

Cover every base, Sad.

First Synth then Dogger viewed their work.

'It could be a disco now, couldn't it?'

'The world feels as though it is sitting on my shoulders in this light.'

Synth mimics the rhythm of a bass drum and high hat with her mouth, her narrow hips bumping the wall on the offbeat.

'Quickly,' I say to Josie as she hovers halfway down the hall.

Why?

'We don't want to miss anything.'

I pushed her ahead of me and the strength of the dry ice, seeping under the tarpaulin, hit us both unexpectedly. I had left the machine on for ten minutes and, judging by the smoke which filled Click's half of the hall, it was nine minutes too long. I flicked the machine's switch and bent down to rub the tears away from Josie's eyes. She was rubbing the eyelids furiously, pulling the skin away from her eyes, trying to stop the irritation. We had both stepped into the control circle without noticing it.

'Don't rub them. Remember what Mum used to say . . .'

I could see her standing in front of the television, crying for attention, big red marks burning deep into the skin around her and Mother saying, if you rub your eyes you'll just make them worse . . .

One hand held Josie's warm, fidgeting fingers while the other faded up the taped music. Satie. A year or so ago, the wackos at the Ecole Du Thérapie in Paris had made a recording of a music therapy session they had conducted with disturbed and violent children. They came up with the humdrum idea and quasi-hippie notion that if you recorded some nature sounds and played them to a bunch of city kids, they would get all au naturel and chill out. Fairly typical woolly thinking by a bunch of neo-Freudians, but there you go. Not everybody can be striding the cutting edge that is Peterson and Sad. But they did have one idea I liked, probably because it was offbeat, but possibly because it had some *milieu* value. They recorded the ambient sounds of birds, wind in the trees, rustling foliage, using synthesisers and samplers, creating an aural wallpaper right there in front of the children. Nice touch but, of course, they should have been recording *city* sounds, not country ones. All they were doing was giving the children a holiday from their hell but always with the sure knowledge that they would be retuning to the streets. *Tease me, tease me.* Far better to equip them with sounds that they could decipher, filter and recognise as part of their daily lives . . . but that's not my problem.

Cheek to cheek looking through the slit in the tarpaulin, Josie and I peered into Click's environment. We saw the lights first. *Pretty, pretty, Curtis . . .* The red, blue and green fairy lights spaced at centimetre intervals along the outer frame of the caravan. They burned through the dry ice, each bulb having its own halo in the gloom. A beacon, I thought, something for Click to find and never get lost, no matter what corner of the hall he strayed to. The fairy lights highlighted perfectly what a good job Blade and Treats had done. With only my rudimentary plans and sporadic direction they had created a mobile home that would not have been out of place on any windswept western shore.

*

It hadn't gone well at first, however. Treats was moody and unresponsive to requests and cripplingly passive to threats, while Blade moaned and complained about how the job could be best achieved with a knife to cut the wire rather than the small (and blunt) wire cutters I had given him. With the hours dwindling before both my patients woke up – the elothine-drine as recommended could only be used for a certain length of time before complications might arise, drip-feeds and blanket baths become necessary – *it's a wonder drug in many ways, Sad, the best non-curative aid a hassled psychologist could ever need. Knocks 'em out.* I decided to ignore the warnings given to me by my Breathhouse colleagues and intervene. I found a knife for Blade, not a Sabatier, as he grimly observed, not even made of top-notch steel, but what it lacked in quality it more than made up in length.

'Fifteen centimetres.' Blade nodded with satisfaction.

But it wasn't just Blade that needed encouragement. Treats, too, was beginning to back off from even half-hearted involvement. I looked through the files in the office for the records relating to the last ped who had visited the unit and found a Dutch *Boy* magazine that the shrinks up at Breath-house had been waving in front of his face or rather his dick, hoping to get some incriminating reaction or erection from him. It worked for Treats. *Give these types a hit of innocent, nubile flesh and they're away.* I gave him ten minutes in the toilet and allowed him to carry the magazine in his back pocket while, and only if, he worked. He was delighted.

'This is hard currency up at the hospital, believe me.'

My efforts to motivate them after their self-worth had been bled out of them up at Breathhouse were rewarded by their attention to detail. The plans simply required a caravan circa 1970 design to be built. *Milieu is concerned with atmosphere rather than precise authenticity.* Three windows, one door, two wheels to be modelled out of wire with a string of fairy lights highlighting the structure's outline. But when suitably mo-tivated, Blade and Treats went much further. A floor inside the model had been created, a latticework of wires criss-crossing from one end of the structure to the other; the separate areas described and photographed by Click, the living accommodation area, the sleeping accommodation area etc were marked out – a string of blue fairy lights for the bed-room, red for the living area and four sets of green lights around the windows and door. After motivation they helped me move Click from his position in the middle of his half of the hall to one of the side walls, whereas before they would not touch him, not quite believing me that he was actually alive. Better still, once the construction had been finished and they helped me wire the environment for sound, dry ice and other electrical effects, they carried Click back into the structure and set him down on the wire floor, in the living accommodation area, folding his arms across his chest as though all of this was some bizarre death ritual, and Click headed for a kind of Valhalla. Best of all was the suggestion I received from Blade which in turn led me to extend the *milieu* into the corridor outside, the red lights acting as an outer edge to the world created around the caravan.

'Where's the caravan meant to be, doctor?'

'Anywhere really. It moved about. There's photographs of everything here from woods to city; from seashore to moun-tainside. Difficult to say, really.'

'Woods?'

'Yes, quite a lot of the time actually.'

'Will you let me go outside?'

No one was to leave the unit, I had been told under strict instruction. It was the terms of the patients' release to me and this was one rule I was not inclined to break. Breathhouse was not Insention, it was not a secure establishment, at least not once in its grounds and once there, with a 15-centimetre knife, Blade might simply jump the wall and go carving. Both Treats and Blade looked at me, knowing that there was some weight attached to my willingness to give permission. To trust or not to trust.

'On you go but leave the knife, Blade.'

'I need it for what I have in mind.'

My toes curled and I bent a scrap of wire all the way round my little finger until I could feel my pulse throbbing at its tip. *A psychotherapist is often required to think on his feet.*

'Okay.'

As for Treats, none of this involved him, and he was happy to slump against the wall, pull out the magazine from his back pocket and quietly absorb the forbidden world.

Colleagues at Breathhouse would be appalled by this sentiment but I envied Treats his simple obsessions, his one-track, non-stop mind. I thought of Josie, not in the unit, but the Josie back home, in the basement, her pale green dress, her trembling body barely visible in the dark cellar but clear to me in my head. Crystal-clear, in fact.

We waited for some time but I did not give in to the impulse that said rush out there, grab Blade and get him back inside before he is discovered. Eventually, he arrived back, dumped an armful of bark on the floor and left again. Again and again he returned with the same load, barks of different colours, greys, greens, browns from different species of trees.

'Where did you get all this?'

He looked at me as though our roles were suddenly reversed and I was the one needing help.

'From the trees, Doctor, every tree around the unit.'

And he was right. I walked out into the corridor to the front door of the unit and saw what he had done, and why he had taken such a long time.

Every tree that I could see, birches, chestnuts, ash, and elms had been stripped of their bark from ground to six feet up the trunk. I was horrified and stunned and needed to laugh at the peculiar sight. I thought firstly of what the Breathhouse lot would make of this, knowing that they would immediately blame it on my inability to control my patients, or see it as some weird and wonderful kind of therapy that I had dreamed up to investigate Click or Fright.

Yes, Sad, you are quite right, tree therapy is particularly 'poplar' on Forestry Commission land. Plenty of scope, you see . . .

Secondly, it could be seen as a rape of nature, a cruel and horrible joke played on God's world by a sick and perverted individual and hardly ready to be considered as a viable preamble to treatment. But thirdly, as I walked back into Click's half of the hall I saw Blade and Treats spreading armfuls of bark across the *wall*, scattering the tree's skin onto the wooden floorboards, all the time their steps getting quieter and quieter. The very environment for a mute becomes muted; our steps no longer echoed. Blade beamed at me and held his knife above his head in triumph. I saw no threat in this, only a patient with an intuitive feel for environment, an understanding of what I was trying to do here. I wanted to hug him but instead I decided to present him when all this was over with twenty centimetres of top-quality Sabatier.

*

I like the music.
Josie leapt into the hall when I drew back the tarpaulin slightly and whirled her way into the dry ice, her arms above her head, her legs kicking out in all directions.
Now you see me.
She crouched down, arms hugging her knees to her chest, and she rolled about the hall. I couldn't stop her, didn't want to stop her.
Now you don't.
A fax spits from the machine in the control circle.
Hey, Sad, ever sent a fax on acid before, it's wild man, just simply wild. I've tried about four times already and I think I've sent the following pages to at least three different places in the world – CIA, Scotland Yard and the Finnish police! Somewhere, anywhere will do. At a crunch, in a crisis, any port in a storm. Somebody's got to read it, eh? Things are picking up here, tripping up here. Ha ha! I'm holding onto the table right this minute, feeling the wood crawl underneath my fingers. I can see into the grains, the imperfections, the splinters, it's all so fucking fundamental. Someone's taken away my eyes, man, and put in microscopes. That's the way I feel. It's taking me back, this feeling, to the growl of Howl and all that. I'm not a 60s kid, I'm 70s and everybody tells me I missed the real times, when it all began, but I don't know about that, don't know about that at all. People might not have been too stoned to think back then, but they sure as hell were too stoned to do much about. it. Oops, says me, acid honesty comes out all the time, hits you between the eyes, slaps you in the face. Who am I kidding man, I'm sitting here gripping the table for dear life and you know what Languid is doing, you know what the sad, beautiful kid is

doing? Talking? Do you think he's talking, an audition for erudition, d'ya think, like he's suddenly found his voice after all these times and he is describing, like Huysman, the tiniest details of his surroundings, extracting finite definitions of nature and the nature of the world? Off the mark, man, way off. He's walking around the room, striding around it, seven large steps for one wall, then six, then nine, then seven again. He's counting them, I know he is, but there is no sound coming from his lips. I tried to count them out loud too but I got lost after four and now he's on his way around again. I've missed the boat, Sad, I guess I'm going to have catch it on the way back, catch you on the way back. Later, Sad, enough tapping on this machine for the moment, eh?

Two bright lights greet my eyes when I step through into Fright's half of the hall. Two car headlights to be exact.

'You got a car, doctor?'

'Yes.'

'You going anywhere in it?'

'Not planning to, why?'

'We could use the headlights, couldn't we?'

Synth seemed ready to strip my car.

'I've already thought of that and anyway there's no stereo in it, I'm afraid, not even a radio.'

She seemed annoyed that I had thought what she had thought.

'You've done a good job, both of you.' Dogger looked as though he didn't care and Synth started to jump on the spot, full of energy, the bass drum and high hat kicking in again. The car was perfect, a close resemblance to my weak drawing of an old Morris, the kind of rounded bubble car that are jokes or collector's items now, depending on your point of view. I gave a halogen light I had procured at a price from one of the orderlies at Breathhouse to each of them and they set about attaching them to the model car.

Synth and Dogger had not worked as well together as Blade and Treats but they got the job done. They were both too absorbed in their own worlds to either relate to each other or to fully concentrate on the task given to them. Dogger's head always seemed to be elsewhere, somewhere in his forlorn past, his destitute present. He wasn't the sort of person that could be taken out of himself easily. *Dogger, Sad, is the kind of patient that is sucked dry by the past, his tragedies leading to anhedonia, nothing to live for but nothing to die for either.* Synth, on the other hand, was rarely in herself, a head and body constantly caught up with some unstoppable kinetic need. She would take a long time to stretch a piece of wire from one end of the car to the next, stopping to tap out some rhythm on the floor, on her head, anywhere in fact. She hummed and sang and busied herself with anything rather than what I had asked her to do, while Dogger's movements were entirely the opposite. *Molasses movement, Sad, don't want to go forward, can't go back . . .*Both doors had taken hours to do and I had to speed up the process by fixing the fairy lights to the roof and panels of the car myself.

'We really have to put a radio inside the car,' Synth had asked.

'Maybe, but first I need some kind of seats. You need something to sit down on if you are going to listen to music.'

That was the kind of woolly reasoning that I hated in other pyschohacks, short-changing and patronising in one fell swoop, but she didn't complain and, at least this way, Synth was motivated to wrap the wire around and around the base of the car in a suitable chair shape until it was strong enough to take her weight.

'Get in, Dogger, we're going to go for a ride and test this stereo.'

Dogger, of course, had backed off from such an invitation and nervously lit and smoked a cigarette. Gently I led Synth away from the car, out of the harsh, white light of the halogen headlamps.

'It's always the same,' she wailed. 'I get near a stereo and some wanker stops me or turns it off or tells me they'll call the police or tells me to fuck off or asks me to get a life . . .'

I grabbed Synth and led her by the arm into the spare

room out in the corridor. I led Dogger, cigarette burning almost unnoticed between his lips, after her. More easily, I asked Treats and Blade to accompany me to the waiting room as I described it. From here, I explained, they would be taken back up to Breathhouse, not before they were generously rewarded for all their work. Blade waved his knife in appreciation and Treats smiled and patted the magazine stuffed into his back pocket. I locked the door behind me.

Suddenly, after hours and hours of constant noise and the sound of metal scraping and scratching the floor, the hall was silent. I drew back the tarpaulin separating Click and Fright, turned off the overhead lights, switched on the dry ice machine and left to find my Josie, who cartwheeled out of the hall, whooping and yelling with her childhood high.

Catch me if you can, I thought I heard her shout.

*

Sad, you're going to have to fax me back and I mean now. Get those transatlantic cables humming or whatever the fuck it is that gets this from here to you. I feel cut off in these damned mountains. I'm a city kid, always have been, always will be. These mountains, the trees all around the cabin, everything is crowding in. You know what I mean, you can be in the biggest space in the world from tundra to desert and you can still feel as though you are in a cupboard, locked, with the key thrown away.

I think Languid is no longer Languid. File x21 is going off the rails and I'm in no fit state to cope with it. You hear me, man, because no one fucking else sure is gonna. This isn't good. I'm still climbing with this acid, there is no levelling out so far and I can't remember when I took the fucking thing. Like a novice tripper I forgot to look at the clock, this being the country and everything, I forgot to look at the clock. I can't believe it. I should have known better. If all else fails and you lose your grounding in the here and now, you're always going to know the time and be able to bring yourself back, stop the trip and get some grip. But I've lost it. I can't move from this table. This fax machine is my orange juice, my only means of getting down. I can't move. Ideas aren't shaking this root, man, psychology isn't shifting this paralysis. And all the time, there goes Languid, here comes Languid. He's tearing the place up. First it was non-stop walking, around and around and around he went and now he's taking everything outside. The chairs, the pictures, the ornaments, even the plates and cups are all going out. And I don't mean he's having a picnic, Sad, this is no picnic, he's just taking the stuff and throwing it out the door. It's getting dark too and God knows where it's all landing but I can hear a lot of crashes and thumps. I can't do anything about it. You want to fax him, type some sense into him, make him stop doing that. Fuck, Sad, he's dragging the fridge now, not even bothering to unplug it, he's scraping the whole caboodle along the floor. There's going to be hell to pay. The Institute has an inventory a mile wide for this place man, a mile wide, and it's going to cost me big time. Half a month's salary is outside already. Shit, and you know the best of it, the very worst of it. He hasn't said one word. Not a grunt, a groan or a whistle while you work. Nothing. I've got to try and move.

*

Click stood in the middle of his part of the hall. Cheek to cheek, Josie and I watched him. These were nervous times indeed and I held onto Josie more tightly than usual, my hand three quarters the way round her tiny waist. Expectation of conclusion. All the best case studies always had the researcher, no matter how formally they were written, in a thrall of edgy expectancy or contained euphoria. It was always there, even, within the smugness of academic language it was always there. My tutor, on reading my thesis on *Domestic Sexuality: The Sexual Family,* said to me, *'You really wanted this to work didn't you, Sad, you really wanted to prove something.'*

He grudgingly passed it.

'Only just, only just. Don't get carried away with ideas. They mean nothing unless they have some practical application.'

I wanted to drag my old tutor out of his Alzheimered retirement and bring him to the unit. My unit, my research, my patients. Ideas meeting the practical head-on, as far as I was concerned. Click hadn't talked yet and that was okay. He had just woken up from a drugged sleep, after days of intensive memory retrieval and he had woken to find himself in an environment akin to the one where he had last had a sense of himself, a sense of living. I call that practical.

We turned on our heels and looked through the opposite slit to see Fright standing in an almost identical position to Click, his painfully thin body shaking, his stubbled head nodding up and down as though he was agreeing adamantly with something that was said. He was silhouetted against the bright beams of the halogen bulbs but I could see him throw his hand into the air with his lips beginning to say something.

I hugged Josie closer to me, my hand slipping down her chest and immediately, incredibly, before my eyes she got too heavy for me, went from ten to fourteen and, where my hand brushed over her bony chestplate, my knuckles suddenly bumped into her breasts. I couldn't find any words for her but without me she managed to say, *It's started, hasn't it?*

'Just about,' I told her, putting her down on the floor while stepping back into the control circle. Gently pushing Josie out of the way, as she bent round my body looking to see what I was doing, I stretched out from the circle not wanting Fright to see me, wanting to keep my anonymity intact, and poured the oil slowly out of the can towards the centre of his half of the hall.

There are, of course, plenty of examples of smell offsetting memory; scent affecting environment and the person's personality along with it. From scratch-and-sniff T-shirts to Sensurround films; from the smell of long-lost home cooking and *Mom's Apple Pie* to that elusive and personal body smell of someone once loved. It was all there in black and white and now it was all on the wooden floor of the hall, in a streak of black glistening in the glare of halogen bulbs.

It had an almost immediate reaction.

Fright sniffed the air and then looked at his feet. The oil spread quickly around him and under the wire frame of the car. He couldn't believe it, his jaw dropped and his eyes rolled in their sockets.

'Jake . . . ?'

He put a hand to the floor and spread the liquid through his fingers, held it up to his nose, wiped it on his Breathhouse uniform. He turned unsteadily on his feet and walked slowly round the car, peering under and over it as though trying to find the leak. The oil had spread so widely and thinly now that it was impossible to tell its point of origin, impossible to escape its stench.

'*Stinky, stinky,*' Josie whispered.

I quickly turned back to the control circle and grabbed Click's first milieu device. He hadn't as yet made any sign of acknowledgement of his newly constructed environment so I threw in his teddy bear, its roughly cut Caesarean neatly sewn by Beth when Click had first arrived. The bear slid along the wooden floor and disappeared into the fog. There was a moment of suspense, a sensation not usually associated with such an institution as Breathhouse. Routine smothered any sense of the unexpected. *You get up, go to work, do what you have to do, go home, go to bed. It's a job like any other, Sad.* Not here, not now, the psychohacks' words echoed meaninglessly in a silence broken only by Fright's muffled exclamations. Then, the suspense broke and action research took hold. The bear skimmed across the varnished floor towards the back of the hall. But not all the bear, just its torso and while it disappeared into the dry ice, the head bumped towards me, its plastic eyes popping out and scattering. Finally the dismembered arms and legs shot up into the air falling through the frame of the caravan. The pondering notes of *Gymnopédies* continued.

Behind me I heard Fright shout and, quickly turning to the tape recorder controlling the music for Fright's half of the hall, I turned on the sound of a car spluttering into life over and over again before it drove off slowly into some distance.

The sounds were looped and, as soon as the car sound faded, it stalled and came back to the noise of the engine starting. Looking over, I saw Fright disappearing under the car, his legs and arms covered in oil, his voice repeating, 'Where's Jake . . . have you found Jake . . . have you found him . . . ?'

Josie hid behind me, her arms wrapped tightly around my waist. I reassured her quickly.

'It's okay, everything's okay. Fright knows where he is, he just doesn't know who I am. It's meant to be like this.'

'Is it?' she asked me. And I just looked at her. I never asked her to say that. Where did that come from?

I was both tired and excited.

Then, if there wasn't enough noise, I heard a crash from the corridor outside and, loath as I was to leave the hall at that moment, I might have to. It could be anyone, but at the back of my mind I teased myself that it was maybe Beth come to help on one of her days off. *I won't be needing you for a few days, why not take a holiday somewhere, you know you deserve it . . .* Or worse, it was the chief pscyhohacks from up at Breathhouse paying the impromptu visit they had always threatened. *We'll come down and see you one of these days, Sad, see what we're getting for our money.* Typical timing. What was probably a slow afternoon up at Breathhouse was the crux of weeks of work for me. A cup of coffee, explanations of the delicate stage the research was at and boot them out in half an hour. Even that was too long. But I couldn't escape it, much as I wanted to.

Of course, it wasn't what I'd thought. From the waiting room across the corridor from the hall, Blade, Synth, Dogger and Treats were battering the door, wrestling with the handle.

'When you going to let us out of here, Sad?'

'When do we get the reward you promised?'

I heard Blade's and Synth's voices and I immediately thought of my foolish gift of the knife to Blade. His voice was the most strident but Synth was hitting a pretty high note. Incredibly, though, it wasn't just the sound of these two voices, it was the impact of four sets of limbs on the door that scared me most. Even if Treats and Dogger were too timid to act themselves, they could be riled enough by the other two. And this was not a time for orderlies, not a time for any outside control to be brought in. Questions would be asked, observations made, and I wanted neither of those at the moment.

'Calm down, I'll be with you as soon as I can.'

*

Sad, get on that phone now and dial this number. Things are not good. There's hardly anything left in the whole cabin. Languid has taken everything out and I'm not talking just the furniture, I mean everything. A minute ago the last piece went out, God knows how he managed it. He took the legs off the two beds, threw them out the window and then dragged the mattress out as well. And you know what he's doing now, you know what he is doing now, Sad, he's tearing the pipes from the sink in the kitchen and in the bathroom, tossing them out to the front of the hut. There's no bath left, Sad, can you believe that, he's ripped the fucking bath out. There's only the toilet left and I don't see that lasting. What is it with this kid? There's nothing, absolutely zilch in his file, in the talks with his parents, nothing that said anything about a tendency to destroy his environment. The guy was meant to be as docile as a deer caught in headlights. Know what I mean? The guy wouldn't react if you jabbed him with an electric cowpoke. And now look at him. I wish you could see him, I wish anyone could for Christ's sake. He's not the boy he used to be, or I was led to believe he was. I've got a fully fledged psycho on my hands and I can't even move from this fucking table. I know, I know, I know what you are going to say and maybe that's why you are not replying, letting me stew in my own juices, that sort of thing. You shouldn't have given him the acid, Peterson, it's your own fault, you've made your bed and now you've got to lie in it. I thought we were closer than that, people at the cutting edge are meant to support each other. Things don't always go smoothly, you should know that. And maybe it is the acid, for him and for me, maybe he's really just sitting there in front of the fire reading a book quietly and I'm imagining the whole thing but I really don't think so. I'm not that far gone, that at least I know. He is reacting to the acid, okay, but he's not singing or talking or shouting or swearing. He's seriously demolishing this property and there is going to be hell to pay. Call me.

*

I rushed back into the hall and ran to the far end where the cord for the curtains Dogger and Synth had put up had been wound around a peg. I let it go and heard above the car noises, the sparse piano notes, the sound of the curtain encircling the car, a quick swoosh of material unfolding, and the patterned flowers were lit up by the halogen bulbs, the silhouette of the model car moving from side to side, Fright's bony frame squirming among the wires, fairy lights and oil.

Curtis . . . Curtis . . .

Josie was tugging at my shirt, unimagined and uncalled for. In the last few minutes she had gained height and age and lost her hair. She was sixteen and about to leave home, the beginning of the long trip from the Josie I had known and grown up with. She was up to my shoulders now, shaven head ready to bounce off my chin, her long earrings waving from side to side as she shook her head disapprovingly.

You have to intervene now. Where's the therapy in this?

'Shut the fuck up. Did I ask you to say that?'

She made a face, got younger and slipped back to age ten, just at the end of the curly hair stage and the beginning of the pale green dress stage, young fat giving way to nothing on her bones. She started to cry and despite everything going on around me – the car roaring its way through Fright's part of the hall, his voice growing more strident, the dry ice tickling the back of my throat, the anxious Breathhouse patients in the other room – I needed to take time to put my lips to the tears running down her cheek, to run my fingers through her hair. There was always time for Josie, didn't matter what grade or night this was, there was always time for my sister.

But as soon as I bent down to touch her, she shot back up in a disorientating rush of age and pushed me against the tarpaulin.

Don't touch me, don't test me, don't use me, she shouted and ran to the other end of the hall.

Click was moving. Preoccupied with Josie, I hadn't noticed his sudden animation. Suddenly he was taking the washing in. I rushed to eject the piano music from the tape recorder and in homage to the neo-musicians from the Ecole du Thérapie I put on an Eno-like soundtrack filled with exotic, jungle sounds, long chords peppered with animal sounds, trees rustling etc. The photographs and writings which he had so furiously and studiously written over the past few days began to be torn from their pegs and then ripped in half, then quarters, then eighths, their fragments thrown up like confetti lit by the red, blue and green fairy lights. This was not good. Not good at all. Click was obviously having a reaction to his environment and sometimes the reaction can be like a kick in the head. Put someone in a field with sheep and they don't always become a shepherd, sometimes they make like a butcher; mutton mania or lambs to the slaughter . . . The initial interaction with environment created in milieu therapy can be a hazardous one and Click had spent so much of his time developing the photographs, the writing, that it was painful to see him intent on destroying the fruits of his labour and the evidence for mine. While he saw his past in the torn and ruined images and notes, I saw my future flying amidst the forest sounds, a beheaded Exit and Panic mixing with ripped shots of the caravan falling with scraps of writing, *Never touch my head . . . I could hear my mother's voice over and over again . . . this body and my eyes have seen everything there is to see of you . . .*

The twelfth rule of psychotherapy is never ever involve yourself with a patient on a personal level.

The thirteenth rule of psychotherapy is when you have to intervene, you have to intervene.

Somewhere I heard the sound of wood splintering and a cheer from several voices. I could see Josie at the other end of the hall, staring malevolently at me, still with her shorn head, still moving away from me, her back sliding up the wall, and

Fright was at the curtains surrounding the model of the wire car. The silhouette made me shudder, his voice made my skin crawl as he continued to call out for his lost brother and his hand furiously rubbed his head as it battered inconsequentially against the curtain. *Why don't you answer me . . . have I done something wrong . . . ?*

In a few minutes there would be no images for me to hold onto. There would be the negatives but I couldn't be sure in the midst of all the paraphernalia in the hall that they too had not been ripped up, and with those gone I would be back to square one and no one would believe that anything had been achieved with Click, another mute destined for a silent life. *Let's see, Sad, you had Click for three weeks and you say you managed to get him to not only learn to develop photographs that illustrated his family life but you got him to write about it? All this after years in institutions with him staring into space and not saying a word. So tell us how did you work this miraculous change in him? Can we see what you've done?*

All I could see is all they would have seen if they had stepped into the unit at that moment. Click's tall body going haywire.

I removed myself from neutrality, from the safety of the control circle. *If you step out of neutral space when dealing with a volatile patient, then be prepared for anything.*

Through the thinning dry ice, Click saw me straight away and reacted like an uncertain predator. He let the photograph of Panic swimming in the mountain pool fall to the floor and he began to circle me, his deep-set eyes not veering from their stare. I remembered my training, the module entitled *How to Behave with Disturbed Patients*, and stood very still, not giving anything away with body language or direct eye contact.

The fourteenth rule of psychotherapy is that in a dangerous situation someone has to remain calm.

I could smell him as much as I could see him, an acrid odour of shit and sweat and, strangely, I suddenly remembered a gap in my preparations for my patient's stay when Beth pointed out that I had not provided toilet facilities. *They're here to get help, Beth, not a bath* . . . The sound of a wood pigeon cooed around our heads while Click's frenetic movements were strangely dampened and muffled, not a sound from his feet pacing the floor around me. Blade had done a good job and somewhere there was a sense of irony that a patient I had barely met or known should react so well to a milieu that wasn't even his own. And then there was Click, not reacting at all well to his environment. *Milieu therapy must allow for the possibility that the patient will reject the environment created for him and seek an alternative.* Typical psychospeak, any heartfelt theory, any headstrong dogma can always, always have a get-out clause – *the exception always undermines the rule, remember that, Sad. Professional myopia is an occupational hazard.* The paper that was Click and Fright hadn't got as far as the appendix or the necessary disclaimer.

Click was the spitting image of his father. Seeing him circle me, watching his taut, coiled movement I saw a dozen photographs of him – in the wood hut, on the wasteland, by the sea, in the pool – the gaunt, harrowed look, the long black hair, the limbs that seemed to have a jerky life of their own. Then there were the photographs of Panic behind the wheel, his explosive rage, ready to kill them all without a thought even to his own safety. There was a reckless, distant look in many of the close-ups of his father's face, so that when Click came closer it was unnerving, to say the least, to see it replicated in his son's eyes.

His breath was stale and putrid, his thin lips parted into some kind of expression, a few rotting teeth catching my eye – a mute having spent a good part of his life in institutions doesn't receive the best of dental care. He breathed on me and passed me by while out of the corner of my eye I could see Josie at the back of the hall. She was ten again, all curls and floral dress and I lost my sense of the immediate, finding warm feelings as I tried to get her to say something. At a wet bus stop, before either of our teens, we huddled and shook together, splashed by cars, waiting and waiting for a bus to take us home. She put one leg over mine and I put one leg over hers; she put one arm around my waist, the other across my chest until we were linked and locked together. We had to laugh when the bus came and went while we fell into a puddle desperately trying to undo our limbs . . . Josie didn't respond. Maybe she couldn't hear me above the noise of the forest, the thrashing of the car in the other half of the hall, or maybe she couldn't see me through the dry ice. It was too much like a game we had played all our lives – cat and mouse, doctor and nurse, good and evil . . .

But, of course, I was getting distracted, I should have been paying attention, should have remembered where I was and what I was doing. *In milieu therapy the doctor as well as the patient must be prepared to immerse him- or herself in the environment created. Anything less could be seen as devaluing the therapy and devalued milieu therapy is not recommended.*

The fifteenth rule of psychotherapy is do not let yourself get distracted.

Remember the terrible affair of the Houton incident, Sad. A renowned Breathhouse consultant psychologist who stepped in to replace a colleague at short notice. One moment he was talking to a very disturbed patient about his need to understand his behavioural oscillation and the next he is looking at the shrubs out the window in the immaculate gardens at the front of Breathhouse. The patient oscillated as he had done on several occasions before, except that he oscillated this time with a large desk lamp. The consultant was never the same again. The head trauma caused by the attack rendered him incapable of either sustained speech or prolonged memory.

While Josie and I interact, Click removes several metres of wire from the rear of the caravan and grabs my hands and quickly winds the wire around my wrists.

*

Hey, Sad, I've finally got myself some smarts, come to some concrete conclusions, or at least possible explanations as to why Languid has refused to talk from the year dot. He's been surrounded by the material and the sophisticated all his life and he has reached breaking point, the point where he can no longer bear to be surrounded by the entrapments of corporeal living. Either that or he's going to go into the removal business when he's a fully fledged man or, of course, he's an innate fledgling psychopath in need of sedation and years of reconstructive therapy. I guess I'm in no position to decide. I'm up from the table now and I kind of apologise for the last fax. I had no right to accuse you of whatever I accused you of, I can't remember anyhow, and the hard copies have been whisked away along with everything else. I know you probably have your own hands full at the moment.

Things are calmer now, the acid's loosened its grip but there are still crazy flickers of distortion going on and everything's got a purple edge to it – the mountains never looked so beautiful – but, of course, the other reason is that I haven't seen Languid for over an hour – all is quiet in the Delong Mountains. I know I should be concerned. If he's fallen over a cliff, my grant and my livelihood are down the pan and I can kiss furthering my career goodbye. But, to be honest, and this is between you and me, Sad, just like all of this is between you and me, I am glad of this hour to get my head together, to assimilate what has happened. I've had plenty of people freak out on me before but the control has always been there, whether it's been a security presence, restraining bonds or a psycho so doped up there is no threat. But it was and still is just me and him and in the Delong Mountains, where no one can hear you scream. Do I sound scared? Do I sound repentant? I don't know, that's for you to decide. But it's not over yet, I haven't given up, I've just been shaken up and, if you're at the cutting edge, you've got to expect a rough ride sometimes. I'm going to go in search of Languid, and have myself a confrontation. Enough of the softly softly, eh? He's going to be coming down as well, even from a full tab and in that state after all that has happened, after his house-ripping exercise, he may well be in the mood to talk. And you know I kind of think I deserve an explanation,whatever way he can communicate it – talk it, draw it, mime it – whatever, but I deserve to know.

I think I'm beginning to sound like his parents.

*

Josie's almost grown up, her hair grown into the length it was when I had last seen her. Seventeen and leaving home. Not for career or further education, just leaving home. *Getting out of here, getting away from you,* as she put it. Something happened, at some point, but it's all so cloudy. I found my notepad and books returned to me one night, lying in a heap on my bed for all to see and from that moment on she wouldn't talk to me, found other, outside things to do, other people to see. Suddenly she blossomed into a social butterfly with girlfriends and boyfriends. A lock went on her door and a barrier went up between her and the rest of the household. The hair was taken off and an attitude put on. There was no conversation with anyone. Just an announcement that she was leaving and wouldn't be back. There were conversations deep into the night that I was never party to, the constant tap tap on my sister's door when one or other or both of my parents would go into my sister's bedroom and stay until voices were raised or tears dropped.

She was like that now, not avoiding my gaze but locking onto it with the look that she sometimes mustered when we played our games in the basement of the house.

I didn't resist when Click bound my wrists with the wire. *In milieu therapy it is sometimes necessary for the professional involved to endure transferred duress where the patient, in becoming accustomed to the recreated environment, exhibits unexpected or violent behaviour. For the professional this is a moment where quick, definitive decisions must be made with regard to both the ongoing treatment of the patient and his or her personal safety.*

Click shook his head from side to side, the mane of jet black hair covering his face. Over by the wall Josie kept her eyes locked on me. When I closed my own eyes and thought of her as she was at home, in the bath, in bed, anywhere rather than the hall, I could bring a smile to my lips, but not to hers. When I opened my eyes, her stare had not wavered; in her hands, a piece of wire she skipped with not like a child but with the concentration of an adult, treading water, marking time.

Click dismantled the caravan wire by wire; the fairy lights piled in a heap on the floor, a campfire of red, blue and green lights. He was doing it carefully, taking the windows out intact, the door from its wire hinges and displacing them all on the floor of the hall. Blade and Synth's construction was quickly reduced to a collection of 2D wire sculptures lying on the floor. *Although the role of the mental health professional may seem unduly non-interventionist at some stages of milieu therapy, he or she can interject questions or statements of relevance to the personal history of the patient.*

'Do you know where you are?'

'Do you know why you're here?'

'Do you know that no one wants to hurt you and that you are amongst friends who want to help you?'

Click wasn't oblivious to the questions. His head shook, his long black hair rising and falling in the dry ice; his bodily movements became more animated. No words, but as Peterson had told me before, there was more to communication than simply words. He twitched, contorted the pale skin stretched across high prominent cheek bones into brief grimaces and vigorously shook his head, all the time, without so much as an audible groan or grunt, wrenching at the wire roof of the caravan.

'Do you know why I built this model for you?'

'Do you know why you are taking it apart?'

'Does it make you unhappy to be close to something that reminds you of your parents?'

Click suddenly threw the remaining wire onto the floor and bent down to scoop an armful of torn photographs, ripped text. Purposefully, with that kind of reined, controlled anger I had seen in sociopaths of various hues over the years, he walked over to me and showered me with the pieces. Scraps of his life fell onto different parts of my body. A branch of a tree, a ripple in water, the mouth of a tunnel and text, phrases and sentences cut short, *but the head camera can lie . . . floundering in my attempts . . . spilling my breath out of my mouth . . .* I nodded my head and smiled.

'I can understand why you did that. I can see reasons for it. You are angry at yourself and your situation, it's only natural that you should see me as your natural enemy. But, I'm not, Click, I really am not.'

I could feel a giggle close to the surface. I heard my voice, its words and admired it for coming out with the sort of self-flagellating crap I had endured for years as a student psycho-hack – the professional ethos that was espoused was that of the ultimate mental health professional doing his all, giving his all for the good of the patient. *You are a vehicle, Sad, on the patient's road to recovery.*

On my thighs was the debris of a caravan life.

Exit sitting in the caravan, a brown veil of hair in front of her eyes . . .

with only the smell of his sweat and a few loose hairs lingering above me . . .

A photograph of the inside of Click's mouth.

But the stare doesn't seem to be going anywhere, at least no where I can see.

A part image of the sea, tide out and distant.

My head camera took a picture of her walking into the sun . . .

The sawn-off tip of Click's erect penis.

The caravan is a haven for no one . . .

Click moved one of the side sections of the caravan and placed it behind me. Josie, without my asking, took out a notepad and pen from somewhere and began to write, glancing up at me occasionally.

'What are you writing, Josie?'

She wouldn't answer, no matter how much I continued to shout the question in my head. When she left, when she slammed the front door of our parents' home, she didn't look back. I went to the window to check for a backward glance. But nothing. No final meeting of eyes through rain-spattered windows, no attempt at one last reconciliation. She left it cold. Left me cold. My mother was wailing behind the door. My father stoically poured a glass of whisky from the decanter. I rushed to my room and wouldn't come out for days. At that moment I believed we were such an ordinary family. I was so disappointed.

The door to the hall flew open. Footsteps echoed.

This was not a good time for a visit by the Breathhouse contingent. I could hear them, their voices pitched between incredulity and suspicion. *Is this what you call close interaction with your patient? We would say you were a little too close to your subject.* They would, I knew, not like what they would see. They might remember from some distant education various ideas about environment and therapy but, as far as they were concerned, the only environments they knew about as viable options for mental health care were the whiter than white hospital, snug cells and comfortable living rooms with 60s chairs, splatters of brown and beige everywhere. In short, only what they worked with was what they would accept. Anything else was out there and too radical. *Therapies come and go, Sad, what the patient needs. What we all need is a consistency of ideas, a set of rules and actions that we can grasp onto in times of difficulty.*

I braced myself, readying explanations, reasons as to my seeming lack of control over one of my patients while the other, to all intents and purposes, was not handling things very well on the other side of the hall. But then I heard voices, and it was not the nasal wines of the interns or the boom of the psychohacks but the edgy hysteria of Synth and the low menace of Blade.

The crashing door had been the Breathhouse inmates breaking out.

*

Hey Sad, I had a vision, a horrible anticipation of a headline scattered across the national press.

Mountain drug experiment goes horribly wrong. Crazed therapist attacks young boy in hallucinatory frenzy

But the truth, as it often is, was a whole lot simpler. I found Languid beside the pile of furniture he had removed from the cabin. Tables, chairs, beds, sinks, plates, bowls, towels, everything that had been ripped out, torn off or pulled up had ended up in a big heap at the bottom of one of the slopes leading down from the cabin. There was a strong smell of petrol in the air and I noticed in his hand was a metal pail. It didn't take much insight on my part to work out what Languid planned and I knew I should be talking him out of his action, talking him down from whatever level he was on; appealing to his better nature, ensuring that he knew such an act of wilful damage wouldn't do him (or me) any good at all. But you know, the thing is, I couldn't; I didn't say a word; there was a whole speech in my head about the harm such an action could do to his chances of effective rehabilitation, the opportunity squandered to become a fully rounded individual etc etc but that's as far as it got. It stayed rooted in my head, unable to get into my mouth and out into Languid's ears. It felt like for the first time in my life I had nothing to say and yet, frustratingly, I knew I had. It was the acid, of course. LSD has always tended to make me introverted as I struggled with visions and rampant trains of thought. Back in flared and carefree days, it always made me introverted while all around people would be jumping into the air, jumping off roofs or finding a whole host of reasons for the universe. Not me. I was stummer than stummer.

But God, Sad, here comes the worst bit, here comes the part that nearly brought on a heart attack, that turned my legs into jelly and any future to zero. When he saw me coming, he poured the contents of the bucket over his head, closing his eyes as though he was in the most calming of hot showers. When he opened them he just stared at me and smiled, and not a psychotic smile. I know the difference between a smile of contentment and an out-and-out I'm going to kill you because I enjoy it smile. Christ I know that difference. But his, Sad, his was a smile as sweet as sweet can be. When I got closer to him he threw the remainder of the bucket's contents over me and I must have still been in slo mo because, before I could even shout or scream or push myself away from him, he had a lighter in his hand which he held over both of our heads. All I could do was close my eyes. Christ, Sad, I realise now

*that I am not good in a crisis situation. I freeze more than that deer in
those headlights. A frightened animal. But you know what, he flicked
the lighter and nothing happened. Can you fucking believe it, I'm
standing there stock still, desperately trying to shake because I'm
shitless with fear, and nothing happens. In my head I was already a
human torch, a sacrifice without a cause. Then he pushes me away,
walks around to the other side of the pile, picks up another bucket and
pours its contents over the cut-up cabin. And, of course, when he flicks
the lighter this time, the whole lot goes up and the heat from the flames
almost makes me pass out as I see jets of red and yellow flying around
his head. And my heart just felt like it was going to trip into some
cataclysmic rhythm while Languid, as cool as anything, walks back to
my side of the pyre and begins to dry his clothes against the fire,
holding his arms out, the palms of his hands quickly looking red hot.
All I can do is stare at him, suddenly seeing x21 or Languid in a
different light – of jumping reds and yellows, burning oranges. Then I
notice for the first time, the length of green hose coming from a rusty tap
sticking out of the ground near the fire. I smell my clothes and find
nothing but the scent of my own sweat. Languid comes over to me,
with that elusive, thin-lipped smile creasing his youthful face, and
says, 'Good acid.'*

*

It was clear to me now what Click was doing. He was
building something around me and I thought it could only
be a hut. He had discarded much of the wire into a pile
where the caravan once stood and he had used some of the
panels connected together to form three sides of the hut. As
he worked I tried to move, to back myself away from his
dream-like state but he blocked my every move. First left,
then right, either way he stood in front of me forcing the
issue. The issue being, as far I could tell how far I would go,
what would I have to do to extract myself from this
situation.

**The sixteenth rule of psychotherapy is in a battle of wills
the therapist must always win.**

I couldn't read him. His eyes gave nothing away, indicating neither true consciousness nor a psychotic break. He swung his head back and forth, the long black strands flicking across my face; he chewed his bottom lip as he moulded the wire to resemble the slats of the wooden hut in his life story. There was concentration, attention to detail, nothing to indicate that he would get physical with me, but not everything could be predicted, as Peterson's fax should have warned me.

He got tired of moving to block me as I tried to edge myself away and eventually he grabbed one of the wire chairs from the caravan, the only one he had not destroyed, and pushed me down onto it. Each buttock neatly halved between the wire. I tried to get up and this time he used his head to butt me back down with a thump into the wire. While I felt a bump swell on my forehead he bent down and used another two spare pieces of wire to bind my legs to the wire chair.

The psychotherapist, when confronted with a patient turning unexpectedly violent, must decide when to re-establish control of the therapy. The moment most often indicated is when the therapist feels his wellbeing jeopardised.

Blade burst into Click's half of the hall, his eyes wild and staring, in his hands fifteen centimetres of Sabatier. Click took several steps back from me, lifted the door from the caravan and stood behind it, stock still. Blade strained to see through the dry ice, picking out first the wire mess on the floor, then the rigid Click and then me.

'What have you done? he shouted.

I could see Josie move closer, between Click and Blade, her eyes alight.

'What are you doing in here? I asked you to wait and said that someone would be along to collect you.'

'What the fuck are you talking about? There's been no one *'along to collect us'*. We've been in there for hours, banging our heads off the wall with Synth fucking tapping the same beat on the door, Dogger moaning on about the end of the fucking world and Treats feeling himself as he looks at that filth you gave him. Who the fuck do you think you are?'

Training, Sad, training. *It is important that, during the critical stages of milieu therapy, outside intrusions are kept to a minimum.*

'Look, Blade, I can see you're upset and you have every right to be upset. But the best thing we can do right now is to work on how we can quickly and safely get you all back up to Breathhouse.'

Defuse, Sad, defuse. But Blade carried on.

'I'm not the one upset. What about the poor guy next door . . .'

'What about him, Blade?'

'What about him, I'll tell you what about him . . .' Blade came closer so that I could feel his saliva speckle my face.

'That guy is in one hell of state, by the way. He's covered, absolutely covered in oil, it's dripping off his teeth, for Christ's sake, all over him. And he can't even get up, he's just sliding about under that fucking model car. And he's like some kind of banshee, screaming at the top of his voice about some guy called Jake . . . the guy is going off the wall, out of his tree and you're the one fucking responsible . . .'

'Blade, listen to me, it's important you calm down and listen. The man in there you are talking about, Fright, is a very sick man and is here for observation and hopefully treatment. He's had a very difficult life so far and his time here is the long beginning in the process of making him better, of making his life better. It's important you do not interrupt the treatment process. It's like . . . how can I put it . . . suddenly changing someone's medication and swapping it for another without any warning, do you understand what I mean?'

'What fucking treatment? I don't see any treatment at all. All I see is a guy lying on the floor covered in filth, surrounded by a fucking disco with a car in it, crying his heart out.

'You don't understand, the progression for his healing is a complicated and delicate business.'

'Tell it to him yourself . . .'

'What do you mean . . .'

Synth and Treats came through the dry ice. They were half dragging, half carrying Fright. Blade was right about one thing certainly, he was covered in the oil I had slicked into the hall, his skin had changed ethnic origin, his facial features were hardly recognisable. His near naked body was cut and in several places the black oil merged with crimson blood. His environment had produced an extreme reaction and, of course, without saying anything I was pleased in many ways to see this but frustrated that the course of action, the direction of control, was being taken away from me. Milieu therapy was not always easy, although there are plenty of examples of a sequence of events leading to a neatly packaged conclusion. Sometimes the doctors' adage did have relevance. It has to get worse before it gets better. There is no gain without pain. I needed to be there with Fright, at that moment, I needed to be there, my ears pressed to lips and be everything he needed me to be. His counsel, his friend, Jake, his father, Jochim or whatever his name was. I had to play the role required of me as a milieu therapist. Now was the time for intervention, the milieu had been established and Fright's regression had authenticated it. I didn't need someone to wave a flag at me and say NOW! I knew I needed to be in his past life for him to have any chance of continuing in a future life.

I tried to tear against the wire holding both my hands and my feet but Click brought the door to the hut over and slotted it into place a few centimetres away from my face.

'NO!' I shouted at him as he latched it to the sides of the metal hut.

'Not now.'

Through the wire I could see the four Breathhouse patients gather round me. Synth ran her fingers back and forth across the wire while Dogger and Treats watched Blade push his face against the wire.

'Get the door off this thing and help untie me, Blade.'

'Oh no, no, no. I'm not to get in the way of the treatment, remember.'

'Can't you see what's happening here . . . Blade . . . Blade?'

I heard Fright's voice.

'Get out and get away, that's what is in my head, get out and get away so I can find my way home, so I can find our room where Jake will be lying smiling and waiting.'

I could see Josie pressing her face against the wire, side by side with Blade, her shaven head bristling along the metal. In her hands were a notepad and pen like the one I had used to mark down the width of her hips, to tally the number of hairs under her arms. She was writing furiously and though I tried to see her in the pale green dress, tried to get into the bath with her, tried to shine the torch between her legs under the bed covers, nothing changed. She wasn't even looking at what she was writing, her stare never wavered from me, not even when Fright pushed between her and Blade, his oily hands finding a grip on the wire.

'I have waited in my room with nothing but the sounds of strangers. And he didn't come back. Do you know what it is like to wait for someone, doctor, truly wait, life in suspension, suspended in a life my father left me. And Jochim. Yes, and Jochim. Big arms, big hands, big everything. *Do you want more of this?* he asked me. And I said no. No, I don't want any more of this.'

One of the most difficult aspects of an unsuccessful milieu therapy is bringing the session to an end. This must be decided by the therapist at his or her discretion.

Click squeezed the tangle of fairy lights through the gaps in the wire until I could see nothing but their glow, haloes fusing with haloes. Around me I could hear the whispers of the Breathhouse patients, the jungle sounds screeching, the car grinding to a halt as the tape finished, Fright's mournful litany close to my face and Josie, above all Josie. Somehow she had managed to squeeze her head through the wire until her face was in front of mine, aglow with reds, blues and greens. I shut my eyes and felt her kiss on my lips, her voice in my ear.

The experiment's over, Curtis.

APPENDIX I

THE RULES OF PSYCHOTHERAPY

The first rule of psychotherapy is that the patient already
knows what's wrong.

The second rule of psychotherapy is a healthy body doesn't
necessarily mean a healthy mind.

The third rule of psychotherapy is never trust what the patient
says.

The fourth rule of psychotherapy is that the end always
justifies the means.

The fifth rule of psychotherapy is that a good and dedicated
researcher shouldn't know how to relax.

The sixth rule of psychotherapy is if the patient looks you in
the eyes they are invariably lying.

The seventh rule of psychotherapy is never lose your sense of
the absurd.

The eighth rule of psychotherapy is never ask questions about
whether what you are doing is right.

The ninth rule of psychotherapy is let everybody know when
you are right and tell no one when you are wrong.

The tenth rule of psychotherapy is always sound as though
you know what you are talking about.

The eleventh rule of psychotherapy is that it is not a science
but a sport.

The twelfth rule of psychotherapy is never ever involve
yourself with a patient on a personal level.

The thirteenth rule of psychotherapy is when you have to
intervene, you have to intervene.

The fourteenth rule of psychotherapy is that in a dangerous
situation someone has to remain calm.

The fifteenth rule of psychotherapy is do not let yourself get
distracted.

The sixteenth rule of psychotherapy is in a battle of wills the
therapist must always win.

APPENDIX II

Extracts from psychotherapist Hilda Folic's notes
on six therapeutic strategies used during
consultations with Josie Sad.

GUIDED IMAGERY

Josie Sad is a twenty-seven year old woman who has
sought therapy due to depression, anxiety and insomnia. I
initialised my standard introductory strategy for dealing with
'first-timers'. I asked Josie to close her eyes and imagine a safe
place. This is a standard meditative technique which allows the
patient to unlock memories. Josie described in some detail a
basement where she used to go and hide from her brother,
Curtis. This safe place was chosen by Josie and not influenced
by me; however, what she describes is a dank, dark cellar, full
of frightening objects and shadows and, while I believe that
she felt, for some time at least, safe in this location, it is not as
secure in its description as locations cited by other patients,
such as a bunker, a toxic waste site or a huge cement building.
When I cue another person into the imagery, the notion that
it is a secure location indeed begins to break down . . .

'I am hiding there, pressed against this old wardrobe,
feeling the nails and splinters on my skin. I'm right against the
wall. I can hear Curtis upstairs, at the cellar door. He's trying
to come down . . .'

I ask Josie whether he manages to get into the cellar, into
her place.

He does.

I ask her to describe what Curtis looks like.

'He's fourteen maybe. He seems quite tall, with very short
hair and glasses. He's wearing the same dirty T-shirt he always
wears, a faded blue one with grease spots on it and a V of sweat

running down his back. He has tight, blue jeans on with nothing on his feet.'

'Can you smell anything?'

'I can smell the oil on the cellar floor, the smell of machinery, of drying grass on the old grass cutter, then there's wood, the smell of creosoted wood. A burning, strong smell. And Curtis.'

'What can you smell about Curtis?'

It is worth noting that asking this particular question in order to guide her further into this particular image produced a strong reaction in Josie – she jerked her head back as though the question had recalled and replicated the smell in front of her.

'It was his smell. Just his, no one else's. It was his smell, of sweat, of unwashed clothes, of sex.'

'Can you describe this last smell any more? How did you get to know this smell?'

'He put his hands down his trousers, wiped his thing on his hand and pushed it under my nose, and said, 'Does yours smell like that?'

HYPNOTHERAPY

I explained to Josie that hypnosis helps in facilitating the reconstruction of personal history and, using hypnosis, I would be able to enhance memories, particularly these early memories with her brother, since I was concerned about the possibility of abuse.

'What smells do you associate with your father, Josie?'

'Antiseptic.' -

'What part of him exuded this smell?'

'His hands.'

'Why did he smell of antiseptic?'

'I don't know, maybe because he was a doctor.'

'And your mother, what did she smell of?'

'Antiseptic.'

'Was she a doctor too?'

'No, but she worked in a hospital.'

'I see. You have a strong memory of this smell of antiseptic. Did Curtis ever smell of it?'

'No.'

'Because he smelt of sex?'

'Yes.'

'Did your parents ever smell like Curtis?'

'I don't know.'

'Try and think of a time when they were close to you, your father bending over to pick you up, your mother leaning to brush your hair. Can you remember a smell then?'

'Antiseptic . . . but I remember another smell . . .'

'Yes, go on.'

'Bubble bath.'

'Were you bathing with your mother or your father?'

'No, I was in the bath, Curtis was beside the bath.'

'What was he doing? '

'He was playing with the bubbles in the bath.'

'Was he trying to touch you at the same time? Did he push the bubbles into your vagina . . .'

'He played with them on top of my body.'

'Did he penetrate you with bubbles or rub them over your breasts?'

'He was playing with the bubble bath.'

'So, he was playing with the bubbles, rubbing them over your body while you were naked in the bath, unable to get away quickly if you wanted to. Did you feel trapped?'

'Sometimes.'

'He trapped you in the bathroom?'

'Yes.'

'And played these games with you?'

'Yes.'

AGE REGRESSION

'How old are you Josie?'

'Ten.'

'What are you wearing?'

'A dress.'
'What colour is the dress?'
'Green.'
'Are you with Curtis?'
'Yes.'
'What is he wearing?'
'Nothing.'
'You mean he's not wearing any clothes?'
'Yes.'
'Where are you with Curtis?'
'Outside.'
'Where outside?'
'In the garden.'
'Are your mother and father there?'
'No.'
'What is Curtis doing?'
'He's lifting up my dress.'
'Why is he doing that?'
'He says he wants to look, check to see if I've changed.'
'And what do you say to him when he does this?'
'I say it's okay.'
'Are you sure it's okay? What do you say out loud to him?'
'Does it always go big like that?
'You mean his penis?'
'Yes.'
'What does he do when it gets big?'
'Nothing. He just stands there, taking notes. Like you.'
'I'm not naked though, Josie. I'm not Curtis.'
'No. You're not.'
'What is he looking for when he lifts your dress?'
'He wants to see if I've got hair.'
    'Why do you lift up your dress? Does he threaten you, say
that he will hit you or tell a lie to your parents?'
    'I want to.'
    'You want to because you feel you would be letting him
down, letting yourself down if you didn't?'
    'I want to. I WANT TO!'

'You need to because you would be rejecting him as your brother?'

'What else was there to do?'

BODY MEMORY

I asked Raymond Pusch, an experienced Body Worker, to take a session with Josie to see if her feelings could be triggered by light touch or deeper manipulation. He reported that, when he massaged her leg, she complained of pain and explained that she had broken it as a child and that her brother had set it for her. He asked how she broke it and she was unable to recall the incident, only the treatment. When he massaged her buttocks, she said that the sensation made her sick. When Raymond asked her why she said this, and he reports that her tone was almost entirely unemotional – patients will often be in this objective state of denial at the beginning of coming to terms with abuse – Josie replied that Curtis sometimes had to hold her buttocks apart for a long period of time while he tried to take the exact dimensions of her anus.

PICKLE AVERSION

I have recently introduced this relatively new technique, used in therapies for post-traumatic stress disorder, which helps patients define and originate feelings and symptoms. After carefully selecting a range of products from my local supermarket, I display these in front of a patient and get their reaction. The results can be startling. Many victims of abuse and perpetrated incest have an aversion to pickles or bananas since they are penis-shaped and, similarly, creams and mayonnaise, in their similarity to semen, can trigger intense emotional reaction in the patient. This abreaction can be seen as evidence of abuse.

I spread mayonnaise on my palm and held half an okra in my fingers and held them up in front of Josie. She drew back, saying, 'That's disgusting.'

DREAMWORK

In a later session, Josie reported a dream to me, which I feel was entirely relevant to her evolving acceptance of abuse. She stated that she dreamt about herself when she was thirteen and Curtis was making her role-play a sexual situation with him, simulating sex by rubbing himself on top of her, feeling her breasts and placing her hand on his penis. The act took place, according to the dream, in the garden shed, a location which she had already identified in an earlier session as a place where abuse did take place and hence the dream can be seen to be both representative and accurate.

FINAL NOTE

Josie has terminated the therapy sessions. She feels that her anxiety and depression are not rooted in her past but in her present and, despite my attempts to assure her that one indeed does affect the other, she is determined to carry on with her life. I have made it clear that my door will always be open when, and not if, she chooses to walk through it again.

Hilda Folic.

APPENDIX III

INDEX OF CLICK'S PHOTOS